THE
FAMILY
BIZ

Also by Alan Orloff

Diamonds for the Dead

Killer Routine

Deadly Campaign

The Taste

First Time Killer

Ride-Along

Running From the Past

Pray for the Innocent (ITW Thriller Award Winner)

I Know Where You Sleep (Shamus Award Finalist)

I Play One On TV (Agatha Award Winner, Anthony Award Winner)

Sanctuary Motel

Late Checkout (Anthony Award Finalist)

Driving the Bugmobile

THE FAMILY BIZ

ALAN ORLOFF

LEVEL BEST BOOKS

To my family and all their biz.

Praise for THE FAMILY BIZ

Chapter One

I came by my dishonesty honestly.

My great-grandfather was a horse thief. My grandfather was a tax cheat. My uncle was a real estate swindler. My father was a con man, a grifter.

And my mother? A *real* piece of work.

That's all in my rearview mirror now. I'm a changed man. Have been for coming up on three years. In fact, today was my one thousandth day out of the life. A milestone, of sorts. And I was celebrating like I had for the past five months. I was driving for Ryde, the fourth-most popular ride-sharing service in the country. I didn't much like the job, but I liked it better than getting evicted. It was one of the more lucrative side-hustles I'd had, at least among the legal ones.

I was trying very hard to keep my life going in the right direction, and if I had to work some dead-end jobs in order to achieve that, then so be it. Anything beat prison.

I glanced into the back seat where my latest fare, a drunk twenty-something, belched loudly as he listed to one side, his shoulder coming to rest against the door.

"You okay back there?"

No answer.

"You need me to pull over?" About three weeks ago, a freckle-faced boy had puked in the back seat. It stank for days, and that was just from too much Mountain Dew and birthday cake. Beer and burgers would smell a lot worse, for a lot longer.

"You awake back there?"

Still no answer, unless you counted a boozy hiccup.

I slowed and waited for a car to pass before pulling into the right lane, then further onto the shoulder. We were on I-66, heading west into the Virginia suburbs, where someone losing their lunch on the side of the highway wasn't as commonplace as it was in other parts of the DMV. Not unheard of, though.

I brought the car to a stop and, checking to make sure it was safe, scrambled out of the car and hustled around to the back passenger-side door. Opened it carefully, not wanting to dump my rider onto the ground. Gently, I hauled him out, supporting him under one arm. "Hey, buddy. You don't look too good. I thought maybe some fresh air might help."

Dusk had fallen, and the dim light wasn't helping his gray-green complexion.

"What's your name?" I pinched his upper arm.

His eyes fluttered open. "Whazzat?"

"You going to be sick?"

He exhaled, and it smelled like a beer truck had overturned. "Where are we?"

I shifted him to one side so he no longer faced me. "I'm taking you home, but it seemed as if you needed to..."

"What? Needed to what?" *Needed* sounded like *needled*.

"You know. You look a little ill. I thought you might need to...you know, feel better."

He finally took my hint and puked all over his shoes, but not before spinning around to face my car. I jumped back to avoid the spatter. I succeeded, but my Camry wasn't as lucky. He'd painted the side of the door with his vomitus.

He hurled again, then straightened and turned around. Looked me in the eyes. "Thanks, man. I needed that." He attempted to wink at me, but it just looked as if he had a piece of dirt in his eye. "Now, can you please take me home?"

"Of course. *Sir*." I wanted to yell at him for messing up my ride, but I bit my tongue. Bad reviews weren't good for business.

I eased him back into the car, made sure he was buckled in. Then I drove him to his home in Vienna, glancing in the mirror every so often. If he was going to hurl again, I wanted to act quickly. We made it there without further incident, and he managed to get out and to his doorstep on his own. Didn't even thank me for the ride.

I deserved a damn good tip, but I had a strong feeling I was going to get shafted.

The glamorous and rewarding life of a Ryde driver.

At least chauffeuring drunks around wasn't going to land me back in prison. I'd done my time.

I'd learned my lesson.

* * *

My next stop was a quickie car wash, the kind attached to a gas station. Eight bucks got the car clean. An hour and a half—and two short fares—later, I decided to head toward home. If I got a convenient rider, good. If not, I'd call it a day. My phone rang just as I'd gotten back on I-66. My mother. I prayed my night wasn't about to get worse.

"Hello, Ma."

"Hello, Chancey. How's my little boy?"

"I'm fine. And I'm thirty-nine, by the way."

"You can't be. That would make me…" I pictured her counting on her nicotine-stained fingers. "… Way too old. And we both know I'm not a day over fifty."

"You had me when you were eleven?"

"How come you don't come by anymore?"

"I came over last Wednesday. Your friend, Harvey, was there. Remember?" I stopped behind a Suburban at a red light. It had a bumper sticker that read: *My Other Car is a Tank.*

"That was Gary. Harvey was the week before."

"I'm busy, Ma. Working."

"Driving around town, picking up strangers? That's too dangerous."

"Compared to what? I spent three years *in prison*. Or did you forget?"

"I told you not to get caught. You need to get back in the game, dear. You'll be happier. Besides, it's the family business. You were born into it. Scamming people is our gift."

The light turned green, and the Suburban accelerated slowly. I eased onto the gas, too. "Was there some reason you called?"

"I could use some help on a thing."

"What kind of a thing?"

"You know, a *thing*-thing." She emitted a raspy cough.

"Forget it, Ma. How many times do I have to tell you, I'm done with that? Please stop asking me."

"Ach, it kills me to watch all your talent go to waste."

A black Beamer zoomed past me on my left. "Most mothers try hard to keep their kids *away* from crime. *Out* of trouble."

"I'm not like most mothers."

She could say that again. "I gotta go, so—"

"Hold your horses, buddy boy. My dishwasher's on the fritz. I need you to come over and fix it. Unless you have some moral objection to *that*."

"Did you look the problem up on Google? It's amazing what solutions you can find there if you poke around a bit."

"You know I'm better with naps than apps." She coughed. "Please, Chancey?"

"Can't you get Gary to take a look at it?"

"Harvey. Harvey's the one who's good with his hands." Another pause, and now I pictured her taking an exaggerated drag on a joint or a long pull on a drinking glass full to the brim with bourbon. "'Course, when he comes over, he ain't thinking about diddling with my *dishwasher*."

"Goodbye, Ma." I hung up before she could describe what Harvey *did* like to diddle with. I seriously considered blocking her number on my phone. When was she going to comprehend that I was really, truly, finished with my life of crime?

Twenty seconds later, Ma called back, and I let it roll into voicemail. A minute later, I listened to the message. *See you tomorrow night for dinner.*

Around 6 o'clock. Bring your toolbox!

Traffic was light, as usual. Fairfax at nine p.m. was dead, which didn't translate into much revenue for me. As I turned into the community where I lived—a mature neighborhood full of vintage apartment buildings and run-down duplexes—my phone beeped with a possible fare. I glanced at the details. I'd passed the pickup point about a half mile back, and the destination wasn't far at all. I was still a little wired from my evening—the call from Mom had just revved me up on top of the puking incident—so I tapped the app to accept the ride. A few extra bucks never hurt. Maybe I'd splurge and make my next six-pack imported.

I arrived at the pick-up point in about three minutes, and my rider was waiting exactly where she should have been, right on the curb. When she spotted me, she waved and stepped forward. I pulled over and waited for her to climb into the back.

She opened the door and poked her head in. "I'm Samantha. Your rider. If you're Chance, that is."

I smiled. "I am. Pleased to meet you. There's a bottle of water in the holder on the door, and I've got some energy bars if you'd like a snack."

"Thanks, but I'm good." Samantha was college-aged, more or less, long and lean, with blonde hair cut short. A tattoo of a butterfly graced the back of her hand, and it seemed to flutter as she removed her shoulder bag and set it on the seat next to her. More fluttering as she fastened the seat belt.

"Going to The Crab Shack?" I always confirmed the rider's destination before taking off. Saved a lot of U-turns and wasted time in traffic.

"Uh, that's right."

"Okay. If you need anything, just let me know. We'll be there in less than ten minutes." I waited for a gap in traffic, then pulled away from the curb. I glanced in the rearview mirror, and Samantha was staring right at me.

"Do you like this job?" She maintained her steady gaze, two intense blue eyes shooting laser beams at me in the mirror.

"It's okay. Helps pay the bills."

"What did you do before this?"

"A little of this. A little of that." A wishy-washy answer, but better than *I made license plates upstate.*

"Married?"

"No."

"Girlfriend?"

"Not really." I'd been driving long enough to have my share of unusual riders, but not too many were as … curious. At least about me. I was getting weird vibes, and somewhere in my brain a red flag started to unfurl.

"Odd. I would think a good-looking guy like you had lots of women after him." Samantha's intensity level seemed to rise. "Have any kids?"

"Kids? No." I changed lanes so I could pass a slow-moving truck ahead.

"You mean none that you know about." Most people would deliver this line with a wink, wink, nudge, nudge. Not Samantha. I punched the gas, passed the truck, and switched back into the right lane. We were about three blocks from the restaurant, and I was beginning to regret my decision to take one last fare for the night.

I risked another look in the rearview mirror. Her eyes were still fixed on me. "Look, is there something—"

"I think we might know someone in common," she said.

"Oh?" I had a feeling things were about to go from mildly uncomfortable to downright unpleasant, based on Samantha's increasingly abrasive tone.

"Yes. Someone who grew up not too far from here. In Maryland. I don't suppose you lived in Maryland, did you?"

"As a matter of fact, I did. And I knew a lot of people there. So, I guess it's *possible* we have a common acquaintance. But I doubt if we ran in the same—"

"Don't you want to know who?"

I was too tired to play games. "That was a different part of my life. One I'd rather not dredge up. Anyway, we're here. The Crab Shack, in all its greasy glory." I hooked a right into the parking lot, not a moment too soon. If I wanted to be grilled about my loserville life, I wouldn't have hung up on my mother earlier.

I pulled up to the front door of the restaurant, saving myself from any further inquisition. Came to a complete stop and unlocked the doors.

Turned and forced my best tip-inducing smile. "Have a pleasant night. I hope you enjoyed your *Ryde*." I hit the word *Ryde* extra hard, just like instructed in the Ryde Driver Instructions. "I, uh, enjoyed our little conversation."

Samantha sat there, still buckled in, staring at me. "Aren't you the least bit curious?"

"About what?"

"About who we know in common."

I'd had a long day, and I just wanted to go home, collapse on the couch, pop open a beer, and watch something inane on Netflix. "Listen, you've probably mistaken me for someone else. You don't know me, and I don't know you. Happens from time to time, someone thinks they recognize me. I guess I have one of those faces." I nodded at the door. "Have a great night."

She made no move to leave.

I wasn't sure which passenger I preferred: the vomiting drunk or Samantha the Rider Who Wouldn't Leave. "We're at the restaurant. Your destination. All passengers ashore, please."

"I didn't pick your ride at random. I used the *Select a Specific Driver* option."

Now the red flag was smacking me in the face. I didn't have a gun with me—I was an ex-con, after all—but there was a container of mace in the center console compartment. I unbuckled my seat belt in case I needed to lunge for it. "What's going on here?"

"You may not know me, but I know you. You're Chance Winston. Almost forty years old. Birthday on August 7. Grew up in Silver Spring. Dropped out of high school. Ran afoul of the law and did time in the joint. Been trying to go straight since getting out." She cocked her head at me. "Should I go on?"

I felt as if I'd been sucker punched, and in some sense, I had been. This Samantha knew all about me. Somehow she'd managed to get me to pick her up with the intent of … what? What could some stranger possibly want with me? I hadn't been lying when I'd said that I tried very hard to forget about my old life. Why did I have a feeling I was about to get dragged right back into it? The faces of a dozen asshole buddies I'd left behind flashed through my mind. Low-lifes, all. "Who sent you? What do you want?"

"Nobody sent me. As for what I want, it's what I *need*." She stared at me, and her twenty-year-old face suddenly seemed a lot younger. And more vulnerable. She looked very much like someone I knew a long time ago.

"I'll bite. What do you need?" If she was after money, the joke was on her. As my mother used to say, you couldn't squeeze drachmas from a rutabaga.

Her lower lip trembled, and her demeanor seemed to shift toward sincerity. Her eyes misted. "I need your help."

"And why should I help you?"

Samantha wiped away a tear. "Because I'm your daughter."

Chapter Two

"Huh?"

"I'm your daughter." This time, she said it much calmer, matter-of-fact. *It's hot in here. I like strawberries. I'm your daughter.*

"You're my daughter?" I'd heard the words, both times, but their meaning was having a tough time penetrating my thick skull. "You're my daughter?"

"Yes. I am. And I need your help. More specifically, my mother needs your help."

I stared at this girl before me, trying to see some part of myself in her. She was attractive, but her looks probably came more from her other parent. "Who's your mother?"

Her pupils dilated for a second and darkened, then returned to their piercing blue. "I guess she was telling the truth. She never told you about me, did she?"

I shook my head, and a wave of sadness washed over me. Samantha seemed like a good kid, trying to help her mother and all, and I'd missed her childhood, completely.

She bowed her head, her shoulders started shaking, and the sniffles followed. I waited her out while I thought about the women—girls, really—I knew twenty years ago.

There were a few.

But only one stood out. Kristal. We'd had a serious thing going, both professionally and personally. We'd run a series of cons together, and after the first couple, she'd moved into my place in order to save money, but we both knew it was more than that. We drank and we screwed and we drank some more and we screwed even more, living together, playing together, working together. She was the best con artist I'd ever seen, then and since.

And, of course, I'd fallen madly in love.

Our arrangement lasted for almost two years, until we had the ultimate fish on the hook. A guy we were poised to take for about a hundred thou. Everything was a go. We knew our lines, had our roles down pat, arranged a place to meet right before we met our mark.

She never showed.

She bolted.

She left my life forever.

She broke my heart.

She crushed my fucking soul.

I never saw Kristal again.

Samantha's sobbing slowed, and she raised her head, and now with Kristal in mind, I had no doubts. Samantha had Kristal's smile, the same ice-blue eyes, the same chin with the faint cleft. I'd always teased Kristal about her pointy nose, and Samantha's was identical. The more I examined Samantha, the more memories of Kristal came rushing back. And they weren't all good ones. After all, she'd left a gaping hole in my chest.

"How is Kristal?"

A small smile appeared on Samantha's face. "How did you know who?"

"You resemble her. A lot in fact."

"You remember my mom?"

"I do." I felt a smile take over my face.

"Well, she's in a shitload of trouble." Samantha stiffened as she recalled why she sought me out. "And you need to help, *Dad.*"

* * *

I'd only been in The Crab Shack once before, and that was, not surprisingly, to eat crabs. The place smelled of Old Bay and fried food, with faux fishing nets covering the walls. A smattering of wire crab pots hung from the ceiling in a lame attempt to give the place a nautical flavor.

The hostess guided us to a table in an alcove adjoining the main room, with a view out to the side parking lot. The place wasn't very crowded, which made sense. The crabs weren't very good.

"Hungry?" I asked Samantha.

"Nope."

"Me neither." I set the menu aside, ran a hand through my hair. "I don't even know where to begin. How did you track me down?"

"Mom wasn't very forthcoming with the details, but over the years, she'd let things slip from time to time. I made a point of asking about you when she'd had a few drinks, so she was a bit looser with the information. I quizzed some of her old-time friends, and I got some info from my grandmother, too."

Kristal's mother, Edith, was a devout Christian, a real holy roller, always praying and carping at Kristal to go to church. On the few occasions I'd actually spoken to her, she repeatedly told me to leave her daughter alone, and that I was a true sinner. That if I didn't change my evil ways, God would punish me. At the time, I dismissed her as a crackpot. When I was wasting away in prison, I realized she might have been on to something. "How is Edith?"

"Not too good. She's dead."

"Sorry about that."

"I'm not. Mom's not either. She was a bitch. Thinking she was better than everyone. Nagging us nonstop about being sinners. Telling us we'd burn in Hell if we didn't do the Lord's work. We got the last laugh. A few years ago, she choked to death on a piece of fried chicken. At a church picnic."

"So," I asked, "are you?"

"Am I what?"

"A sinner."

She smiled, and again, I saw Kristal smile. Was this how it was going to be now? Me seeing Kristal in everything Samantha did? "I guess that depends on who you ask."

I nodded. She was a wiseass, too, just like Kristal. "How old are you, Samantha?"

"First of all, everyone calls me Sammi. And I'm nineteen. Born on the Fourth of July."

I did the math, and it wasn't out of the question. I was with Kristal around the time Sammi was conceived, but it was pretty close to the time when things ended. Of course, I could tell Kristal was Sammi's mother just by looking. But that didn't necessarily mean I was her father. Kristal was a professional con artist, after all. Even though I'd trusted her with my life twenty years ago, sometimes people changed. I had, so maybe she had too.

"You still there?" Sammi rapped her knuckles on the table.

"Huh?" I snapped out of it. "Sorry. Was thinking about your mother, a long time ago. What kind of trouble is she in?"

"Oh. We're done talking about me now? You just found out you have a daughter, and you've moved on to somebody else?"

My face flushed. It had been a while since I'd had a conversation with a teenage girl. Like since I was a teen, probably. "Sorry if I was rude. Please, tell me about yourself."

She waved a hand in the air, and once again, the butterfly on the back of her hand fluttered. "Just messing with you. Let's talk about Mom. She's in some deep shit and needs your help."

"Why me?"

"I heard stories. She never mentioned you by name, of course, but she was always going on about how *my father* was this twisted genius and all, and that I got some of his mad skills. Well, we need some of those skills now."

"Is that true?"

"Is what true?"

"That you got some of those skills."

"Well…" She looked over my shoulder at a passing server, then refocused on me.

My gut clenched. Had Sammi taken up my family business, too, even though she probably didn't even know she was part of my family? "What do you do?"

"What do you mean?"

"You know, do you go to school? Do you work? Do you sing for the

Washington Opera?"

"I don't go to school. Too boring. And I got my singing voice from my mother, so no opera." She shrugged. "As for working, I guess you could say I do a little of this and a little of that. Whatever comes along. You know how it is, right?"

"That sounds like what your mother did when she was your age." Hard to believe the girl sitting across from me was the same age as Kristal was when I ran with her. Kristal had seemed mature and worldwise, while Sammi seemed, well, like a typical nineteen-year-old. Naïve and impetuous. I mean, she tracked me down, thinking I would just jump in and help her? For all she knew, I could be a psychopath. "Does 'whatever comes along' include things that might get you in trouble? Things on the wrong side of the law?"

Just then, the server came to the table.

"Can I get you something to drink?" she asked.

I nodded to Sammi.

"I'll have a beer. Whatever's on tap."

The server eyed her. "Gonna have to see some ID."

Sammi scowled. "Make it a Coke, okay?"

"Right." The server turned to me. "And for you?"

"Water with lime, please."

The server rolled her eyes, disappointed we weren't going to be ordering fancy drinks, and stalked off.

"Now, where were we?" I asked, ready to hear about Sammi's run-ins with the law, ready to be reminded of some of my own poor choices.

"Maybe we should go back to talking about my mother and her problem. That's why I'm here, you know."

"Look, if I really am your fa—"

"You are!"

I recoiled, surprised by the intensity of her response. I thought about debating the point, telling her that while it was *possible* I was her father, it wasn't a slam dunk. But there was no sense doing that, not now. She believed I was her father, and nothing I could say would dissuade her. She'd known me as an abstraction for so long, and to finally see me in the flesh must have stirred up some strong emotions.

I tended to be more cynical. As far as I knew, Kristal and Sammi had cooked up this scheme to separate me from my money. I'd let a paternity test make it official. Trust, but verify. "Listen, Sammi. Allow me to offer you some advice, having lived it. If you *are* following in your mother's footsteps—at least what she was up to when she was your age—then I strongly suggest you stop. I didn't, and I had my life taken away from me for three years. *Three years.* Believe me, you really appreciate freedom once it's gone."

Sammi closed her eyes and pretended to snore.

Wiseass. Yeah, she was definitely Kristal's kid.

I didn't have to put up with attitude. I stood and slid my chair out, making sure it screeched across the floor. Her eyes flew open.

"I guess I'm too boring to help you. Good luck." I started to leave.

"Wait! I'm sorry. Please!"

I turned around slowly.

Sammi sprang to her feet. "I'm sorry. This is all so stressful. Please sit down and listen. Mom really does need your help. She's in big, big trouble." With that, the tears started flowing, and I realized Sammi had been trying very hard to keep it together, but in true nineteen-year-old fashion, she tried to deflect her worry with sass. But she'd misread her audience: me.

I put an arm around her and felt her bony shoulders tremble as she sobbed. She was almost my height but only about half my width. Just like Kristal had been. A terror in a trim package. After a few moments, I guided her down into her chair and sat back in mine.

"Okay. I'm listening. Tell me about your mother's situation."

Before she could get started, the server returned with our drinks and clanked them down on the table, a bit of water sloshing over the side of my glass. "What can I get you to eat?"

Afraid they might toss us out if we didn't get something more than a soda, I ordered a warm brownie à la mode, two spoons. I figured Sammi could use some comfort food, and that particular dessert had been one of Kristal's favorites.

The server rolled her eyes again and added a slight, disgusting shake of the head as she left to help another table. One that would generate a much bigger tip, most likely.

Sammi ripped the narrow white paper band holding the napkin around the silverware, unfolded the napkin, and blew her nose into it. Then she wadded up the napkin and set it down on the table. In addition to having Kristal's pert nose, she had her mother's impertinent manners, too. "She's been with this guy, Granger, for a while, and he moved in a few months ago. Wears old guy shirts, you know, the kind they wear to play golf. Thinks he's retro or something. For the most part, he pays attention to Mom and leaves me alone. Treats me like I'm a piece of furniture, but I'm okay with that. Really."

Sammi paused, took a breath. Looked at me as if she was trying to gauge my reaction. I kept a poker face, but whenever someone said they were okay with something, then tacked on a *really*, I always doubted them. "Go on."

"He and Mom are working some game on this rich investor or something. Not quite sure because Mom wasn't telling me anything about this job, which was unusual. Even though she's my mom, she always tells me what's going on, that's part of what makes her great. Doesn't treat me like a kid, the way Granger usually does. Be seen and not heard, and all that shit. Anyway, about a week ago, Mom comes home crying. Alone. Without Granger."

Sammi stopped abruptly and took a sip of her Coke. Not surprisingly, she shared her mother's talent of talking for long stretches uninterrupted—at a high rate of speed.

"Does this Granger have a last name?"

"Granger *is* his last name. Duane Granger. But I've never heard anyone call him Duane, and I have a feeling if you did, he'd slug you." Her words had a sharp edge, as if I were an idiot for not knowing Duane Granger's full name. *Teenagers.*

"He's violent?"

"No. Not really."

"Which is it? No or not really?"

"He's never hit Mom, if that's what you mean."

"But you wouldn't be surprised if he did?"

She shrugged, and I had my answer. "Can I finish now?"

"Go on."

"It took me a while, but I pried it out of Mom. She and Granger had already sunk a ton of money into this con—money they had to borrow. Mom thought their mark caught on, and the only way she saw to keep the con alive was to come up with some additional seed money."

My stomach sank. Throwing good money after bad wasn't generally a good business decision.

"Things went sideways big-time, and…" Sammi started sniffling again.

"And what?"

"Bottom line. Mom borrowed *more* money. And then that asshole Granger stole it."

"He stole it?"

"I think he did. I haven't seen him since, so I'm guessing he's in the wind. Mom won't tell me the details. But…I've never seen her like this."

"Maybe she'll realize she needs to throw in the towel," I said. "Give up on this job. Give up hustling people altogether."

"On the contrary. First, she's going to track Granger down and get that money back and probably tear off his balls with her bare hands. Then she'll get *really* nasty."

I remembered the face Kristal made sometimes when we argued, fangs and crazy fierce eyeballs, and my own balls shrank reflexively. I didn't doubt for a moment that Sammi's fear of her mother going off the deep end was completely warranted. "How much money does she need?"

"Counting the extra fifty thousand Granger stole?"

"I thought you didn't know any details."

"*Many* details. Mom vented a lot, and I picked up a few things. You'd have to be deaf not to."

"How much money does she need, total?"

Sammi scrunched up her face, thinking. Then she blurted out, "Three hundred fifty thousand."

"Holy Christ. That's a lot."

"Yeah, it is. And there's one tiny detail I haven't told you yet. The guy who loaned all that money to my mom wants it back. With the interest she promised him. If he doesn't get it, he said he'd kill her." Sammi's voice caught. "And he said he'd kill her daughter, too."

Chapter Three

Pretty much all I knew about nineteen-year-olds these days was what I'd seen on TV, and honestly, how accurate was that? Real life didn't have a canned laugh track. I wasn't sure if Sammi was being overly dramatic in that teenager way, or if someone had truly, honest-to-god threatened them. I did know this: you had to take threats like that seriously, regardless. "Did you actually hear this guy say he was going to kill your mom and you?"

Sammi had gotten very still, which was more unnerving than if she had started crying like a scared infant. "Yes. He called, and Mom had him on speaker. I was in the next room, but she must have thought I had my earbuds in. These were his exact words. 'If I don't get my money, I'm going to kill you and your girl.' I'll never forget them."

I sat back, thought. If a law-abiding citizen received a threat like that, they'd hang up immediately and call the police. But those who operated on the shady side of the law didn't have that luxury. They had to be more creative or elusive or defensive. Or they had to just plain get out of Dodge.

"Your mom say anything about taking an extended trip? Until she figured something out?"

Sammi looked at me with disgust. "I thought you knew her. She'll never give up on something, especially not this. Not something that matters as much as this does to her. She *hates* to lose. And she hates Granger with the intensity of a thousand suns."

Poetic, but I couldn't help but think back to when Kristal and I split, when she *did* give up on something. Or rather someone. *Me.* I guessed I hadn't meant that much to her, in the end.

"Any idea who this guy is?"

A head shake. *No.*

"Any idea how much time your mother has to repay him?"

"A week? Ten days? I don't know for sure. What difference does it make? We don't have the money!"

I exhaled. I usually subscribed to the *you made your bed* philosophy, and if it had been solely Kristal in trouble here, I might have turned away and let natural consequences run their course. She knew the score going in; we all did. But Sammi was an innocent here—if her story could be believed—and she was my blood—again, if her story could be believed. Either way, it warranted further investigation. And the first step was to determine if she was telling the truth.

From out of nowhere, the server appeared with our dessert. She plopped it on the table and tossed down two spoons. "Anything else for you?"

"No thanks," I said.

"Just holler when you want the check." She turned on her heels without waiting for any type of reply.

Sammi picked up a spoon, pushed around the whipped cream on top of the ice cream, then set her spoon back down without sampling the sundae. "So? Will you help us? I don't know where else to turn."

"I need to check out a few things first."

"What kind of things?"

"Give me your phone number, your mom's number, and while you're at it, the name your mom is going by these days." I had a feeling she wasn't using the last name I'd known her by. She'd ditched that one the same night she ditched me.

"Her last name is Young," Sammi said. "Mine too. That's our *real* name."

Uh huh. When I was with Kristal, she was using Johnson as her *real* last name—at least that's what her driver's license said. I never saw her birth certificate to know what her *real* real name was. I gave Sammi my number, and she texted me all the contact information I'd requested, mumbling to herself as her thumbs danced across the screen. When she finished, she said in a pleading voice, "*Now* will you help us?"

"I'm going to sleep on it."

"Sleep on it? What if something happens while you're sleeping?"

"Seems unlikely."

"There's no telling when my mom might try some crazy stunt to get the money. She could be out right now robbing a bank."

"Banks aren't open at night."

"You know what I mean. Argh!" She slapped the table with her palms.

"So text her. See what she's doing right this very minute." I flashed Sammi a patronizing grin.

She frowned, and I could practically see her mind working to come up with some other reason why I needed to jump into action immediately or at least *commit* to jumping into action. "Okaaaay." She tapped on her phone, reviewed her message, then hit send.

We waited for a reply.

In the meantime, I asked her to take a selfie with me, father and daughter. She made a face. I asked again, and she shook her head. I asked—nicely—a third time, and she told me no fucking way. I reminded her that she was the one requesting *my* help, and she stared at me, obviously noodling things through. Finally, I got tired of waiting and just snapped a picture of her scowling at me.

Kristal still hadn't responded to Sammi's text.

"Nice weather we're having," I said.

No response. With my spoon, I carved out a big chunk of the brownie, making sure I got some ice cream, whipped cream, and fudge sauce, too. The warm brownie had caused the ice cream to melt, and it was a gloppy mess, dripping everywhere. I stuffed it into my mouth and winced from the sugar rush. I chewed and swallowed. "How about those Nationals?"

Sammi shot me a look, then went back to staring at her phone. A minute later, it dinged, and Sammi read Kristal's text aloud. "She's drinking wine and watching Netflix."

"Sounds like we're safe for tonight. No grand theft in the plans."

"You don't understand. She *always* says she's drinking wine and watching

Netflix whenever she's doing something she doesn't want me to know about."

"Then what does she say when she's really drinking wine and watching Netflix?"

Sammi glared at me. "Are you going to help us, or not?"

"Like I said, I need to think about it."

Sammi barked something I couldn't quite make out, burned a hole in me with her steely blue eyes, then jumped out of her seat and flounced out of the restaurant. I thought about chasing after her, but figured she could find her own way home.

I finished the brownie sundae, scraping the bottom of the plate to get the last of the hot fudge, paid the check, and drove straight to my place, ignoring two potential Ryde fares.

I'd had enough excitement for one night.

* * *

Some people had dogs, others cats. I kept tropical fish. I'd always wanted a dog, but when I was younger, it was never practical, knowing I might have to bolt on a moment's notice to get out of a jam. Living like that wasn't fair to a dog.

Of course, since I'd become a free man again, I could have gotten a dog. I had no reason to think I would be bugging out now. It was hard to fathom what kind of predicament a Ryde driver—and sometime landscaper, handyman, courier, warehouse picker, drywall hanger—could get into that would require him to escape under cover of night, leaving everything behind.

But I guessed old ways of thinking died hard.

Now, I sat backwards in a chair and stared at the tank as I nursed a beer, replaying my conversation with Sammi at the restaurant. What was the real story? Sammi had all but admitted that she followed in her mother's footsteps, namely that they're a couple of con artists. How did I know I wasn't their next victim? But did that make sense? I knew about their backgrounds. I knew all the tricks of the trade. Wouldn't I be the hardest type of person to con? Or because of my overconfidence, would I be the easiest?

I watched the fish swim around for a while, not a care in the world beyond where their next meal was coming from.

Midnight approached, and I was plenty tired, but I wanted to do a little research before turning in. I felt I owed Sammi an answer tomorrow, and if Kristal really was in trouble, there wasn't time to waste.

I booted up my laptop and tried Googling Kristal, using the name Sammi had given me. Sorted through the search results, clicking here and there, diving deep in spots, giving a cursory glance in others. After twenty minutes chasing down possible leads, I stopped clicking.

Nothing substantial to go on. Aside from a few ambiguous mentions, Kristal had not left an electronic trail. Which was pretty hard if you were a regular Joe—or Jane—in today's society. You'd have to really want to stay anonymous to keep such a low online profile.

No Facebook. No Twitter. No Instagram. No nothing.

At least nothing on the names Sammi gave me. Undoubtedly, Kristal would have set up fake profiles on social media, probably created a bogus website or two to support whatever scams she'd been running over the years. I knew because I'd done the same thing. And one of the nicest, most liberating things was saying goodbye to an alias you've used for a while. A little melancholy, maybe, but on the whole, I felt free whenever I'd "kill off" one of my personas and move on to another.

You could reinvent yourself.

You could erase your bad history.

In effect, you were getting a do-over on life, at least on some level.

I was sure Kristal had more of a sordid history than I'd ever be able to track down using Google, but I figured it was worth a shot.

I tried to come to grips with tonight's revelation. As I did, my anger grew. How dare Kristal keep this from me? As the father, I had an absolute right to know about my child, didn't I? Holding back on something like that was criminal. If—when—I saw Kristal, I was tempted to rip her a new one. A *large* new one.

I shut down my computer and went to rinse out my empty beer bottle in the kitchen—really just a kitchenette that opened out into the living area—when I heard a soft knock at the door, followed by a not-so-soft voice.

"Chance? You up?"

I set my bottle in the sink and headed for the door. Because I lived in a cramped, converted garage at the back of my oddball landlord's property, I didn't have far to go. I swung it open, and my oddball landlord, Hobie Harrison, strolled right in.

"Saw the light on. Hope you don't mind a little company." Hobie grabbed the chair I'd been using and dragged it over next to the sofa. Sat down, kicked off his flip-flops, and put his feet up on the scuffed coffee table.

I flopped down on the sofa. "Don't you ever sleep?"

"Sure, I sleep. Just need three hours a night, though. Probably the only advantage of being old. That and getting a discount at the movies."

Hobie had to be at least seventy, although he kept in pretty good shape. "Want a beer?"

"No, thanks. Already consumed my share for the day." He spread his arms wide, gesturing to the place I'd called home since I got out of prison. "It's all shaping up nicely."

Hobie always said that, and I could never tell if he was serious or simply mocking me. I hadn't changed a thing since the first week I'd moved in, three years ago. "Thanks."

"You're the best tenant I've ever had."

"Aren't I the only one you've ever had?"

"Not if you include my Uncle Smitty." Hobie pointed to one corner of the place, where an old coatrack stood. "That's where he died, right over there. Massive coronary. That was about two weeks before you moved in. He hadn't even unpacked all his stuff yet."

Every time I thought I'd heard all of Hobie's stories, he came up with another one. "Sorry to hear that."

"Eh. I didn't like him much. I was only letting him stay here until he patched things up with Aunt June. He was a dipshit with a gambling problem. And he smelled bad." He winked at me. "Now you, I like. You've been doing real good staying straight, and I admire that. It ain't easy, but I guess it's because you have a good work ethic, big brass balls, and a very caring landlord."

"Thanks. I think." Hobie was always extending a helping hand to ex-cons who needed a boost to get their lives turned around. I'd gotten the sense he'd done something bad when he was young, and was, in his words, giving back. I admired *him* for that.

Hobie reclined, clasped his hands together, and rested them on his stomach. He had a full head of bright white hair and a scraggly beard and wore surfer clothes no matter the season. Today's T-shirt read, "Hang Ten, Mofos," and it looked as if it had been new last decade. "How was your night? Pick up any interesting riders?"

Hobie had this uncanny ability to know when something noteworthy had transpired. He called it his gift, but sometimes I wondered if he hadn't bugged my car or apartment somehow. One afternoon, after he'd surprised me with some knowing comment, I'd actually spent about an hour combing both, searching for tiny electronic spying devices. "As a matter of fact, I did."

He leaned forward, anxious to hear anything lurid or sensational. As usual.

Not one to disappoint, I told him all about Sammi.

By the time I'd finished, Hobie was on his feet and pacing the small living area. "Holy cats! You've got a daughter. And you never knew about her. That must blow your mind."

I pulled out my phone, called up the picture of Sammi I'd taken. Showed it to Hobie.

"Wow. Just wow. She looks exactly like you, man. The spitting image. Especially the scowl."

I took my phone back. Examined the picture. Our features did look similar, but the only person I saw in Sammi was Kristal. "First off, there's been no confirmation she's my daughter. And second, yeah, it kinda does blow my mind. I mean, there's a mini-me out there. From what I could tell, she's a good kid. Her career path might need a little redirection, but basically, she seemed on the ball. Smart, attractive, clever." I smiled. "That does sound like a kid of mine, doesn't it?"

Hobie stopped pacing and headed for the fridge. Brought a beer back and popped it open. "Your story made me thirsty." He guzzled about half the bottle, then belched. "So, what are you going to do?"

"What do you think I should do?" I knew Hobie was going to tell me, whether I asked or not, so I figured I'd let him go first.

"Glad you asked. You're a nice guy, Chance. Sometimes too nice. And I guess she really could be your kid, but…" He shrugged. "You should find out more about the situation. If you discover something fishy's going on, then cut bait. You know how most of these things go. Someone's out to separate you from your hard-earned cash." He tipped his beer and swallowed the rest of the bottle. "I don't have much on my plate the next few days, so if you need someone to ride shotgun, I'm your hombre."

"Thanks. I'll let you know."

Hobie rose and dropped his empty bottle into the recycling bin with a clank as he made his way to the door. "Goodnight," he said, eyes twinkling, then added, "Pops."

He left, shutting the door behind him.

I remained on the sofa, trying to come to grips with tonight's revelation. Was I really a father? Sammi's father? The timing seemed to work. Sammi looked an awful lot like Kristal, eerily so, and although I wasn't sure I saw it, Hobie was convinced she looked just like me. I examined the selfies we took, searching for the tiniest clue that she really was my flesh and blood.

What kind of father would I have made?

Certainly, as a twenty-year-old, I was a fuck-up. Irresponsible. Immature. Selfish. Would having been thrust into the role of father accelerated my maturity? Or would I have just screwed up Sammi? Kristal wasn't any more mature than I'd been, but she'd raised Sammi on her own, and if appearances counted for much, she'd done a good job.

But *had* she raised Sammi on her own? Maybe there *had* been a father figure involved. Maybe this Granger guy had been more of an influence than Sammi admitted.

I realized I hadn't asked Sammi about any of her upbringing. Where had she grown up? Had she moved around a lot? What kind of childhood traumas had she weathered? Had Kristal ever had a stable, long-lasting relationship with a man? So many questions. No answers.

One thing I did know. Kristal had raised Sammi like my parents had raised me—to be a con artist. I wasn't sure how I felt about that. Conflicted, to say the least. I mean, being quick on your feet and clever and ruthless had kept me alive as a young adult, and it had paid the rent, but ultimately, I regretted it. I wished I'd channeled my talent in a more productive, more socially accepted fashion. Ripping off people and running from the law was not the way to achieve enlightenment and self-actualization.

It was the way to prison. Or worse.

I wished someone had swooped in and changed my career path when I was nineteen. I could have avoided prison. I could have pursued a career, a main hustle, and avoided the perpetual side hustles.

Back to the decision at hand. For argument's sake, I assumed Sammi was my daughter. Would I help her, based upon what she told me?

Yeah, I would.

And if she wasn't my daughter? Kristal was still her mom, and I'd cared for her—a lot, back in the day. Would I help Kristal out? After what she'd done to me?

That answer wasn't as clear, but if I had to help Kristal in order to help Sammi, then so be it.

After their current situation was resolved, *then* I could provide Sammi the type of guidance a father should provide. I could help her break free from her current path using my own experiences and poor choices as object lessons. What to avoid. What *not* to do.

And Sammi would heed my fatherly advice and find some honorable way to make a decent living.

Because all nineteen-year-old girls listened to their fathers.

Yeah, right.

Chapter Four

Twenty years ago

Krissy slammed the apartment door behind her, and for a moment, I thought the doorframe might splinter. She slammed the door—on occasion—when we'd get into an argument, but I think this might have been the first time she'd slammed it because she was euphoric.

We'd run home from the Blues Festival and were still panting as we flopped on our second-hand futon, side-by-side. The futon had so many stains it looked as if the fabric had come from a Holstein cow.

"Three hundred twenty-seven dollars." Krissy held up the bills and fanned them out, then fanned me with them. "Best haul yet."

We'd worked the crowd at the festival for about three hours, pickpocketing unsuspecting victims. We'd target the tourists in their designer clothes, artfully remove their wallets or purses from their pants or pocketbooks, take a few bills, then either put the wallets back or hand them over, with a "Hey mister, I think you dropped this."

They'd take a quick look inside to make sure their money and credit cards were still there, see bills lined up, then a sigh of relief as they offered up a genuine thanks. One guy even gave us a twenty-buck reward, on top of the forty we'd pilfered.

Service with a smile.

"We're getting much better at this, wouldn't you say?" Krissy had developed a great touch. Light and quick, oh so quick.

"Yes, I would say. You're a fast learner, all right."

"No one is ever going to catch us." Krissy's smile hadn't dimmed a watt. I knew she got off on the possibility of getting caught, and her adrenaline was running as high as I'd ever seen it. I enjoyed the thrill of it, too, but I'd been at it a lot longer. I'd been caught before, too. Nothing but a hand slap, but the experience had tempered my excitement. For me, it was just a way to make a few needed bucks.

"That's not the right attitude. We aren't invincible. We can be caught. Don't forget that, or it will happen a lot sooner than you think."

Krissy threw the money up in the air, like confetti, and tilted her head upward so several bills landed on her face. She brushed them away with a laugh. "Don't worry so much. You sound like my old man."

She took my hand in hers. She had slim wrists—slim everything, really—but she was a lot stronger than she looked. "We make a great team, don't we?"

"That we do."

"So, what's our next caper?" She turned toward me, face aglow with eagerness. Krissy was a fun-loving girl, and she went from zero to bubbling over with excitement in three seconds flat. One of the things I loved about her. But life wasn't all fun and games.

"Caper? This isn't some old-time Cary Grant movie where the crooks always end up rich and happy. These aren't capers."

"Sounding like Dad some more." She let go of my hand, kicked off her sandals, got up. "Wanna get high? Drunk?"

"No, I don't. Maybe we should talk about this a little bit."

Krissy pushed out her full, ripe lips, and her pout never looked sexier. "If we're going to have some kind of conversation," she threw air quotes around the word, "then I'm going to need some fortification. Wine?"

"No, thanks."

She plodded across the small living area and into the kitchen.

I kept my eyes on her and tried to concentrate on the matter at hand. We'd been living together for three months now, and at first, it was mostly a way to save money on rent and food, and have a handy sex partner. Grins and giggles, as Krissy always liked to put it. And things hadn't really changed over those three months. We'd pull a handful of penny-ante jobs to cover expenses, maybe splurge on some wine or some weed. Every once in a while, we'd take some bullshit server job or stock clerk job, but those rarely lasted more than a few weeks. Yeah, we'd skim a little off the top or swipe some stuff from the storeroom, but I guess we just got bored. And what could you do with half a dozen economy packages of AA batteries? Stand on the street corner and sell them?

Living on the edge in a rundown shithole of an apartment with secondhand stained furniture wasn't boring. Not when we had each other.

But I knew that, unless we were extremely careful and utterly disciplined, we'd get caught. It had happened to most of my family members over the years, and while I considered myself smarter and more capable than any of them, I wasn't completely divorced from reality. Committing crimes was dangerous. Part of the allure, sure, but a risk that had to be managed.

Krissy returned with a tumbler full of red wine poured over a few ice cubes. We bought the cheapest stuff available—actually, we got an older friend to buy the cheapest stuff available because we were only seventeen. But wine was wine— either red, white, or rosé—and we didn't know the difference between merlot or pinot grigio or cabernet or some other French word. Didn't matter much to us as long as it got us where we were going.

She snuggled next to me, emptied half the tumbler in two large gulps. Held up the glass. "Sure you don't want any? It's yummy."

"No, thanks. Look, today was great, but every day is not going to turn out like this. Every job isn't going to be successful. And what we've been doing is small potatoes. When the jobs get bigger, they get more complicated. And that means more planning and more discipline."

She put her hand on my thigh. I shifted slightly. I was trying to have a conversation.

"And there's something else I've been thinking about. A lot."

"Oh, now you're a big thinker?"

"It's been bothering me."

"What has?"

"Ripping off people who don't deserve it."

"What are you talking about?"

"There are plenty of shitheads in the world, right?"

She cocked her head at me funny. "Yeah. So?"

"So, we should be targeting them. Assholes. Thieves. Rich lawyers. Politicians. You know, people who deserved to get taken down a peg."

"Some kind of Robin Hood thing?"

"Not exactly. But..."

"When did you develop a conscience?"

I shrugged. "Seems like they might even have more money. And it would definitely be more fun, right?"

Krissy smiled and raised her glass to me in a mock toast, then she tilted her head back and drained the remaining wine. "Speaking of fun."

She took my hand, pulled me up off the couch. I started to talk about how we needed to work together to achieve our goals, but she placed a slender finger on my lips. "Shh."

She tugged on my arm, hauling me toward the bedroom. "I want to show you something." She giggled. "Actually, I want to show you a few things."

* * *

The next morning, I texted Sammi and arranged for us to meet. I suggested a coffee shop not too far from where I lived, a place where I knew the owner would give us a quiet table in the back so we could talk. Sammi countered by suggesting we meet at the National Zoo, saying it was the perfect place for a father to take his daughter. I could practically see the sarcasm dripping from the words of her text.

I went along, though, and now we were sitting on a bench near the tiger exhibit. Sammi held a giant mass of pink cotton candy in one hand and plucked snatches from it with the other. A cup of soda was wedged between her legs. She'd wanted the cotton candy, a bag of peanuts, some animal crackers, and a Coke. I'd negotiated her down to the sticky pink confection and a drink, figuring even that was enough sugar to fuel an entire kindergarten class.

"Come here often?" I asked.

"First time. Mom was always too busy to take me places, especially cool places. Never went to the zoo. Never went to the circus. Never went bowling or to Chuck E. Cheese or played soccer or took ballet or learned how to play the cello."

"You wanted to learn how to play the cello?"

"No. But I would have liked to have been asked, you know? I missed out on my childhood, always getting dragged to this place or that. Do you know we moved seven times before I turned ten? Tough to make friends that way."

I felt a pang in my stomach. Regret? Loss? The shame of being a bad father? I mean, I didn't take her anyplace cool either. Of course, I hadn't even known I was Sammi's father. Another pang, and this one was anger directed at Kristal. "We don't have a time machine. All we can do is move forward." I nodded at the tiger enclosure across the walkway. "Don't live in the past. Ever forward. Like a tiger."

"You mean caged up until you die?"

"I'm new at this fatherly advice thing. Give me a break, okay?"

Sammi glanced at her phone, for the twentieth time in the last three minutes. "Can we get on with this?"

"Sure. Just to recap. Your mom borrowed three hundred and fifty thousand dollars to run a scam, and now the guy she borrowed it from wants it back. With interest. The money from the original loan is gone, as part of this scam your mom and Granger were running, and Granger stole the rest. If the loanshark doesn't get his money back, soon, he's threatened to kill you and your mom. That sum it up?"

"Yup." Sammi slurped some of her Coke.

"Is there any possibility your mom can save the con?"

"None whatsoever. Mom says they caught on and told her they'd be calling the cops if she tried to get any of their money back. Said they had recordings and everything. Three hundred thousand, down the drain."

I didn't remark on the incredibly sloppy work exhibited by Kristal and Granger. Letting that much money out of your control, even if you thought your con was a mortal lock, wasn't a wise move.

Sammi stuck her drink back on the bench between her thighs. "You can say it."

"What?"

"Mom fucked up, big time."

Kristal was in a heap of trouble, with no clear way out. I'd been in similar situations, and I knew how she must have felt. Scared, anxious, frantic, determined, and hopeless all at the same time. "What can I do?"

She cocked her head and smirked. "I don't suppose you have half a million dollars lying around."

"I drive for Ryde. I don't have fifty bucks lying around."

"Then find Granger, for starters. Mom thinks that maybe this loanshark, Norbert something I think is his name, might accept the fifty thousand he took as a down payment. Buy us some more time."

"Your mother borrowed money from Yelton Norvetch?" I'd been out of the game for a while, but even I knew Norvetch by reputation.

"Yeah, that's the dude's name. Norvetch."

"He's not a nice man."

"No shit."

We sat in silence. I was picturing Norvetch doing terrible things to Kristal and Sammi. I didn't know what Sammi was thinking, but I had to assume it was along those lines, too.

She grabbed my hand, and hers was still a bit sticky from the cotton candy. "Please help us. I don't know where else to turn. You cared for Mom once. And I'm your daughter. Family is everything, right?"

My throat felt dry. Family was important. And if I'd had my way, I would have married Kristal. Before she disappeared on me, of course. As for Sammi, if she was my daughter... "I've given this whole thing some thought, and I am willing to help, but—"

Sammi squealed and started clapping. "I knew you would. I just knew it."

"Hang on."

She slowly stopped carrying on. "What?"

"There are conditions."

She gave me a large helping of side-eye. "Such as?"

"Look. This life might seem glamorous, exciting. I know it did to me when I was your age. It seems fun, pretending you are who you aren't, stepping into some other persona, but it's only temporary. You can't really hide from yourself. And when you finally look into the mirror and see who you really are—five years later, ten—trust me, you don't want to feel like I did. Like you wanted to punch that asshole in the face for wasting the best years of your life."

Sammi rolled her eyes, as if she'd heard this speech a thousand times before. Had Kristal delivered some version of it on occasion? "Okay, I get it. You're sorry you conned people. You're sorry you went to jail. You're sorry you drive for Ryde and have fifty bucks to your name. What does all that have to do with helping us?"

"After we extricate your mom from this mess, I want you to promise that you're done with all this. No more scamming people. No more grifting."

Sammi sat still again, as if she were some prey for one of the nearby tigers and didn't want to be spotted. After a full minute, she slowly turned to me. "If you save my mom and me, I'll do it. I'll go straight."

I nodded. I didn't trust her for one second; a con artist's words were made of spun sugar just like the cotton candy Sammi had devoured, but it was a start. If I saved Kristal, then I'd force my way into Sammi's life. I had that right, didn't I? That responsibility? Once involved, I'd do my best to help her live up to her potential. Show her a different path to happiness. My experience had to count for something, didn't it? "Okay, then. There's another condition. I'm in charge. I'm calling the shots here. All of them."

Sammi introduced me to her pouty face. "But you don't know all the details."

"You can fill me in."

"Come on, Chance. I may be nineteen on the outside, but inside, I'm, like, thirty."

I eyed flecks of cotton candy around her mouth and the flip-flops adorned with pink sequins she wore. "Uh-huh. You asked me to help, so if you really want my help, you need to let me do it my way." I smiled, patted her hand. "Don't worry, I'm sure you'll be plenty involved."

Sammi sighed so loud I thought the tigers might recoil. "Okay. But I have one condition for you."

"Oh? What?"

"You can't tell Mom you're helping out, at least at first."

"Why not?"

"She'd go ballistic. Through the roof. She'd be pissed that I asked for help at all, and she'd fucking flip out if she knew I asked *you*. She'd kill me before Norvetch had an opportunity to."

"Does she hate me?"

Sammi shook her head as if I were the village idiot, and maybe I was. "It's the opposite, Chance. She never stops talking about you, and if she found out you knew about her messed-up situation, she'd never forgive me. She can't stand to show weakness."

"Oh. So, it's all about you."

"Of course. It always is."

I waited for some ironic smile, but she looked dead serious. I might have been feeling bad about missing out on Sammi's early childhood, but I wasn't so sure about her teenage years. I might have dodged a bullet there. "You want to be involved in this? Fine. What should be my first move?"

She was ready with her answer. "Follow Mom. Make sure she doesn't do anything stupid."

"How is following her going to get her money back?"

Sammi gave a half-hearted shrug.

"Why do I get the feeling you're not telling me everything?"

Another sigh. "Okay. I think she's going to do two things. She's going to try to scrounge up money from anybody she can, but I doubt she'll come up with much. And she's going after Granger. To get his money. You need to protect her, mostly from herself."

"I thought he disappeared."

"Evidently, Mom thinks she can track him down. They were together for about a year, and she thinks she's on his wavelength. Or some such bullshit. She doesn't tell me everything, you know."

I didn't know, but it was Kristal's style to play things close to the vest, only parceling out info when and where it was needed. I had a feeling that was a trait Sammi shared. "Is Granger dangerous?"

"He's a douchebag, but he's not what I would call dangerous. Although sometimes his BO is bad." She gave me a fake smile. "He's nothing you can't handle, I'm sure."

"People can be deceptive." I paused a beat. "As I'm sure you well know."

She waved her hand as if she were shooing gnats. "When can you get started?"

I didn't have too much on my plate at the moment. "How's first thing tomorrow morning?"

"How's in an hour?"

"Well, I—"

"There's nothing more important than this. You can drive around drunken losers next week."

I stifled a laugh. I could tell Sammi was used to getting her way. Just like her mother. "Okay. You win."

"Of course." She swiped her phone screen, then started tipping and tapping. "I'm sending you a picture of him and his car."

"Fine." I opened the texts on my phone, and the face of a good-looking guy with a pleasant smile stared back at me, which didn't really surprise me. Kristal's type. I used to fit that mold, but after I got out of prison, I'd let myself go a bit. From the looks of him, Granger hadn't spent any time inside. It was in the eyes. Prison dulled that internal spark.

"Get it?" Sammi asked.

"Yep. All set. If there's anything else you think might be helpful, please send it along."

"I will. And you'll let me know how things are going, right?"

"Of course. I'll keep you informed every step of the way. Because it's all—"

"About me. Yes, I know." She bounced off the bench, leaving her soda and cotton candy detritus behind.

I remained seated. "Go on, I need to make a call."

She cocked her head, probably unsure if I was stringing her along, as if I might just spend the rest of the day strolling around the zoo gawking at the animals. "Okay. But don't waste too much time. Mom could be getting into trouble this minute." She stood before me a moment, then lunged in for the most awkward hug in the history of hugs. She wrapped her arms around me and gave me a quick embrace. Her fingers traced a sticky cotton-candy trail across my neck.

I barely had the chance to hug her back before she straightened and stepped back.

"Um, goodbye, then," she said, giving me a wiggly-fingered wave.

"Goodbye." I responded with a feeble wave back, still trying to catch my breath from being caught off guard.

Sammi turned and took off down the paved pathway. I watched her go, a proud father, even though I had absolutely nothing to do with her growth and development, aside from being there at its very beginning.

Maybe.

I removed a Ziploc bag from my pocket, unfolded it, and set it on my lap. Then I carefully removed the straw from her cup, placed it inside the bag, and sealed it up. Ready to send, along with a DNA sample from me, to the lab for a paternity test. The way I collected the sample wouldn't hold up in court, of course, but I didn't care about that. I just needed to know if Sammi was my daughter.

I slipped the bag into my pocket, got up from the bench, and headed to my car.

I had someone to follow.

Chapter Five

I'd learned the streets of the DC area quite well over the past five months, driving for Ryde, so I took a few shortcuts on my way to Kristal's apartment in Wheaton, MD. Off of Connecticut Avenue, a couple miles outside the Beltway. Her building was tucked away in an enclave of garden-style apartments, four or five adjacent complexes melting into one amorphous grouping of moderately priced dwellings. It was the type of community found in just about any area of the country. Anonymous. Generic. Mundane.

The perfect place to blend right in. I bet Kristal didn't even know her next-door neighbor.

I parked across the street from her building and slumped down in the seat. I opened up a newspaper—old-school—and read the Sports section as I waited for Kristal to get going. Earlier, Sammi had texted me some more information she thought would be helpful. A photo of her mom's car, a list of some of her usual hangouts, and the names of a few friends, in case I bumped into them. It was all fairly random, but I guessed it wouldn't hurt. She also said she'd let me know when her mom left the apartment. She ended her barrage of texts with a smiley-face emoji with two hearts for eyes.

I examined the apartment building. Uniform in its nondescript beigeness. Two stories. Most of the balconies seemed to double as storage areas for bicycles and other crap. For the most part, the parking area was full of older American cars, with a smattering of newer foreign models. The landscaping, such as it was, seemed designed not to get in the way of anything. All in all, it reminded me a lot of the place Kristal and I lived in together for those eight months. The rent was low, and we got what we paid for. The bathroom faucet dripped, no matter how many new washers I put in. The refrigerator ran hot and cold—literally. And the walls were so thin we had to whisper when we hashed out some of our schemes.

We were so in love, we didn't care about any of it.

It wasn't much of a kitchen table—it really was just an old folding card table we'd liberated from a dumpster—and technically it wasn't in the kitchen, only the back two legs of a folding chair touched the peel 'n stick vinyl kitchen floor, but we kept up the illusion as some kind of weird homage to growing up in a real house with a kitchen large enough for a table.

I was drawing diagrams on a clipboard, over and over, trying to explain our next scam to Krissy. It was only ten in the morning, but she was already on her second glass of "fortified grape juice," and she was having a tough time concentrating.

"Okay, look. We need to get this down, or it will never work."

"How many times do we need to go through this?" She rolled the bottom of her glass on the table, watching the crimson liquid swish back and forth.

"As many times as we need to." I pointed to my latest diagram. "Here's the intersection. You'll be waiting here," I pointed to a spot a foot off the curb, in the right-hand lane. "And try to stay where the driver can't see you, either out the window, or in the side view mirror."

"Can't see me. Right."

"Wait until you see Hufnagel's car, okay?" We'd identified a rich asshole telecom lobbyist as our target, and we were staking out a spot near the garage where he parked for work. I pointed to an area on the sidewalk, fifteen feet away. "I'll be here. Watching your every move."

"You always do like to watch me, don't you?" She smiled, and I was reminded of the devil.

"Krissy. This is serious."

"Sorry." She sipped from her glass, then her gaze drifted over my shoulder, out the grimy window. "Nice day today, huh?"

I slapped my pen down on the clipboard. "Do you want to do this? Make some serious money? Or do you want to keep putting your hands in old men's pockets, reaching for their wallets and who knows what else?"

Her head snapped back. "I told you I'm paying attention. Get on with it, okay?"

I stared at her a beat. She stared back. I picked up my pen. "When the light turns green, you need to time it just right. And whatever you do, don't take any unnecessary chances. This is dangerous enough without taking crazy risks."

She grinned her devilish grin again. "Since when do I take crazy risks?"

"Uh huh." I exhaled. Maybe I was being too anal about all of this. We'd been over it a dozen times, covering every conceivable contingency. Underneath the alcohol and the practiced nonchalance, Krissy did have an impressive capability to absorb stuff. At some point, I'd just have to trust her.

"Are we done yet, teach?"

"If you think you've got a handle on things, sure, we're done."

"Good." She stood, undid the button on her skimpy jeans shorts, and shimmied out of them. No panties on underneath. She pulled off her t-shirt. No bra on, either. Then she straddled me, where I still sat on the chair. "Well, teacher, I've been a bad student, haven't I? I think you need to discipline me. And I'm practically incorrigible, so you'd better discipline me hard."

I gave her as much discipline as I could muster.

Twenty minutes later, I disciplined her again.

* * *

At ten the next morning, we were in position—Krissy on her bike, hugging the curb, me on the sidewalk, leaning against a wall, acting chill. Ten minutes into our wait, Hufnagel's dark green Jaguar pulled up into the right lane next to Krissy's bike. Turn signal blinking. I saw the muscles in her long, lean legs tense and knew it was go time.

The light was red, and there was a No Turn On Red sign posted, but Hufnagel inched forward, ready to make the turn as soon the light changed. A straggling man with a cane was the last pedestrian to clear the crosswalk, just as the light for the cross-street turned yellow.

The light turned green, and the Jag started its turn.

And Krissy started her turn, too.

The car and the bike were barely moving when there was a loud thud, and then

Krissy's bike was down, and she was down, too. The car slammed on its brakes, and Robert Hufnagel hopped out and ran around the front of the car. "Are you okay?" he called to Krissy, who remained sprawled half in the street, half up on the curb.

She didn't say anything, and then I flew into action, running up beside her. "You hurt?"

Krissy looked at me, eyes moist. "My leg is killing me. And my neck, too."

I knelt. "Just take it easy."

Hufnagel stood there. "I didn't see you."

"We should call 911," I said, phone already in hand.

"Okay, sure," Hufnagel said, after a moment of hesitation.

"Hold on," Krissy said. "I don't think I'm hurt that bad. I don't want all the fuss. And I think they charge you for ambulance visits, don't they? I can't afford that." Then she looked over at her bike, lying on its side, four feet from the Jag's bumper. Her face went wild. "My bike! Oh shit, I need my bike."

"Hang on a minute." Hufnagel went over, picked up the bike, and hauled it onto the curb. "Let me move my car out of the intersection, and I'll be back."

"Don't run off, buddy!" Krissy said, still sitting on her butt on the curb. "Would you mind taking a picture of his car and license plate, just in case?" she said to me.

"Absolutely." I made a big show of taking the pictures. I snapped one of Hufnagel, too. I didn't think he'd take off, but we needed to play our roles. While he moved the car, I knelt again and pretended to console Krissy.

"We got him, I can feel it," Krissy whispered.

"Let's not start counting our chickens," I said. "Once we've got the money in our pocket, then we can celebrate." I examined her knee. She had scraped it a bit. "Does this hurt?"

"Nah. I'm tough."

"That you are." I glanced at Hufnagel, who'd parked in a loading zone twenty yards away. He circled his car around the front and examined the right side, where he thought his car had hit Krissy's bike. They hadn't actually collided; the loud thud he'd heard was Krissy smacking the car with her palm. "Okay, here he comes." I went back into caring-stranger mode. When Hufnagel got within earshot, I said, "Maybe you should have that knee looked at. You never know with knees."

Hufnagel came up, ignored me, and spoke to Krissy. "You sure you're okay?"

"I'll live," she said. "But I'm afraid my bike wasn't so lucky."

He took a step toward it, gave it the once-over. "Doesn't seem so bad."

I joined him at the bike. Bent down, ran my fingers along the frame. "I don't know. Looks like the frame's bent." I did know; Krissy and I had carefully bent and dented the frame beforehand. "And once the frame's bent..." I added for good measure.

"Maybe it is a little." He frowned, then tilted his head at me. "Do you know her?"

"What? No. Why?" I asked, an edge to my voice.

"Never mind." He glanced at his watch, an expensive gold model, peeking out from French cuffs.

I went back to Krissy and helped her up. She groaned appropriately as she straightened. If conning people didn't work out, she could make it as an actress, with that talent and her good looks. She kinked her neck to the side a few times, wincing like a pro, then limped over to the bike and gave it a longer examination than I had. "It's totaled."

"Totaled? Really?" Hufnagel said. "Looks like you could get it fixed." He glanced at his watch again. Drops of perspiration appeared on his receding hairline. "I really need to get going."

"What about my bike?" Krissy said.

"Look, I sympathize, I do. But you bicyclists need to be more careful, you know?"

Krissy's eyes narrowed, just as we'd role-played. "This was your fault, buddy. I had the right-of-way."

"That's not how I saw it. The light changed, and I made the turn. You came out of nowhere—not even a bike lane here, by the way—and smashed into me. Unfortunately, car beats bike every day of the week."

She reached for her phone, tucked into her pocket. "I'm calling the cops."

"Go ahead. Your word against mine." He jutted his chin out, challenging.

I stepped forward and raised my hand tentatively, as if I didn't want to really contradict anyone. "Actually, I saw the whole thing."

Hufnagel spun in my direction. "Yeah?"

I pointed to the nearby building. "I was leaning on the wall there, drinking my coffee. I, uh, noticed the girl on the bike..." I flashed Krissy an embarrassed smile,

"...and then the light changed, and she went ahead and you just kinda plowed into her, without looking."

"This is some kinda scam, isn't it?"

"What?" Krissy's face got red. "A scam? You practically kill me and then accuse me of a scam? I am calling the cops, and then I'm going to get a lawyer, and I'm going to sue your ass into next week. Hell, into next month!" She started limping toward Hufnagel, as if she were going to get right up in his face and let him have it some more.

I intervened, putting a light hand on Krissy's shoulder. "Hold up, hold up. Let's just take a breath." I gave Hufnagel a knowing, I'll settle her down nod. "I don't think you should escalate things. That will be bad for both of you. And boy, once the lawyers get involved, nobody wins except the lawyers. I'm sure there's a way to settle this thing that will make each of you, well, if not happy, then at least not totally pissed off."

I backed up, smiled at Krissy. "Sound okay?"

She pouted, then gave me a tiny nod.

I looked at Hufnagel. "Keep the cops and lawyers out of this?"

"I am a lawyer." He sighed. "But, okay." Then, to Krissy, "What would make you not pissed off?"

"My bike is ruined, and I need a new one."

"How much is a new bike?"

"This is a good model. I'd say about $900."

Hufnagel reacted like he'd been socked in the gut. The number shocked me, too, because Krissy and I had agreed that $400 was about the cut-off for an on-the-spot, quick-and-dirty settlement. Anything higher was problematic, for two reasons. One, it was unlikely Hufnagel had more than $400 on him, and two, once you got above $400, the feeling of getting royally ripped off kicked in. People who felt they were getting taken advantage of—no matter how wealthy they were—tended to dig in their heels.

I held my breath, waiting for Hufnagel's response, although I had a good guess what it would be. I was getting pissed off myself, thinking that Krissy freewheeling it might blow the deal. Four hundred bucks was a lot better than zilch.

Hufnagel stared at Krissy, then glanced at me. He took a deep breath, as if he were trying to calm himself—which I'm sure he was. If I was in his position, I might just blow my stack. But I knew he was doing the mental calculus, balancing the amount of his time it would take to defend himself, and the sheer inconvenience, multiplied by the likelihood that a judge would find him guilty, to come up with his answer.

"Nine hundred seems like a lot." He reached into his back pocket and pulled out his wallet. I exhaled. We had him.

He opened and flipped through the bills with his index finger. "I've got $650 right here. That enough to get a new bike and make this go away? I'm late for a very important meeting."

We blew that $650 in a week, but we had fun doing it.

My buzzing phone interrupted my reminiscence. A text from Sammi. *Mom is on her way. Good luck!* This time, she followed it with an emoji I couldn't make out.

Kristal emerged from her building through the center exit. She wore jeans, a white blouse, and black boots, with a black purse thrown over her shoulder, nothing remarkable in the least, but my breath caught. Her blonde hair flowed back over her shoulders as if she was going eighty miles an hour. When I was with her, it always seemed she was.

She turned down the short sidewalk between the building and the parking lot, clicking her remote as she walked to her car. The lights on a sleek black Audi flashed, and a moment later, she hopped in.

She gunned the engine, then reversed out of the spot and sped out of the parking area.

I waited a few seconds, then started my engine and followed.

I had no reason to think Kristal believed she was being tailed, but I didn't want to take any chances, so I hung back a bit. If I lost her, I figured I could ask Sammi to text her mom and find out where she was. It wasn't a perfect contingency plan, but there was no telling what might happen if Kristal found out I was following her, and with her temper, physical violence wasn't out of the question. Better to risk losing her than losing a limb.

She headed south on Connecticut, under the Beltway overpass. Even though it was early afternoon, traffic was heavy. More and more, it seemed, traffic was thick no matter what time of day. But it moved okay, and there was a minimum of bleating horns. This wasn't New York, after all. I kept several car lengths behind, changing lanes every couple of blocks, in case she was keeping an eye on her rearview mirror.

She put her turn signal on, so I changed lanes to get behind her. When she got the green arrow, she turned left, and I followed the traffic, also turning left. The cat and mouse continued, for another few turns and another few miles. Finally, Kristal pulled into a decrepit strip center and parked in a handicapped space. I hung back at the mouth of the parking lot, engine running.

She hopped out and strode toward Paddy's Pawn Shop, long legs eating up the sidewalk. I inched my car up until I got a decent view inside the store. Kristal seemed to be waiting patiently for the dude at the counter to finish up with a customer.

After selling what seemed to be a saxophone, the customer finally left, and I got a good glimpse of the guy working behind the counter. Pudgy, balding, what looked to be a full sleeve of ink on one arm. Kristal stepped forward. She leaned over the counter, and the man also leaned forward until their heads met.

The intimate conversation only lasted about thirty seconds. Then Kristal straightened abruptly, pointed at the guy, and seemed to shout something. He yelled back, and there were some ugly hand gestures, and then Kristal stormed out of the pawn shop.

It was tough to tell at this distance, but her face had turned a couple of shades darker. She slid into her car and slammed the door, started up her engine, and roared out of the parking lot.

Whatever had transpired in the pawn shop hadn't gone her way.

I took off after her, and she upped her speed to about ten miles per hour above the limit, darting from lane to lane, passing slower-moving vehicles. I had my hands full trying to keep up, but driving as much as I did had honed my skills substantially. We were heading farther up-county, and the traffic thinned.

Which meant she could go faster. Which also meant I had fewer cars to hide among. I found a Suburban going at a pretty good clip and ducked in behind it. Every so often, I'd swing wide into the adjacent lane to make sure Kristal was still ahead of us.

About ten minutes later, she turned off the main thoroughfare, and I did the same. A couple of turns later, she pulled into the lot for Amigo's.

Judging by the twenty or so Harleys parked out front, Amigo's was a biker bar. Kristal's Audi didn't really fit in, and she must have realized it because she ignored a number of parking spaces in front and drove around the side.

I stayed on the street, pulled up tight on the curb, so I had a view of the front door, but couldn't see exactly where Kristal had parked. The bar was little more than a square brick house that had been converted into a bar, and if there hadn't been a big throwback neon *Amigo's* sign out front, you wouldn't know the difference.

Aside from the row of hogs, of course.

A moment later, Kristal came chugging around the corner. In her jeans and boots, she could certainly pass for a biker mama. I, on the other hand, would have a tougher time blending in, so I decided to stay in the car and let my imagination run amok.

I didn't have enough time for my imagination to even get in gear. Kristal came charging out of the bar less than two minutes after going in, and if possible, she looked even more pissed-off than before. She disappeared around the corner of the bar, and I started my engine. I had a feeling I might have more trouble keeping up with her now.

Her car came barreling around the corner, hit a patch of gravel, and fishtailed out of the parking lot onto the street. She spun the wheel around and steered back in the direction she'd come, flying right past my front bumper with about three inches to spare. I'd barely had time to duck so she wouldn't spot me. I jammed my car into gear, quickly pulled a U-turn, and sped after her, my own tires squealing.

The pattern continued for another hour and a half.

Kristal visited a car title loan place. Another pawn shop. A dry cleaners. A diner. And yet a third pawn shop. At each destination, she'd pop in for a few minutes, then emerge as if she was escaping prison.

A couple of times during the afternoon, Sammi had texted me, wanting an update. Each time, I'd been vague and non-committal with my response. Told her nothing much was going on. No need to confirm her fears about how desperate her mother really was. Besides, it was tough to relay any details when I didn't *have* any details.

At least Kristal hadn't pulled up in front of a bank, donned a ski mask, and darted inside carrying an AK-47. Yet.

I riffed on that idea, and for a brief moment, imagined she'd robbed each establishment she'd visited. But nobody had come chasing after her, and if she was going that route, she would have picked some bigger, wealthier targets. And if she *had* somehow scored big, she would have quit. My very first assessment still stood. She was after some quick cash, and whatever she was peddling, nobody was buying.

I didn't know how much longer Kristal would keep trying—being threatened with your life and the life of your child was mighty strong incentive, for sure—but at some point, she'd have to realize her strategy wasn't working. She'd have to come up with a different way to score some cash.

I didn't think that was a good thing. More desperation would lead to more risks, more carelessness, more danger.

After the last fruitless visit—AAA Liquors—Kristal's energy seemed to wane. She trudged back to her car, and from my vantage, I thought I could detect tears on her cheeks. This time, Kristal didn't floor it out of her parking space. She gently backed up, like pretty much every other driver around.

Something about seeing Kristal so visibly upset—and crying—brought back some memories. She hadn't cried often when we'd lived together, but when she had, it always seemed to cut right through me, especially those times when I knew there was nothing I could do to ease her pain.

I felt the same tug now that I'd felt on those occasions—to help her, in any way I could.

Kristal drove south, and her pace had slowed; now she kept more or less to the speed limit as we headed back toward Wheaton.

If Kristal had been looking for Granger, she hadn't found him. And at most of the places she went, it didn't seem like she was really looking for him.

It wasn't too hard to guess how Kristal had been trying to increase her bankroll at each of her stops. At the pawn shops, I assumed she was trying to sell something of value. But what? She hadn't carried in an oil painting or a tray of silverware or a trombone. I had a hard time believing any con artist had much of value besides money. Tough to throw a piano in the back seat when you were skulking out of town in the middle of the night.

At the car title place, she'd probably put her Audi in jeopardy.

At the other places, her motives were unclear. Was she trying to collect a debt from somebody? Kristal never struck me as the type to loan money. And certainly not enormous sums of it.

Dealing drugs? Not really in Kristal's character, at least back then. I guessed desperation changed people's character, but still, drug dealing seemed unlikely.

Other cons? Possibly, but the places she went—the pawn shops, the biker bar, the dry cleaners—all seemed small potatoes. If you were going to run a con, you picked larger fish. Make it worth the effort. You had to go where the money was.

I really had no idea what Kristal was after, but I felt sorry for her, racing around town, trying to scrape together some dough.

It was almost five o'clock, and the traffic thickened the closer we got to the Beltway. When we hit University Boulevard, however, instead of turning west, Kristal turned east. Evidently, there was at least one more stop to make.

This time, no seedy strip shopping center, no biker bar. This time Kristal pulled into a driveway next to a small brick Cape Cod in a neighborhood full of small brick Cape Cods. Two empty planters flanked the front door.

I parked across the street, two houses down, and watched in the rearview mirror as Kristal got out of her car and casually strolled up the walkway to the front door. No jogging, racing, or stomping. Her demeanor had changed entirely.

She rang the bell, and the door opened a moment later. She went inside without a glance backward.

I slumped down in my seat and waited, adjusting the mirror so I could keep an eye on the front door. Was this what private detectives did all day long? Follow cheating spouses around and wait in their cars? I couldn't think of too many more boring endeavors. Of course, I drove people around to make a buck, so maybe I didn't have much of a leg to stand on. Or ass to sit on, as the case may be.

I texted Sammi with an update.

Outside a house in Rockville. Or maybe Kensington. Someplace. Your mom's inside. Still no new info.

She texted back. *I think I know that house. Creepy guy lives there.*

Me: *Dangerous?*

Sammi: *No. Just creepy. Thanks, Chance. Talk later.*

She followed that with a smiley-face emoji.

Fifteen minutes later, the door to the house opened, and Kristal stepped out, big smile on her face. She started to leave, then spun back around on the porch to say another goodbye. A man came out onto the porch to give her a hug.

When they broke apart, I got a good look at the guy.

Medium height, pasty complexion, and one of the biggest beer bellies I'd ever seen.

But I *had* seen it before.

That gut belonged to Jake Petrucci.

Chapter Six

I'd known Jake a long time. In fact, it was Jake who introduced me to Kristal. Jake and I had worked a couple of small things together, and when I had a job that needed a female touch, he'd brought Kristal into the gang. The three of us had collaborated on a number of cons, and after Kristal disappeared, Jake and I worked together on some others. At times, our working relationship was a bit rocky. In truth, Jake was a jerk.

I'd lost touch with him—prison had a way of ruining friendships—but evidently Kristal had not. Was Kristal's visit today just a friendly drop-by, or was something else in the works? Was she trying to enlist his help in this situation? Or was she trying to scam him?

I stayed slumped in my seat until Kristal passed. I could keep tailing her, but to what end? I didn't think following her to another pawn shop or quickie loan place would do much to expand my knowledge of the situation.

Whereas I was reasonably confident a conversation with my long-lost buddy Jake would add a whole lot to my understanding of the situation.

I hopped out, looked both ways like a good boy, and crossed the street.

When Jake answered the door and saw it was me, his pleasant smile first turned to amazement, then morphed back into a huge grin. "Oh my God! If it isn't Chance Damn Winston in the hot damn flesh!"

Hearing him shout out my name triggered a bad memory, something that had happened after the last job we'd pulled together. As I recalled, I wasn't completely happy with how the take got split up. Seemed like Jake grabbed a little more than his fair share. Nothing huge, something on the order of a couple hundred bucks, but still, not cool. I pushed it back into the dark recesses of my mind. I'm sure the statute of limitations on being peeved by something so small had long expired. "What's going on, man?"

Jake leaned in for a bro-hug, but I stuck my hand out for a fist bump. I ended up punching him in the stomach. I'm sure he barely felt it.

"Come in, dude." Jake led me into his house, and we walked down the hall into a large living area in the back, next to the kitchen. Messy and cluttered, just like the Jake I remembered.

He gestured to a worn couch. "Have a seat. Get you something to drink? Beer?"

I waved it off. "I'm good."

He sat in a leather recliner opposite me. Still smiling. His t-shirt rode up in front, making his belly seem larger than it was. And it was already plenty large. I imagined he'd been pounding beers for the last couple of hours. "What brings you around? Now? After all these years?"

I considered staying polite, simply an old friend catching up, then thought about the two hundred bucks he'd ripped me off for. "Guess."

He feigned ignorance. Shrugged.

I didn't say anything, just raised an eyebrow. "You're smarter than that, Jake. Put two and two together."

He exhaled. "Okay. You're here about my previous visitor, right?"

We both knew the truth, but I gave him a curt nod anyway.

"Why are you following her? Trying to pick up where you left off." He tilted his head back and silently counted to himself. I could tell because his lips moved. "What, about twenty years ago?"

"I heard she might be in some trouble."

He roared. "And you're going to swoop back into her life and save her? Ha, that's rich. You were an asshole then, and you're an asshole now."

Takes one to know one. "Why was she here?"

"Fuck you." Jake didn't move, just stared at me, issuing some kind of unspoken challenge. Were he and Kristal a thing? She looked better than she had nineteen years ago, while Jake looked about two hundred percent worse. Even if Kristal had lost all her marbles, she wouldn't go for a guy like Jake.

"Seriously. Someone asked me to help, if I could. I haven't even spoken to Kristal."

"Someone? Had to be Sammi." He shook his head. "Figures."

"What's that supposed to mean?"

"Don't get me wrong, Sammi's a great girl and all, but she doesn't know when to mind her own business. She's always sticking her nose where it don't belong."

I narrowed my eyes at him. "How well do you know her?"

"Well enough."

The smug way he said it made me want to break a few of his teeth. I sucked in a deep breath. "Okay, then. Back to Kristal. Did she tell you exactly what's going on?"

"If she did, why would I tell you?"

"Like I said, I'm trying to help her."

"Says you." He dug his phone out of his pocket. "Maybe I should call her, tell her what's going on."

"Sure, you could do that." I settled into the couch, stretched my arm across the back. "But Sammi seemed to think I'd be more effective if she didn't know I was involved, at least for the time being."

Jake pursed his lips, and I could practically hear the gears grinding in his head. He lowered his phone. "Well…we should do what's best for Kristal, right? Okay. I'll hold off on calling her." He quickly added, "For now. But I'm going to tell her you came by sometime, you know. Doesn't seem right otherwise."

"Sure." I gave him a plastic smile. "So, about Kristal. Why did she stop by?"

"She's in a really tough spot. Her thing fell through, and her partner ditched her, holding the bag. The empty bag. Kristal came by asking if I could lend her some money."

"And did you?"

"I would if I could, but being a graphic artist doesn't pay so great."

"A graphic artist?" I remembered he used to draw cartoons with silly captions and leave them lying around. Most of them featured talking penises.

"Surprised? Really? I always considered myself to be artistic. I've gone straight."

"Is that right?"

A sly grin appeared. "Well, straight*er*. I still partake when something good falls into my lap."

"I don't hustle anymore," I said.

"Oh? Then what *do* you do?"

"This and that. Mostly drive for Ryde."

He raised an eyebrow. "That like Uber?"

"Yeah, but worse in every respect."

Jake nodded, not sure what to say to that.

"Did Kristal say how she's going to get the money she needs?" I asked.

"Not really. She tried to keep calm, but I could tell she was really wound up underneath. Said she had a few more things to try. Then she joked that the next time I might hear from her would be on a long-distance call from Argentina. She wasn't chuckling when she said it, though."

"Do you know Granger?"

"Yeah, I know him. Worked together some."

"Before you went straight?"

He winced. "Right. If you listen to Kristal, she'll say she was really into him, but they were always fighting about something. Sammi hates him. Even before he rabbitted with their money."

"I don't suppose you know where he went?"

"Not a clue. If it were me, I'd be in Katmandu sipping mint juleps or whatever they drink wherever that is." Jake sighed. "I really feel for her. She is so good at what she does, and from what she described, she had this whale on the line for a boatload. Some investment scheme. Her mark was a real shithead, I gather."

The people we set out to scam were usually shady lawyers, sketchy business execs, or worse. People who straddled the line of the law. One benefit for us? They weren't as eager to get the police involved after we'd shafted them for fear of their own dirty exploits being discovered. "Will you do me a favor? For old time's sake? I mean, we did use to be friends, right?"

"Yeah. We did." He made an aw-shucks face. "Still are, really. We went through some times together, didn't we? I'm just bustin' your balls a little, that's all. What we do, right?"

Not really. "Sure. Could you let me know if Kristal contacts you again? What she says? What she's planning?" I rose, and Jake struggled a bit but eventually hoisted his bulk out of the chair.

"Okay. And you do the same, will ya?"

I made a forefinger-thumb gun and shot him. "You got it."

I left out the part about hell freezing over.

* * *

In the past twelve years, Ma had been progressively downsizing. She'd started in a traditional Colonial house, then moved to a smaller contemporary, then down to a townhouse. With each transition, her neighborhood got progressively worse. Now she lived in a shotgun shack one step up from a hovel, in a part of town I didn't like visiting any time of day.

She would deny that her downward mobility was due to decreased income, but she'd been working fewer jobs, smaller jobs, and less lucrative jobs. Basically, she was getting old, and her skills were aging fast, too.

Unfortunately, that didn't deter her from trying to tackle things that were too big and too complex for her. As the saying went, her spirit was willing when nothing else was.

I didn't have time to change clothes, nor did I have time to go home and pick up my toolbox, but I managed to get to my mother's house only ten minutes late. When I walked in, dinner had already started.

Ma no longer used the dining room for dining. Instead, she'd converted it to storage for the detritus of her many multi-level marketing schemes. It was full of hairbrushes that untangled anything, miracle cleaning supplies, scarves made of exotic non-wrinkle fabrics, and supplements that could cure any ailment known to man or beast. Plus, there was a pallet-full of stuff from the Franklin Mint. She claimed that one day she'd use most of it in some kind of hustle, but I think she just liked buying crap advertised on TV by washed-up game show hosts.

The lack of a dining room meant that meals were usually eaten in the family room, on a card table in front of the TV, but whenever more than two people ate a meal, she had to haul out a second one. Now the two flimsy tables were shoved together and covered with a cheap vinyl tablecloth she bought from the clearance aisle at the dollar store.

"Well, look who it is," Ma said, not bothering to get up. Smoke curled up to the ceiling from a cigarette she held between two fingers. She gestured with it to a guy sitting next to her who resembled Colonel Sanders, fluffy white hair on his head and scraggly white hair on his face. "This is Morty. Morty, this is one of my sons, Chance."

Morty nodded and said something with a mouth full of meatloaf.

I hadn't heard Ma mention Morty before, but honestly, I never paid much attention to the names of her many *beaus*. I nodded back and was about to take my seat when I noticed an extra place set at the table. "Who else is here?"

On cue, the toilet flushed from down the hall, and a moment later, my brother Peck sauntered into the room wearing his usual smirk.

"What are you doing here?" If I had known Peck was going to be around, I wouldn't have come. Not my favorite person.

"I live here," he said, pulling out his folding chair and sitting in it.

"Since when?" I was a little peeved that no one had bothered to tell me. On the other hand, I didn't really want to know all the details of my dysfunctional family's goings-on.

"Since a couple of weeks ago," Peck said. "I'm between living arrange-ments."

"Where's your car?" It wasn't parked outside.

"I'm between vehicles at the moment, too." He picked up his fork and pointed it at me. "I don't know why Ma called you, though. I can fix her dishwasher just fine."

Ma coughed loudly and spoke before we could start arguing. "Thanks to both of you for volunteering to help your mother out. But the fact is, the dishwasher started working again on its own, this morning." She stuck a forkful of mashed potatoes in her mouth, but that didn't stop her from continuing to order us around. "Now, Chance, have a seat so we can enjoy a pleasant family dinner, okay?"

Morty nodded. "I'd like to get to know your boys better."

I sat, ignoring Morty, and glared at Peck. He glared back. Lately, he never passed up an opportunity to knife me in the back. We'd been feuding since I told him I no longer wanted to be involved in the family's shady enterprises. He saw it as a lack of loyalty. I saw it as my salvation.

"How's the driving going? Ryde still in business?" Every time he mentioned my gig, his smirk grew.

"At least I get a paycheck." I grabbed the serving platter and took a couple of slices of meatloaf. It looked drier than Ma usually made it, and that was saying something. "Morty, could you pass the potatoes, please?"

Morty struggled to hand over the bowl—it was pretty heavy—and I plopped some onto my plate with an ice cream scoop. They looked much wetter than usual.

"Food's delicious, Arlene," Morty said. "And the company is even better." Then he actually winked at Ma. I could tell the patter of a guy hoping to get laid, and that thought practically turned my stomach.

"Thanks, hon." Ma patted his arm, took a last, long drag from her cigarette, then stubbed it out on her plate, right next to some peas. "You're so sweet to me."

I glanced at Peck to see if he was also nauseated, but he didn't look up from his food. He was my older brother by two years, and as a kid, I idolized him. I followed him around, did whatever he asked, no matter how embarrassing, and took all the shit he rained down on me. Until I turned fifteen, when he got caught taking our neighbor's car for a joyride, and my respect for him dwindled.

I wasn't disappointed he took their car; I was crestfallen he'd gotten caught. My brother—my brilliant, clever, capable, devious, perfect brother—was no better than the lowlifes getting busted nightly. I still loved him—he was my brother, after all—but he'd tumbled from the pedestal and from that point on, I never had any trouble telling him no.

He never liked being told no.

Ma and Morty stopped making googly eyes at each other, and Ma turned to me. "Want a biscuit?" She pushed the plate my way.

"Thanks." I took a biscuit and bit into it. Hard as a rock. Ma's cooking, awful on her best nights, had deteriorated, right along with all her other skills. Sad to see, and I was just dreading the call I knew I was going to get. Ma in jail after she'd messed up some scam and got caught.

"Your mother tells me you got in on a ground-floor opportunity, driving for an up-and-coming ride-sharing outfit," Morty said. "That's what I like to see, an enterprising young man."

"Yeah, he's enterprising, all right," Peck said. "He could be more enterprising if he'd listen to his mother and brother."

"Now, Peck," Ma said. "Let's not get into that right now." She theatrically tipped her head in Morty's direction, followed by an eye roll, but Morty didn't notice.

"Now seems like a good time to me," Peck replied. "I'd like to know why Chance here thinks he's better than us."

Ma jumped to her feet, pulling Morty up with her. I hadn't noticed while he was seated, but he was about five inches shorter than Ma. She rubbed his shoulder. "Hon, would you do me a favor? Can you go out to my car and get a bottle of wine I left there? I'd like to make a toast."

"Of course. Of course." He slid his chair back and shuffled out of the room, down the front hall, and out the door.

Ma waited until the door closed before starting in. "Listen, you two. Morty doesn't know what I do, and I want to keep it that way."

Peck raised his arms, spread them wide. "How does he think you can afford such luxury?"

The sarcasm passed right over Ma's head. "He thinks I work as a receptionist in a vet's office."

"You don't even like animals," Peck said.

"That's beside the point. Don't say anything about what I really do, I mean it."

"Should we also not mention Gary or Harvey?" I asked.

Ma glared at me. "I enjoy socializing. Sue me." She pointed a bony finger my way. "I could really use your help on a job, kiddo. It's a big one. The pull-it-off-and-retire job."

"I already told you no, a million times." I jutted my chin at my brother. "What about him?"

Ma waved her hand. "Naw. I need someone who's quick on his feet. With a silver tongue." She smiled at Peck. "No offense."

"None taken," Peck said.

"Your talents are better used elsewhere."

"Whatever." Peck gnawed on a biscuit.

One son insulted, Ma turned back to me. "What do you say? Gonna help your old ma?"

The front door opened, and Morty poked his head in. "Couldn't find it. Could it be in the trunk?"

"The trunk! Yes, look in the trunk," Ma said. "And try to be thorough."

"Will do," Morty said and ducked out again, closing the door behind him.

I tried to keep my voice down. "Honestly, Ma, I don't believe you. If I get caught again, I'll get sent back for a long, long time. Is that what you want? Seriously?"

Her face melted. "Of course not, dear. I would never want you to go back to prison. Practically broke my heart when you went in before." Her face brightened. "This time, don't get caught."

She started laughing, and Peck joined in, and the both of them kept cackling like idiots until Morty returned. Slowly, the laughter petered out.

"I didn't find any wine," he said. "And I turned that car upside down."

"Oh, I guess I was mistaken. Thanks for looking." Ma chuckled, then clapped her hand over her mouth in a vain attempt to quell her laughter.

Morty took his seat but seemed perplexed. "Did I miss something?"

Ma giggled again. "Nothing, really. Just a little *inside* joke."

With that, Peck started howling again, and Ma did too. A moment later, Morty started laughing right along with them.

I failed to see the humor, so I got up from the table and left. I doubt anyone noticed.

Chapter Seven

I was wrong; Peck noticed. He came bounding out of the house in pursuit, reaching me before I got to my car.

"Hold up, dude. I need to talk to you." He had a piece of food stuck in his front teeth.

"What?"

"It's serious."

I sighed. "What is it?"

"It's Ma."

I glanced at the house, saw Ma peering at us through the window. I turned my back on her, although there was no way she could read my lips at this distance. "What about her?"

"She's getting older. More, uh, what's the word I'm looking for?" He tilted his head up, as if his answer would be dropping down from the sky.

"Manipulative?"

Peck laughed, and I got another glimpse of the food in his teeth. "Yes, she is, but that's not what I was going for."

"Stubborn? Illogical?"

"True and true. But that's not it."

"More promiscuous?"

He shrank back in mock horror. "Hey, that's my mother you're talking about."

I'd had enough games. "Come on, Peck, what's on your mind? Spit it out, or I'm leaving."

"Bottom line, she's not happy."

"When was she ever happy?" Ma rode the emotional elevator, and it rarely stopped on the floor marked *Happy*.

"She's worse than ever. And we can help her. We can help her a lot."

"How?"

He gestured, first at the house, then at the surrounding neighborhood. "Look at this place. It's a dump."

"You're talking about your house, too, you know."

"We both know I only moved in here to keep an eye on Ma. Help her out. Keep her from burning the house down or something."

That and he didn't have a place to live of his own. "Thanks for your service, hero."

"No need to be an asshole."

Pot, kettle. "How can we help Ma?"

"She needs to feel useful. To feel like there's some meaning in her life. She needs to accomplish something."

"Tell her to knit a quilt."

"Stop screwing around. This is Ma we're talking about. I thought you might care about that."

Peck started back inside, but I guessed I needed to hear him out. Ma *hadn't* seemed herself lately. "Hold on, hold on."

He stepped back toward me. "We need to help her. She keeps going like this, she'll be ready for the old folks' home in six months."

I imagined Ma in a home, trying to fleece all the other residents in Three-Card Monte. "What do you suggest?"

"I suggest we help her regain her former glory. I suggest we help her with the con she's working on." Peck crossed his arms and stared at me as if he'd challenged me to a duel. Maybe he had.

I felt the heat rise on my cheeks. "Now, who's screwing around? I can't believe you two. You think I want to risk doing time again? I'm happy to help Ma in any and every way I can. As long as it's legal. If you think Ma won't do well in a nursing home, think about how well she'd do in *prison*."

This time, Peck brushed past me and kept on going.

I didn't stop him.

* * *

When I got home, Sammi was standing outside my front door, playing on her phone. When she saw me, she stuffed it in her pocket. "Where have you been?"

"At dinner," I said. "Why are you here? And maybe a better question, how did you find me?"

"I thought we were going to meet and discuss our strategy."

We hadn't made any concrete plans to do anything. "How did you track me down?"

She waved her hand in the air dismissively, exactly like Ma did. "Piece of cake. I'm pretty resourceful, you know." She put her hand on a hip. "Can we go in? I'm getting eaten alive by all these bugs."

"Sure."

We went in, and Sammi flopped on the sofa. I sat in a chair. "I'm afraid I don't have much to tell you. I followed your mother around today, and I'm not any closer to figuring out what she's up to. Maybe we should tell her I'm willing to help, if I can."

"No. Not yet. She will totally freak, I'm telling you."

"Okay, what's your bright idea?"

"Find Granger. He's got our money."

"Any idea where he might have gone?"

She shook her head. "Mom was always saying how creative you are. Maybe there's some other way to get some cash, quick."

Seems like everyone wants me to get back into the game tonight. "Look, Sammi, I don't hustle people anymore. I've gone straight."

Sammi's lower lip quivered, and she started blinking rapidly. A moment later, the sobbing began. I moved from my chair and sat next to her on the sofa. Put my arm around her shoulder. Didn't say anything, just held her. The father who showed up nineteen years late. Better late than never?

I hadn't consoled anyone in decades, and it felt terrible. And somehow rewarding, at the same time.

When Sammi ran dry, she gently shrugged out from my embrace. She inched over on the sofa and stared at me with red, wet eyes. "If we don't get the money, Norvetch is going to kill her, you know. And me too. There's no way Mom is going to be able to save us, not this time. We are goners."

"Did your mother ever prepare you to run?"

Her lip started quivering again.

"You know, the works. New identities. Move to a different country. New lives."

"Trust me, I know all about running. We've done more than our share. Used fake names, stolen identities. But we got tired of it. So, we moved back here, where she grew up, and she thought she'd get out of the game, like you. But she couldn't really work a regular job. Didn't have the, what-do-you-call-it? Temperament? We do what we need to in order to get by. We're careful, though. Make-up and aliases, most of the time. Most of her recent marks don't know Mom's real name or what she looks like without a wig. But Norvetch? He does. And if we run, he will find us. And he will kill us." She swiped some tears from her eyes.

I'd been in plenty of tough situations over the years, and I'd felt hopeless and desperate before, many times. And I'd always been able to handle my emotions. After all, I got what I deserved. But when it came to other people in despair or in pain or in trouble, people who I cared about, well, that tore at my heartstrings more than anything.

And now, a daughter I'd just discovered? Bawling her eyes out, believing that in short order, someone was going to kill her and her mother?

I'd have to be a monster not to be moved by that.

"Okay, okay. Why don't I see if I can get a line on Granger on my own, without following your mother around? Maybe he hasn't gone far. Fifty thousand is a fair chunk of cash, but it's not buying a yacht and sailing the world money."

"You'll do that?" She sniffled once, and her eyes brightened.

"Yeah."

"Thank you, thank you, thank you." Sammi dabbed at her eyes with the fabric of a sleeve. "If you can get that money back, then we can buy some time with Norvetch and…" She trailed off. Exhaled. Took a deep breath.

"And we won't have to run scared, at least not yet."

"Okay, then. Tell me everything you know about this Granger character. And don't leave anything out, no matter how small."

For the next thirty minutes, Sammi rattled off anything—and everything—she could about Duane Granger. And Jake had been right—Sammi hated his guts from the moment she met him. I took notes and asked some clarifying questions, but for the most part, Sammi put on quite the filibuster. When she was finished, she slumped back into the cushions. "See? A ginormous asshole from the beginning."

I glanced at the clock, and it was approaching eleven. "It's getting late, and if I'm going to get started early, I need to get to bed." I stood and stretched, trying to loosen my stiff back.

Sammi got up, too. "So…?"

"What?"

"Can I help?"

"With what?"

"With tracking down Granger."

"I don't think that's a good idea."

"Why not?"

"If I find him, things could get unpleasant."

She scrunched up her face. "Granger *is* unpleasant. I'm used to it."

"I meant dangerous."

Sammi clenched her jaw.

"Besides, I was hoping you could tag along with your mother tomorrow. If I'm tracking down Granger, I can't be following her. Make up some excuse about how you need some mother-daughter bonding time or something."

"Why don't I tell her I want her to take me to Chuck E. Cheese? Sheesh. I'm nineteen."

"Then why don't you tell her you'd like her to take you drinking?"

"You're so clueless."

"Then enlighten me."

"Never mind. I'll figure something out. Text me how things are going, and I'll text you whenever Mom sneezes."

"I see you get your sense of humor from your mother," I said. "Unfortunately."

She stuck her tongue out at me.

"Nice." I stepped over to the door to let Sammi out, but she didn't move.

Instead, she stood there, twirling a sprig of hair with her fingers. "Chance?"

"Yeah?"

"It's late. Would it be okay if I crashed here? On the sofa? I'm really no trouble."

My lips parted. "I…uh…"

"Please?"

"I don't know, Sammi."

She yawned, and I could practically see her tonsils. "I'm feeling sleepy, and it's a long drive."

Since when was half an hour a long drive? "Well, okay, I guess."

It seemed like the fatherly thing to do.

* * *

The next morning, I showered and dressed as quietly as I could. Sammi was still sacked out, and there was no need for me to wake her. I figured I'd hit a coffee shop for some breakfast and then start hunting down Duane Granger. I left a note for Sammi in one of her shoes—even a clueless nineteen-year-old would find it there—telling her to lock up when she left and headed out myself.

Hobie was waiting for me right outside my door, sitting in one of those low-to-the-ground beach chairs. He wore his ever-present board shorts, and his tanned legs extended straight, feet ensconced in a pair of day-glo orange Crocs.

"Morning, Bucko." He squinted against the sun, looking up at me.

"What are you doing here?" I asked, voice barely above a whisper.

Hobie got the hint, and he lowered his voice. "Overnight visitor still asleep?"

"Yeah. My, uh, daughter." Spoken out loud, those words sounded mighty strange. *My daughter.* Usually, people had nine months to get used to the idea of being a parent. "How did you know?"

"I saw her arrive last night. Kept an eye on her while she waited."

"Making sure she didn't try to make off with anything?"

Hobie looked offended. "Au contraire, mon frère. Just making sure she was safe."

"Right. This is a real rough neighborhood."

Hobie shrugged, then tried to get up, but fell back down into the chair. After two more failed attempts, he finally made it to standing. "It's hell getting old."

"What about all that yoga you do?" Every other morning, it seemed, Hobie was out on the back patio—right in front of my place—doing all kinds of weird poses in a green spandex get-up. Like an AARP version of Gumby.

"Can you imagine how decrepit I'd be *without* it?" Hobie took my elbow and steered me around the patio and through the gate into the front yard. "So, what's on your agenda today?" His voice returned to normal volume.

"Gonna grab something to eat, and then I've got some errands to run."

"Hey, me too." Hobie grinned. "Mind if I tag along?"

"Got a lot to do. And it's going to be boring, so…maybe another time, eh?" I started to move past him to where I'd parked on the street. The last thing I needed was another person to watch out for.

Hobie didn't leave my side. "That's okay. I've got nothing better to do."

I stopped, turned. "Ordinarily, I'd welcome the company, but…" I held my palms up.

"Oh, cut the crap, Chance. I know something's up. Your daughter airdrops into your life, then you're off at the crack of dawn—"

"It's 8:45."

"Relatively speaking. When was the last time you were up this early?" He raised an eyebrow. "I figure you can use the help."

"You have no idea what's going on." I cocked my head, again wondering if he had my place bugged. "Do you?"

"Well, I *might* have had a fairly lengthy conversation with Sammi. While she was waiting for you. Seemed rude to let her wait all by herself, you know?

Delightful child, by the way. Now come on. You can buy me breakfast as a thank you."

* * *

After a thoroughly mediocre breakfast at Denny's—Hobie had a weak spot for Grand Slams—we began our quest. Finding someone who didn't want to be found was a lot harder than finding someone in general, naturally, and I didn't have much to go on.

Sammi had given me some of Granger's favorite hangouts last night during her monologue, so I figured that was as good a place to start as any. According to her, he spent a lot of his time at a menswear store called Cushwell's, but she had no idea why—whether he worked there or just did a lot of shopping there.

I parked on the street and fed some change into the meter. Hobie and I walked the half block to the store, passing two wireless phone stores and a gelato place. When we opened the door to Cushwell's, a tiny bell dinged—not an electronic simulation of a bell, but an actual bell, old-school style.

There was one large guy sitting in a chair in the back of the store, but otherwise, there were no other customers.

An immaculately coiffed gentleman in a perfectly tailored suit stepped out from behind the cash register. "May I help you?"

His face soured when he got a full look at Hobie, who'd entered behind me, wrinkled t-shirt, raggy shorts, orange Crocs.

"Oh dear," he said. "Oh my. You've certainly come to the right place. How may I help you?"

For a moment, I thought he was going to pass out, but somehow he managed to return a smile to his face.

"We'd love your help. But I think we're more in the market for information than for clothes," I said.

The man looked Hobie up and down again. "If you say so."

Hobie didn't react, just drifted off toward the sports coat section.

"I'm looking for Duane Granger," I said.

The sales guy smiled faintly. "I'm afraid I don't know anyone by that name."

I guessed that shouldn't have surprised me. It was entirely possible Granger wasn't using his real name. It was also entirely possible this guy was lying, covering up for Granger. I pulled out my phone, called up the picture of Granger that Sammi had texted me, and showed it to the sales guy.

I caught a flicker of recognition on the man's face before he slipped back into his poker face. "I'm sorry."

"I owe him some money. And I'm a guy who always likes to repay his debts."

"I see. How much money do you owe this gentleman?"

"Quite a lot, in fact. Enough that I'm sure he'd want me to find him."

"What makes you think I would know him?"

I glanced around the shop. The guy in the chair was gone. "I was told he frequents this place, although I wouldn't know why. Do you know why someone might have told me that?"

"We do have the finest selection of menswear around."

"I didn't get the impression he's a snappy dresser. Maybe there's some other reason?"

"Not that I would know." One corner of the man's mouth twitched. "But, if I should happen to run into this Mr. Granger, I'll be sure to tell him you're looking for him." He tilted his head at me, as if he was trying to see inside one of my ears. "Who shall I say stopped by?"

"Names are such an artificial construct, don't you think?" I gave him a cold smile. "Just tell him I've got something he's due, okay?"

The sales guy's eyes narrowed, and his jaw clenched. He clasped his hands behind his back and rocked on his heels as if he were a manservant waiting for his next order. "I shall pass along your message." He paused. "If I ever meet this man, of course."

"Of course." I caught Hobie's eyes—he was perusing the dress shirts—and nodded toward the door. On our way out, I heard him tell the guy to let him know when their next sale would be.

We walked to the car in silence, and when we got there, two guys were leaning against the side of my car. One was the guy who'd been sitting in the shop. He wore jeans and a polo shirt and had a pair of wraparound mirror sunglasses resting on the top of his head. The other guy was in a slick nylon warm-up suit. Each one was bigger than me and Hobie put together.

Next to me, I sensed Hobie tensing up, but when I glanced at him, he looked cool as a cucumber. Or as cool as one can look in orange Crocs. He slowly moved to his left, closer to the guy in the warmup suit.

"Morning, boys," I said. "Something we can do for you?"

The guy in jeans pushed himself off the car to stand upright. "As a matter of fact, you can. Just a small thing, really."

"What's that?"

"You can stop asking around about this Duane Granger character."

"Who?" I asked. Out of the corner of my eye, I noticed Hobie continue to drift to his left. And maybe a step closer to the dude in the warmups.

"I certainly hope you're not like the last guy who gave me lip." The goon stepped toward me and pointed a finger at my face. I'd never seen a hand so large, and I could only imagine the damage it could inflict if he balled it into a fist and smashed me in the nose.

"Who asked you to warn me?" I asked.

"None of your fucking business." He jerked his hand toward me, and I flinched, instinctively. He just smiled and patted my cheek softly, and I felt like kneeing him in the groin, but didn't think that was a wise, long-term play. "We understand each other, don't we?"

I nodded.

"You drop this whole Duane Granger thing, and everyone will be happy."

The guy in the warmups had stepped closer to the dude who was in my face, and Hobie had edged behind him. Our eyes met, and for a second, I thought Hobie was going to try to attack from behind, some wild-ass assault sure to get both of us killed. Instead, he lost his balance and tripped into the guy in warmups. The guy spun around and shoved Hobie, who stumbled back into the side of my car. "Watch what you're doing, asswipe," the guy shouted at Hobie. "Jesus!"

The dude in jeans ignored the commotion behind him and bared his teeth at me. "Let me add one thing. If I hear that you're still messing with this, I won't be as nice the next time we meet." He jerked his head at his pal. "Come on, let's let these guys enjoy the rest of their day."

They sauntered off down the sidewalk, message delivered.

I went over to Hobie, who now leaned against the car like the goons had. Except he wasn't trying to be intimidating. He was leaning against it for support as he tried to catch his breath.

"You okay?" I asked.

"Just give me a minute," he said, gaze following the progress of the two musclemen as they turned the corner at the next block. When they did, he straightened and smiled. "Never better." He held out a wallet. "I believe this belonged to one of those gentlemen."

I stared at him. "You lifted that guy's wallet?"

Hobie shrugged. "Lifted? Found? Semantics, really. Better I found it than some low-life who might try to use the credit cards or steal his money, right?"

"Sure."

He dug through the wallet and removed a driver's license. "Trent Ulrich. Lives in Hyattsville. Twenty-seven years old." He slid the license into his pocket.

"Maybe we should get going, in case Trent realizes he's missing something and decides to come back for it. You can continue your examination in the car."

Chapter Eight

Five minutes down the road, and Hobie had finished rifling through the wallet. "Sixty-four dollars. Two credit cards. One ATM card. One Hungry Hank's Subs customer card, with three punches to go for a free sub. Some other useless crap."

"Where'd you learn how to do that?" I asked.

"What?"

"The pickpocket trick."

"That was nothing. Saw an opportunity and took it." Hobie stared at the side window, away from me.

I didn't know much about Hobie's background. Every time I'd asked, he'd deflected with some ambiguity or vague response. Sometimes he'd offer an answer that directly contradicted something he'd said the last time I'd asked. I knew that when he was younger, Hobie operated on the margins of the law—doing what exactly, I didn't know—but that he had some sort of epiphany along the way and went straight. Devoting some of his time and money to helping those like him—myself included—survive by also going straight.

I preferred to judge a man through his actions than by what crap came out of his mouth. I was used to people spinning tales, from outright lies to slight shading of the truth. After all, I grew up in a family of liars and con artists, I plied their trade for years, and I spent time in prison. In my jaded world, it was the truth that stood out from the bullshit—like orange Crocs in a sea of black wingtips. "You displayed some real talent there. I'm guessing that wasn't the first time you lifted some dude's wallet."

"I don't really recall." He kept watching the world go by out his window. "Besides, that was a long, long time ago. Different place. More importantly, different person."

"Well…good job."

A pause. Then, "Thanks."

* * *

We checked out a couple of other places on Sammi's list but came up empty. No Granger. But no heavies out to warn us either. We stopped at a Dunkin', and I sent Hobie in to get us some coffee. While Hobie was inside, I texted Sammi for my new best bud Jake's number, then gave him a call.

"Hello?"

"This is Chance."

"Whoa. Don't hear from you in ten years, then hear from you twice in two days. That's quite a coincidence," he said. "I almost didn't answer—didn't recognize the number. I hope you're calling to tell me that you've solved Kristal's problem."

"Nope."

He sighed. "Then what do you need?"

"You can relax. All I need is some information."

"Try Wikipedia."

Jake had never displayed much of a sense of humor back when I knew him. Things hadn't really changed. "Do you know a guy named Trent Ulrich?"

Silence on the phone.

"Jake? You there?"

More silence, then, "Yeah. I'm still here."

"Well? Know the guy?"

"Why do you think I know this cretin?"

"How do you know he's a cretin unless you know him?"

"Fine. Looks like an Olympic shot putter. Square head. Square neck. Not too tall but plenty damn wide. IQ a bit short of triple digits. Mean as a junkyard dog that hasn't eaten in a week. That the Trent Ulrich we're talking about?"

"So, you do know him."

"Unfortunately."

I bet he wouldn't be happy we boosted his wallet. "Who's he work for?"

"Depends."

"On what?"

"Who's paying him the most. Like every crook I've ever known."

"He was with another guy, just as big."

"Had to be K-Bar," Jake said.

"K-Bar?"

"Yeah, like the knife."

"First name K, last name Bar?" I said.

"Laugh it up all you want, but he's practically a carbon copy of Ulrich, except ten times as smart and twice as mean. They're a pair, I'm telling you." He clucked his tongue. "Why do you want to know about these guys?"

I told Jake about our little run-in.

He gave a low whistle, "If you know what's good for your health and well-being, you'll steer clear of those guys."

"Then what happens to Kristal?"

"If she's involved with those two—or more specifically, someone who felt the need to hire those two—she's in deep shit. You *have* to persuade her and Sammi to stop looking for Granger and hit the highway without looking back. I'm serious, Chance."

"Thanks for the info. Talk to you later."

I clicked off and stared into space. Kristal and I had discussed contingency plans in case one of our hustles blew up, and we had to pull up stakes in a hurry. As nineteen-year-olds, we'd always romanticized it, the two of us, in some foreign land, living under assumed identities, enjoying life to the fullest. Two refugees making the best of things. But that was twenty years ago. And we'd had each other. Two young kids who didn't know better. Now, reality intruded. Being on the lam involved living in a lot of fleabag hotels and venturing out only at night, wearing dirty wigs and too much make-up.

I had a strong feeling Kristal wouldn't be up for the challenge. And if she wasn't going, neither was Sammi.

Hobie emerged from the shop with a couple of coffees and a box emblazoned with the familiar orange and pink logo. He got in and handed me a cup. "Got some donuts, too. A dozen, to be exact."

"Think that's enough?"

"I didn't know what you wanted, so I got an assortment." He opened the box, and I got a blast of blessed fried dough aroma. "It's okay. Trent's buying. It's the least that asshole can do after shoving me, don't you think?"

"Got a chocolate glazed?" I asked.

"Coming right up."

* * *

After we each downed four donuts for lunch—in the car, as we drove—we decided to take a break. We didn't have any good leads, and I needed some time to think. I said goodbye to Hobie at his front door and walked around back to my place. I was mentally braced for Sammi to be lurking, but she was nowhere to be found. I felt a little disappointed about that. I was also *very* surprised I felt that way.

Inside, she'd left me a note in response to my note. *Thanks for letting me crash, Dad! I owe you two Pop-Tarts.*

I balled up the note and tossed it into the trash.

I'd barely removed my shoes when someone knocked on my door. Had Hobie forgotten something? But it wasn't the harsh triple-knock that he favored. Another knock.

I padded to the door and checked the peephole. Then I swung the door open to face my visitor.

Kristal stood there, wearing a manufactured smile. I'd seen her yesterday, of course, but that was at a distance. Today, close up, she looked amazing. Not twenty years older, but twenty years better. Her skin wasn't quite as flawlessly smooth, and her face had filled out a fraction, but she still possessed that unquantifiable *aura*. Simply put, she was a goddess, and she'd been mine. "Aren't you going to invite me in? After all, you've been following me around town for who knows how long."

"Come in." I opened the door wide, and Kristal whooshed in, as if she were air escaping a popped balloon. She did a quick lap around the living room, circling like a dog, then plopped down onto the sofa, exactly like Sammi had yesterday.

She gazed up at me, piercing blue eyes. "So, what's new?" she asked casually, as if we'd seen each other last week and she wanted a quick catch-up before moving on to more pressing matters.

I stared down at her, dumbfounded. Surely, she recognized the absurdity of the situation. I waited for her to crack, for her to break down and apologize for running out on me. Apologize for keeping my daughter a secret from me for twenty years.

I kept waiting.

She waited, too, a vague smile on her face, some unanswered question floating in the air. Innocuous. Innocent. And wholly incendiary.

I played along. "What's new? Nothing. What's new with you, Kristal?" I sat in the chair next to the sofa, offered my own vague smile. Inside, my heart pounded in my chest. Kristal, in the flesh. Up close.

She shrugged. "Nothing much. Moved back to town. Working. Trying to lose a few pounds. Oh, and someone's going to kill me if I don't come up with four hundred thousand dollars. So, you know, same old, same old."

"I heard it was three hundred and fifty thousand."

"Rounded up." She dropped her smile. "Why are you following me?"

"How did you find out?"

"Jake Petrucci called me."

Figured. Once a slimeball, always a slimeball. "I heard you were in some trouble and, well, I thought if there was something I could do…"

"You got four hundred grand?"

I gestured to the walls of the converted garage I called home. "What do you think?"

"Then I don't see how you can help me." She picked at a loose thread on the sofa. "How did you hear I was in some trouble?"

I remembered a few conversations when we were together that went like this. We each had information the other wanted, but neither wanted to divulge any details. Hardly the bedrock of a successful relationship. As I recalled, we were both quite good at this dance. "Around. How did you find out where I lived?"

"Around."

"Right."

"I also heard—around—that you weren't hustling anymore. That you'd gone straight." She laughed. "That certainly must bug the shit out of your mother. If she's still alive, that is."

For some inexplicable reason, Kristal liked my mother. Always had. "She's still alive. And she's only gotten worse."

Kristal fell silent, gazed off.

On the outside, she seemed cool, but I could only imagine what was going through her mind. Worried someone was going to kill you. And your child. Plus, having to suffer the indignity of asking someone you ran out on for help. I mean, that had to be why she was here, right? If she just wanted to bust me for following her, she could have called. Jake had my number.

"Why don't we cut the shit, okay?" My tolerance only lasted so long.

"Sure. Let's just give it to each other straight." Kristal got up, and I rose too. She stepped close enough so I could smell her shampoo and pushed me up against the wall. For a moment, I thought she was going to start pummeling me.

Instead, she kissed me. Long. Hard. Hungry. I resisted at first, unsure what was going on, then I decided to go with the flow. Our tongues danced like they had twenty years ago. On some level, it felt like it had been just yesterday. On another level, we were different people living different lives in a different time. She stepped back and hit me with another smile. This one genuine.

Then she sprang forward and slugged me in the gut. I doubled over, from the pain mostly, but also from the surprise. After struggling to catch my breath, I finally straightened and brought my arms up in self-defense. "What the hell?"

Kristal smiled again and raised her fist, then stopped abruptly.

I flinched. "Funny. You didn't have to slug me."

"Maybe. But it felt good."

"To you, maybe," I said. "Do me a favor, don't do it again."

She gave me a big shit-eating grin. "Sorry. No promises."

I felt my anger rise. "I should be the one slugging you."

"Hitting women? Not your style."

"How could you not tell me about Sammi? My daughter. Jesus Christ, what did I do to make you so angry with me?"

Kristal didn't answer, not at first. She licked her lips a couple of times, and opened her mouth once, as if she was going to answer, then shook her head. Obviously, whatever had caused her to keep such a colossal secret from me wasn't something that could be answered with a single sentence. "I'm sorry, Chance."

"That's it? 'I'm sorry, Chance.' That's what you say if you accidentally step on my toes." I felt the anger bubbling up inside, and I couldn't get the image of a mushroom cloud out of my mind. "We're talking about a child of mine."

Kristal didn't answer. Instead, she took a slow tour of the room, then settled back into the couch. She seemed calmer.

"I'm sorry, Chance. For everything." She looked at me with her baby blues, and my insides fluttered. Then I regained control. "I know it's a little late for an apology, but that's all I can do now. You don't know how often I wanted to reach out to you over the years, but…" She sniffled. "But there never seemed to be the right time. And it's not so easy to tell someone, oh, by the way, we had a child together five years ago. Or ten. Or fifteen. I am so terribly sorry, Chance. You have to believe that."

"Why now? Why come to me and apologize now?"

"You were following *me*, remember?"

"I thought we were being straight with each other," I said.

"Well, here's the straight scoop on Sammi. She's a great kid. A real gem. I wish I could say I had a lot to do with it, but…she's her own person, you know. Sweet. Smart. Determined. When she sets her sights on something, you know it's going to happen. Lord knows I don't deserve her. And to think, she's…" Her expression darkened and gained intensity. Nostrils quivered, face crimson. I could feel the heat rising from her skin. "I should slug you again. Conspiring with her behind my back? She might seem like an adult in many respects, but she's not even twenty. She's got some grandiose ideas about things, and she doesn't always have a firm grip on reality. Which is understandable. She hasn't *seen* the reality we've seen, has she?"

"She wanted to help you."

"I don't need your help. I don't want your help." She drew in a sharp breath, then exhaled. "I want you to stay away from Sammi, at least in the short term. Until I've got my situation figured out. Then we can work out some kind of arrangement so you can see her."

"Kristal," I said gently, trying not to work her up into any more of a lather. "She's almost twenty. An adult. She can go where she wants and see who she wants. That includes me, her father."

"What do you know about it? About raising a child? You're not her father. You're just her sperm donor." Kristal turned and stared at the wall. Deep in thought? Or afraid to say more?

"Me not being in her life was one hundred percent your fault. Not mine."

She stared at me, then started crying.

I remained in my chair. Anyone else, I might have gone over to console her, lent her my shoulder to sob on, but I was pissed. The more she sat there feeling sorry for herself, the more furious I became, knowing she robbed me of such a significant part of my life. If I had been raising Sammi, it was entirely conceivable I would have chosen a different line of work. One where going to prison wasn't a possibility. I'd been a reckless young adult, but I wasn't a complete idiot.

Everything would have been different, and I would have known my daughter.

And the cherry on top of my emotional sundae? Sammi was in dire trouble. Without some miraculous intervention, she would be out of my life as quickly as she'd entered it. Hiding in Montana or Mexico or Madagascar.

Or worse.

I wanted to dive in, go after Kristal, *demand* to know why she did what she did. Not just why she disappeared, but why during the nineteen years since, she never told me I had a daughter.

I tried to tamp down my anger, tried to focus on a possible solution to the problem. Tried not to hate the person sitting across from me. Not succeeding. If Kristal hadn't still been hustling, she never would have put Sammi in peril. How could I *not* hate Kristal?

Yet. There she was. My Kristal. My goddess. Back in my life, however briefly and for whatever reason.

Finally, she stopped crying and peeked at me through her fingers. I didn't know what she expected from me, but I sat there, stock-still, a hard shell on the outside, seething on the inside. I wanted to hear the real reason she'd come by, and I was afraid if I went ballistic, I'd scare her off.

Slowly, she collected herself. Wiped some tears from her face. Hand-combed her hair. I waited until she stopped fussing before speaking. Tried to soften my voice, not sure I succeeded. "Why did you take off?"

Kristal seemed to measure her thoughts, and I wasn't sure if she would ever speak again. At least to me. Then she nodded to herself and started talking. "I was a mixed-up, confused kid. Found out I was pregnant about a week before we were supposed to pull the trigger on our job. I mean, I flunked out of high school, couldn't hold a real job, and we were hustling people for rent money. Playing house, you and me. I could barely think straight as we prepared—I'm surprised you didn't even notice," she said. "Although you were pretty oblivious to things. Actually, I should rephrase that. You were oblivious to things that didn't have anything to do with our plan. You were *very* focused on getting the job done, and getting it done right."

So many thoughts—and emotions—flooded my brain. I tried to calm down and only let one through at a time, not wanting to bombard her. "Uh huh. I can understand being scared. But running away from your one source of support—me? Not sure I understand that part."

"Well, now, sure. My decision seems awful. But back then?" She shrugged. "I did what I thought was best at the time. I figured my life was messed up, and I didn't want to drag you down with me."

"Messed up?" I tried to come up with a way to phrase my next thought so it wouldn't seem harsh, but I wasn't thinking too clearly. "You didn't have to keep the baby, you know. At the very least, it should have been a joint decision."

"Fuck you. Sammi is the absolute best thing that's ever happened to me. I should have expected a comment like that from you. You always could be a pompous shithead at times. *At times*, I wondered why I stayed with you. Back then, you didn't care about much more than yourself."

"Now, Kris—"

She put her hand up. "You know about her now. Maybe you can make up for lost time. If we can somehow squirm our way out of the mess I made."

And full circle. Back to the elephant in the room. "Sure. Any ideas how you might be able to do that?"

She glared at me. "Look. I know I fucked up. You don't need to be condescending."

"I wasn't trying to be."

"You got that tone you always used to get. It's one of your tells, Chance. Don't forget, it may have been a long time ago, but I still know you better than anyone else alive. And I know you think I'm trying to hustle you." She rose. "It was nice seeing you. I hope that—somehow, sometime—you'll be able to spend some quality time with Sammi. It would be great for her. Only don't do it behind my back. And not now. Definitely not now. I'll call you in a few months, and we can work out some details." She paused a beat. "Goodbye, Chance."

Kristal walked out of my place, and I didn't make a single move to stop her. I did say goodbye, although she'd already closed the door behind her.

Right now, I hated her.

Right now, I loved her, too. Always had.

Chapter Nine

That night, Krissy and I popped open a bottle of champagne. Cheap, but it would do double duty. Serve as celebration while putting us on the path to getting drunk. We'd reprised our bike scam four more times and got paid off on three. That was better odds than the 50-50 I'd predicted. The one guy we couldn't hose? A bigwig's assistant who just happened to be driving his boss's Lexus. As soon as he got out of the car wearing his JCPenney polo shirt, I knew we didn't stand a chance. In fact, we didn't even try on that one.

We didn't bother with glasses. Krissy held the bottle up in the air. "To us!" Then she took a big gulp and passed it to me.

"To us!" I drank, and then we collapsed onto the futon. Scamming people all day long was hard work. But lucrative. We'd pulled in just over two grand, and our marks had deserved it.

"We make a great team, and we proved it once again." Krissy gave me the bottle, then took my hand. "If we do this one day a week, we'll be golden."

Mathematically, yes. But practically? "I don't think it works like that."

"What do you mean?" Krissy sat up a bit. Her smile dimmed.

"After a while, people will get wise. Seeing us out there all the time, you dumping your bike. They'll figure it out. And someone's bound to report what happened. Couple reports, the authorities will start to watch out for us."

"We'll go to different places. This is a big area with lots of intersections, you know. And lots of rich assholes." Her voice had an edge to it. "Hell, we could even go to different cities."

"Sure, we could move around a bit. But I'm afraid it will eventually catch up to us. In the con world, as in the rest of the world, innovation is key. Don't worry, we *can come up with new cons. Or even new twists on old cons. The sky's the limit." I glanced at Krissy, saw her pout, and felt bad about bringing her down. This bike con depended on her acting, and she did a great job. And here I was harshing her buzz. I could be a dick sometimes. "Let's just celebrate what we did today, talk about tomorrow tomorrow."*

She shoved the bottle into my hands. "First, you get on my case about how I handled Hufnagel. I knew he had a fat wallet. I knew we could get him for more than four hundred. Now you're telling me that we've got to be cautious. Being cautious is for accountants. Being cautious is for pussies. Being cautious is something my dad always told me. We've got something that works, we should be exploiting it. We need to be bolder, not cautious."

"We need to be careful."

"Fuck you, Chance." Krissy jumped off the futon, stomped to the bedroom, and slammed the door. Then I heard the lock button click. I was fucked.

* * *

For the next two weeks, Krissy barely spoke to me. After that first night, she let me back into our bed, but our sex, while still frequent, lost some of its intensity. I pleaded with her to talk to me so we could clear the air, but she kept insisting nothing was wrong. She was perfectly polite to me. She wasn't mean. She even would laugh at some of my jokes. Just like always.

I might not have been the best reader of women, but I wasn't completely illiterate. There was a definite chill in the air, a decided icy undercurrent. I knew she was pissed at me and what she perceived as my controlling ways. And I knew—mostly because she kept mentioning it—that I reminded her of her father's worst traits.

I'd read that some women date and marry men who remind them of their fathers, but I thought that was supposed to be a good thing.

I spent my time working up another scam. One that had a much, much higher ceiling. One that wasn't cautious.

This one wasn't some two-bit hack that would net a few hundred bucks and would need to be repeated ad nauseam. No, this was the kind of scam that would set us up for a year. This was a scam that even my family would be proud of.

At this point, I wasn't involving Krissy in the planning. Her acting skills would be key when it came time to pulling it off, but she didn't have the patience to conduct the research to map the scam out. So, I spent a lot of time planning and making notes.

Finally, the day arrived. I'd choreographed everything out to the millisecond, and Krissy and I had rehearsed it until we had it cold.

Before we got out of bed that morning, she took my hand, intertwined her fingers in mine. "I'm not feeling it, Chance. I don't think we're going to pull this one off."

"It's big league. Natural for you to have doubts, but isn't it what you've been after me about? Take more risk? Go for a bigger score?"

She stared at me, and I could see something in her eyes. Not sure what, exactly.

"We'll get it done, have a little faith," I answered, trying to bolster my own confidence, too.

"If you say so." She forced a weak smile. "I love you."

"Love you, too."

We needed two cars for our scheme, so we split up that morning, after a rousing session in bed.

And then I waited for her at the designated meeting place.

For ten minutes.

For twenty minutes.

For half an hour.

After an hour, I gave up on the con and went back to our place. All her stuff was gone, my worst fears realized.

She'd bolted.

Out of my life.

* * *

I rolled out of bed the next morning around ten, still groggy from only four hours of sleep. I'd stayed awake, tossing and turning and pacing and thinking, until about six, when finally my body and mind caved in.

I was torn. I didn't want to get involved in Kristal's mess, not really. And it seemed, at least on the surface, Kristal didn't want me involved either. So far,

I'd only been following people and asking some questions. Almost got beat up in the process. But nothing I'd done had been illegal. The more deeply I became involved here, though, the more likely that wouldn't continue to be the case.

I'd been straight for three years—1002 days, to be exact—and I was afraid if I slipped back, I'd slip back for good. Working side hustles and living in a shithole wasn't much fun, and with the promise of riches that perpetually drove the con artist, I knew it wouldn't take too much materialistic success to turn me back to the dark side.

On the other hand, Sammi.

My daughter.

Appearing in my life, dropped from heaven. How could I just stand by and let bad things happen to her?

I couldn't.

Which led directly to the next series of questions. How to extricate her, and by extension, Kristal, from the mess they were in? Despite my conflicted feelings about Kristal, she was Sammi's mother, and if something happened to her, Sammi would feel the effects forever. The kid had lived with one parent until now, but it would be awfully nice if she got the treat of having two parents in her life. Besides, she needed a good parent—me—to counter all the twisted shenanigans brought on by her mother.

It sure was weird thinking of myself as the steady parent.

I took a nice long shower, turning the water as hot as it would go. Which meant it got barely warm—the plumbing in the converted garage wasn't the most efficient. As I got out, someone was knocking on the door. I wrapped a towel around my waist and went to answer it.

It was Sammi. I opened the door, and she walked straight in as if she owned the place.

"Forget something?" I asked.

"Mom and I got in a huge fight this morning, and she just stormed out." A lot of that going on.

"What was the fight about?"

"The same thing we've been fighting about for days. To run or not to run."

"Which side is she on?"

"I know she talked to you last night. When she got home, she was a total wreck, and it took me forever to find out what happened. I know she said she doesn't want your help. But you have to ignore her. She's trying to look out for my best interest, but my best interest does not include moving to some small town in the desert and wearing nasty wigs the rest of my life. But that's exactly what's going to happen if you don't help us. We'll be gone. Forever." She stopped talking, leaving the implied, "and you'll never see me again" hanging in the ether.

"I honestly don't know how you think I can help. And you didn't have to drive all the way over here. You could have called."

"On the phone? Gross. Besides, I am better at persuading people in person."

"I don't know, Sammi. I really don't—"

She didn't let me finish my sentence. "I know you've done a great thing, going straight and all, and ordinarily I'd really admire that. I mean, I'm only twenty, but I can tell what a shitty life it is, one small score after another, but never really hitting it big so you can retire." She paused and twirled her hair the way Kristal used to when she wanted something. "But you were really good at what you did—if Mom's stories were anywhere near accurate."

I had been pretty damn good at ripping people off—my main hustle had been hustling. I knew exactly where this was headed, and it wasn't going to be a short conversation. "How about if I get dressed and then we can continue this, uh, discussion?"

She looked at me, and it seemed like she noticed I was wearing only a towel for the first time. "Sure. No prob."

Normally, I got dressed in the living area, because there was barely enough room to move in my so-called bedroom, but I managed to get dressed in there, while mostly sitting on the bed. When I returned to Sammi, she was checking things out, and her movements were feline, more lioness than house cat. She stopped to examine the lone picture I owned, with her back to me.

"Okay. Now, where were we?"

I startled her, and she spun around, dropping the picture. The glass shattered as it hit the concrete garage floor in the one space not covered by a thin throw rug.

"Oh, my God." She bent to pick up the picture.

"Leave it alone—you don't want to cut yourself," I found myself saying, probably the first parent-like thing I said after finding out that I actually was a parent.

Sammi straightened. "I'm so sorry, Chance."

"Don't worry about it. Just glass." As long as the picture itself wasn't harmed. It was of a much younger me with a much younger Kristal, taken at some concert. We both looked buzzed, but happy. That's how I liked to remember the time I spent with her.

"Here, have a seat, and we can talk." I gestured to the sofa, and Sammi took her place, in what was fast becoming her usual spot. "I didn't have any luck finding Granger, although I did get a friendly warning to butt out."

"Forget him, for the moment. I've got another idea." Sammi licked her lips.

"Your mother doesn't want me to have anything to do with you right now. Someday, yes, but right now, she wants you to stay away from me and close to her. I can't say I blame her. We—I—should have told her about my involvement from the beginning."

"She's overprotective. And wrong." A sense of urgency came across with her words. "Chance—Dad—if we could just pull a job, one more time, one last time, then everyone will be happy. Mom and I won't have to go into hiding. No one gets their legs broken. And you get to connect with the daughter you never knew you had, and that daughter gets to connect with you. Win-win-win. The only loser is the poor schmuck we rip off. All we have to do is make sure we pick some scumbag to burn."

I noticed how easily Sammi switched everything to *we*. "I thought I made myself clear. I'm not in the business anymore."

"These are special circumstances."

She had a point. "Hypothetically, suppose we somehow can get buy-in from your mother. In your ideal scenario, who am I supposed to go after now, if not Granger?"

"I told you, forget him. The money he took won't save us, not in the long run. It's just a stay of execution. I've got a way to get *all* the money we need."

Had she been planning the Granger bait-and-switch all along? Was I being played by a protégé of one of the greats? "Go on."

"Guy's name is Nathaniel Freeman. He's a so-called self-made multi-millionaire. Owns a string of massage parlors and a chain of Qwickie Marts—unrelated. Totally loaded, verified, for real. He's also been accused of a billion things. Sexual assault, money laundering, prostitution. His fancy lawyers always get him off. Or he pays big settlements. Either way, he's not afraid of breaking the law if he thinks it will benefit him. We've researched this guy every way to Sunday. Or Tuesday. Or next Friday, or however that saying goes."

"Sunday," I said. "I don't suppose you have an angle in?"

"As a matter of fact, I do. Several possibilities, in fact. The guy has an ego the size of Ohio, which always makes things easier."

"I'm listening."

"You sound awfully interested in the details, especially for someone who's not planning to get involved." One corner of Sammi's mouth twitched.

"Why do I get the feeling you're going to go ahead with this, whether I get involved or not?"

A cord on Sammi's neck tightened. "Because I am. Freeman is a fuckhead, so I can kill two birds. Take him down and save our skins. Another win-win."

"But, and I mean no offense, you're not even twenty years old. I've got socks older than you."

"If that's an offer to help, I accept." She bowed her head slightly. "If not, then I can manage on my own. I may still be a teenager if you go by the calendar, but we both know I'm a lot older than that experience-wise."

"How do you think your mother will react to your idea?"

"We don't even have to tell her, until it's over. Then we can hand her a pile of cash, she can repay her debt, and we can go back to knitting scarves and baking chocolate chip cookies."

Sammi didn't strike me as the knitting type. "We've got, what, four days before Norvetch comes looking for his money? Good cons take a lot more time than that to develop."

"What if I told you we've had our sights on Freeman for a long time? Doing some advance work and planting some seeds."

"Who's 'we'?"

"Me, Mom, a few trusted others." She drew out the word *trusted*, and her inflection sounded exactly how I remembered Kristal talking, when she was trying to make a point.

"Others? Like who?" I prepared myself to hear a bunch of names from the past. Cons Kristal and I had worked with, most of whom I'd consider anything *but* trusted.

Sammi rattled off some names, none I knew. "Part of your regular crew?"

"I wouldn't call them our crew, but yeah, Mom's worked with them. They're good at what they do. Specialists, you know?"

"And are they prepared to jump in and help now?"

Sammi slowly shook her head. "Nah. They wouldn't get involved unless Mom was running the show, and she's too emotional right now to be thinking straight. Granger ripping her off sent her over the edge."

"Who's going to call the shots?"

She smiled at me. And her smile grew and grew.

"I don't know, Sammi. I haven't been in the game for a while. I'm liable to be quite rusty."

"It's like riding a bike. Once you know how, you always know how."

I remembered Kristal and our bike-riding scam and had to suppress my own smile. "You ride often, do you? Your mom teach you how?"

"Actually, I never learned. But you get my drift. And I'm sure you must know a few friends who could help us out, too." She looked at me with puppy-dog eyes. "What's your answer, *Dad*? If you're not going to help me, I need to know now. Because I'm doing this, with or without you."

"Give me a minute, okay?"

"I'd be happy to give you—"

I held up my hand. "How about a little quiet so I can think?"

She rolled her eyes and shut her mouth. Then she got up and started pacing again, a large cat on the prowl. I closed my eyes to shut her out so I could concentrate.

I didn't want to relapse—that's how I viewed it, conning people was a sickness. It had been quite a struggle, to decide to go straight, and to stay straight. It felt like I ate beans and rice for ten straight months and worked eighteen hours a day doing shit work just to afford that. My wardrobe consisted primarily of clothes I bought before I went to prison, and I lived in some old man's converted garage with the smallest hot water tank in existence. But I was clean. I didn't have to look over my shoulder—for the law, for other hustlers looking to separate me from my bounty, or from victims looking to get back what belonged to them. For the past three years, I didn't have to sleep with one eye open.

Now, I was being asked to flush all that down the toilet. To go back to my old, evil, self-crippling ways. To risk returning to prison, and this time, for longer than three years.

The carrot? If I was successful, I'd have a chance to get to know my daughter. As long as I managed to get her out of her current jam. Maybe more importantly, in the long term, anyway, I might be able to get her on the right path before she wasted twenty years like I had.

And if she was truly planning to go ahead with this, with or without my help, I knew her chance of success would be greater if I was involved. Much greater.

Of course, the idea of reconnecting with Kristal hadn't escaped me, either.

I opened my eyes, and Sammi had already returned to her seat. She stared at me, expectantly.

"Okay. I'm in."

She shot off the sofa and practically dove at me. Enveloped me in a hug before I could even stand. "Thank you, thank you, thank you." She disentangled herself. "You won't be sorry. You'll see. Together, you and I will rock this town."

Something in her tone, how she said the words, with her youthful exuberance, spurred an odd thought. Namely, that Sammi saw this not so much as a way to save her skin—and her mother's, too, of course—but more as a fun adventure to be shared with her newly-found father.

That kind of attitude could get us all killed.

What had I just agreed to?

Chapter Ten

Sammi had wanted to stick around and help get me up to speed on what they'd started with Freeman, but I didn't want it all dumped on me in a jumbled heap of paper and thumb drives. I wanted it in a neatly organized bundle. I told her to go home, gather whatever they had, and try to distill it into a few pages of coherent summary.

Mostly, I wanted her out of my hair for a while so I could conduct my own research and get in touch with some of my buddies who were still hustling.

I booted up my laptop and Googled Freeman. As you might expect of a high-flying, flamboyant entrepreneur, there was no dearth of information. He started a number of businesses in his early twenties, and they all failed, but he kept at it, coming up with new ideas and somehow getting them funded. His chain of neighborhood massage parlors—supposedly legit with no happy endings—offering decent massages at lowball prices caught on, and he made his first few millions. Then he parlayed that into a pet food delivery business, which he sold to another company that ran it into Chapter 11, and an after-school tutoring/childcare service, The Tutor Squad, still in business. All the while, he bought up struggling independent convenience stores and rebranded them into a chain of Lightning Strike stores to take on 7-Elevens.

All of his business models focused on customer service and convenience. There were no hi-tech plays, no business-to-business relationships. He focused on giving the end user—the customer—a good product or service to make things more convenient. After all, a person's time was finite, and in this particular affluent market, time didn't equal money. Time was more valuable.

I continued sifting through all the links, clicking and scrolling and reading. After the first half-dozen, most were simply rehashed accounts of the same basic information. I found pictures of him at charity galas and cultural events, always with a different—stunning—woman on his arm.

Finding personal data was a bit more difficult. He'd been divorced twice and was currently single, and he had two children, who, by one account, were both estranged from him.

Red flag number one.

I dug deeper. It seemed that at one point, Freeman had been sued for age discrimination. One of his senior execs had been fired, and she claimed it was because she was too old, in his eyes. Even though he was in his mid-fifties, judging by the age of the women in the photos, anyone over thirty-five was too old, in his eyes. I found a tiny snippet later, in another article, which seemed to indicate the suit had been settled out of court.

Rich people settled a lot of things out of court.

I got up to stretch my back. Walked over to where Sammi had dropped the photo, knelt, and picked up the broken glass, careful not to cut myself. I put it all in a paper bag and put the paper bag in the kitchen trash can.

When you lived in a converted garage the size of mine, you only had room for one table, so I moved my laptop to the side and smoothed the photo out. Examined it. Kristal and I were definitely at a concert, and it had been taken sometime during the early stages of our relationship. I don't remember the venue, or the band, or much else about the night, except for the fact we ended up in my bed before it was over. I'm pretty sure it had been the first time.

Back then, only rich people had cell phone cameras, so pictures weren't nearly as ubiquitous as they are today. Back then, photos were physical objects—and treasured as keepsakes. To me, they seemed to carry more meaning than today's digital images.

I'd carried this photo to prison, and to all the places I'd lived since. It was my only tangible connection to Kristal, and it was one of the only true pieces of evidence I'd ever been happy in my past.

I got up and placed it on top of one of the kitchen cabinets, where no one could carelessly set a drink down on it and where it wouldn't get accidentally swept up with the detritus of a fast-food meal heading into the trash. At some point, I'd have to get another frame for it. Right now, however, I had more important things to do. It had been a while since I had anything important to do, and although Sammi and Kristal were in danger, having something important to do felt good.

I returned to the table and my research, digging deeper and deeper, falling into rabbit hole after rabbit hole. On a cursory look, Freeman appeared like many entrepreneurs. Brash, impulsive, work-hard, play-hard. People seemed to fear him, and he seemed to enjoy that reputation as a bit of a bully. Judging by many of his quotes, Sammi had been right about the guy's ego—ginormous. I found multiple examples of him tweeting or calling a press conference to dispute things people said about him that showed him in a bad light.

There were various accounts by ex-employees—those who hadn't signed confidentiality agreements, presumably—that confirmed the public's perception of Freeman as being a bratty twelve-year-old with a fifty-million-dollar net worth.

Running good cons started with knowing your marks inside and out, better than they knew themselves. Finding out what made them tick. Their motivations, their hot-buttons, their secret desires. Information, the more detailed and personal, the better. Sometimes it took months to gather this kind of valuable data. Unfortunately, we didn't have time to infiltrate Freeman's inner circle or ingratiate ourselves with someone close to him. We were going to have to make some assumptions and keep on our toes. Pay attention to the inevitable changing tides.

Based on what I'd found, though, I think it was safe to assume that Freeman was a greedy, insensitive bully who didn't like to lose.

Good qualities for a mark and a good place to start.

I called and arranged a meeting with my buddy, Bear. He had some skills we would need.

***

With a nickname like Bear, you might expect a 250-pound behemoth of a man with an abundance of back hair and a handshake that would crush all your bones. Or a creature that lumbered along. My friend was the opposite. My Bear might have weighed 120 pounds if he'd just made three trips to the buffet. Which was weird because Bear could put away the food. I don't know where it went after it went down his gullet, but it didn't stick to his frame.

I asked him once where the nickname came from, and he muttered something about calling the fattest guy in the room "Slim." I never bothered asking again.

I hadn't seen Bear in years, but I'd kept track of his doings via social media, at least in a broad sense. He still wasn't married. He still was a bit odd. He still was a computer geek.

He was a buddy from my old life, the one I'd been trying hard to leave behind, so I'd never reached out to him. I was apprehensive, afraid of what emotions I might dredge up if I revisited my dark past, but this wouldn't be the only time, not if I was going to keep my promise to Sammi. I needed a way to come to grips with this one-off con without getting frazzled each time I did something illegal, immoral, or just plain foolish during its course.

Knowing my audience, I suggested we meet at the Tasty Foods Buffet in Annandale, but Bear insisted we meet at a small coffee shop in Chantilly. Even when I told him I'd be buying, he didn't waver. This was disturbing. Bear passing up a free all-you-can-eat meal? What had happened to him?

I plugged Haz Bean into my phone's GPS app, snapped the phone into the dashboard holder, and took off. Fifteen minutes later, I found the café smack in the middle of a strip center, which itself was located in an entire square mile of strip shopping centers. A home improvement store anchored one end, and a discount baby store anchored the other.

Bear was waiting for me at an outside table. When he saw me approach, he popped to his feet. I went for a handshake, but he slid in for a guy-hug. "Dude! Long time."

"Yeah. Long time." Because of our height difference, I was speaking to the top of his head.

An awkward moment later, we broke apart. Bear kept looking me up and down. "So that's what it looks like going straight, huh? It's definitely an argument in favor." He gestured to an empty chair across from his. "Sit, sit."

We took our seats, and I jutted my chin at a plastic tray in front of him with a small stack of half-eaten pastries. "Started without me? I told you I was buying."

"Not exactly." A couple got up from a table near us and walked to their car. "Hang on a sec."

Bear got up, stepped over to their table, and proceeded to clean up after them, nesting their trays and consolidating all their trash. He took it all over to a trashcan and dumped it in, setting the trays on top. It also didn't escape my attention that he returned to our table carrying a doughnut with a bite missing on a napkin. He set it on his tray with the rest of his partially eaten food.

Was Bear in such dire straits that he needed to scrounge food? I leaned in and lowered my voice. "What the hell? I said I was buying. You don't have to eat other people's leftovers."

He clucked his tongue. "Not for me. For some homeless guys, I help out. There's a lot of food here that goes to waste. I collect it and drop it off for them on my way home."

"Doesn't seem too sanitary."

Bear looked offended. "I cut out the germy parts first, of course. Better than starving."

He had a point. "Nobody stops you?"

"I know the owner here. He lets me hang out for as long as I want, using the wi-fi and meeting people. Sometimes I stick around for four or five *hours*. I do some cleaning up, help him out here and there, and he looks the other way about me digging through the trash. And in addition to what I gather, he gives me the surplus and day-olds. He's cool, you should meet him."

"Maybe sometime. Do you want something of your own to eat?"

"Thanks, but I ate before you got here. Three eclairs and a cinnamon roll. Oh, and a cream cheese bagel, too. If you're hungry or thirsty, go ahead."

If I was worried about Bear having changed, I could let that rest. "That's okay, I'm good. I didn't come for the food; I came to talk to you."

"And a sweet talker you are." He kept shifting positions in the chair as if he were sitting on walnuts. I couldn't imagine him fidgeting like that for four or five hours. Didn't he frighten the customers? "Speaking of sweets, did I ever tell you about the time I was at this charming café in New Orleans? And their heavenly beignets? I must have polished off two dozen."

If I didn't cut to the chase, Bear would talk in circles and tangents—and crullers and cupcakes—until he went hoarse. "Kristal's in some serious trouble, and I think I need your help."

"Kristal? Your Kristal?"

I hadn't thought about Kristal being *my* Kristal in two decades. "Know any other Kristals?"

He shook his head. "Just checking."

"Have you been in touch with her lately?" I'd been living with Kristal for a while before Bear arrived on the scene, and together we'd only worked with him once or twice, so I didn't figure he had really bonded with her, but I thought I should ask anyway. There was a lot of stuff that—evidently—I hadn't been aware of.

"No. The minute she disappeared from your life, she disappeared from mine, too." Bear cocked his head. "How come you didn't look me up after you got out?"

I wasn't sure if I wanted to get into it with Bear. I was probably closest to him before I got arrested, and on some level, I assumed he knew my reasons. But just because those reasons were clear in my head, didn't mean they were clear in his. Bottom line, we were friends, and I divorced myself from him when I got set free.

"It's a fair question, isn't it?" Bear asked.

I swallowed. Before I went to prison, I wasn't very good at apologizing. After I got out, it seemed that was all I did. "Sorry, man. I guess I wanted a clean slate. Totally clean. Hell, I wouldn't have even spoken to my mother, except she kept calling me."

"I know. She means well, she really does. And she loves you, even though she doesn't show it very often."

My insides began to churn. "How do you know so much about my mother and her feelings toward me?"

"Dude, I'm tight with Peck. He throws a lot of work my way. Hell, I eat dinner—if you call it that—at your Mom's place once every few months. Of course, I always stop at McD's on the way home to get something edible."

I felt blindsided, mostly because I was. "What kind of work do you do for Peck?"

"I don't work *for* Peck. He introduces me to those who want work. He's the middleman. Like a matchmaker."

"Let me guess. He gets a cut of the action."

"Sure. Way the world works. A referral fee. Like in real estate."

"Except this is in shady dealings."

"You say potato. I say pomme de terre. They both taste good out of the fryer, though." Bear picked up half a chocolate-covered doughnut and took a bite.

"I thought that was for the homeless."

"The chocolate will melt before I leave, so…" he said, mouth half full. "You know how much I hate waste."

"Do me a favor, will you?"

"Sure." He took another bite of the doughnut.

"Don't tell Peck—or my mother—that you talked to me, okay?"

"Sure, boss. Although family is important, and I hate to think you're on the outs with yours. Can't you see past some of their past trans—"

I interrupted Bear's filibuster. "Okay, okay. Let's get down to business. Kristal is, as Sammi says, in deep shit."

Bear held up his hand. "Who is Sammi?"

"Sammi is Kristal's nineteen-year-old daughter." I paused, unsure how to continue. If Bear agreed to help us, he'd probably meet Sammi, and she would probably blab, so I might as well lay all my cards on the table. "Evidently, she's my daughter too."

Bear's eyes went wide, and his mouth dropped open so far I could see bits of chocolate icing on his molars. "Holy shit." He grinned. "I mean, congratulations on becoming a father."

"Thanks, I guess." I waited as Bear mumbled "Holy shit" over and over. "You done yet?"

"Holy shit, holy shit, holy shit. Now I'm done." A sheen of perspiration covered his forehead. "Holy shit, you're a father!"

"*Maybe* I'm a father. You remember Kristal, right? Con artist extraordinaire? This could all be bullshit."

"Yeah. Sure. Okay. Right." With each word, he settled down a notch more. "So. What kind of trouble is she in and what kind of help does she need?"

"She owes a lot of money to a very bad man. One who's threatened her with severe bodily harm if she doesn't pay him back, and soon."

"Who's the heavy?"

"Yelton Norvetch."

"Ouch. That's major league, all right. Can't believe Kristal got tangled up with him." Bear's expression sagged. "What's your thinking?"

"Still working on the details. Evidently, Kristal has some kind of bogus investment opportunity she can dangle in front of some rich schmuck. If he bites and forks over some dough, then she can repay her debts and get out from under this goon."

"Sounds like a plan. How is it working with Kristal again?"

"I'm not exactly. Sammi contacted me. Kristal doesn't know anything about it."

Bear let out a low whistle, and a lady two tables over looked up. He waved at her, then turned back to me. "Doesn't sound like a recipe for success."

"Sammi knows the details, and we'll let Kristal know when we've got everything all set up. Then she won't be able to say no. Are you still doing what you do so well?"

"I couldn't stop if I wanted to. Computers are in my blood."

"Good. We'll need all the usual technical support. Hacking, website design, etc. You remember the Westheimer job? The bogus filings and all the ginned-up documentation? The slick fake website? Can you handle that? We're on a very tight time frame."

Bear pulled out his phone, tapped a few keys. "Let's see, let's see. I think I can squeeze you in." He set down his phone and smiled. "I'd fit you in no matter how busy I am."

"Thanks, pal."

He tipped his head at me.

"Okay. Here's what I think we need to get started." I reeled off half a dozen things I needed to know about Freeman. Mostly information not available publicly. I knew most databases were no match for Bear. If it could be hacked into, he could do it. Hell, I bet he gave the Russians lessons. I also asked him to troll the dark recesses of all the social media sites to discover any rumors, innuendo, or hearsay regarding our mark. You didn't know what information might come in handy until you found it. Bear had a great feel for what I was looking for.

When I finished outlining my request, he simply nodded. "You got it." He leaned back and clasped his hands behind his head as if he were vacationing at the beach. "You know, it's great to have you back in my life, Chance. It's been empty without you. Now it will be like old times. You and me against the fricking world." He leaned forward and picked up another partially eaten pastry, turned it over to examine it, then stuffed it into his maw.

Great to have you back in my life? My stomach did another somersault, and I didn't think it was from watching Bear eat someone else's garbage.

Chapter Eleven

Bear would be a great help in whatever hustle we designed, except he wasn't exactly the type of person we'd want interfacing with actual people. His strength was working with computers and data and all those behind-the-scenes things that were essential, but that didn't require any type of finesse, tact, personal grooming, or basic manners.

When it came to acting a role, Kristal was the Academy Award winner, hands down. But I didn't know the extent of her current involvement with the scam, and we'd be screwed if she'd already claimed one role when we needed her to fulfill another, especially if she'd already contacted Freeman. And there was always the very real possibility Kristal would tell me to go screw myself, furious I was still working with Sammi over her objections.

In other words, I needed a capable backup, and fortunately, I had someone perfect in mind.

I swung by my place to pick up Hobie. He'd called while I was talking to Bear, and said he had something urgent he needed to discuss with me, something that couldn't be discussed over the phone.

When I pulled up in front of his house, he was leaning against a lamppost, waiting for me. He bounded over to my car and hopped in. Fastened his seat belt. Then he turned to me. "Hey, Chance. What's going on?"

"What's going on with you? What's the emergency?"

"No emergency. Just bored."

"Seriously?" I tried to keep my voice even. "I've got a lot of things to do today."

"You snuck out of here pretty early, you know."

"What are you talking about?"

"I figured after our encounter yesterday, with those two, uh, gentlemen, that you'd want a wing man with you."

"Well, you thought wrong." I hit the button to unlock the car door, hoping Hobie would take the hint. "I think I'm good today."

He didn't unfasten his seat belt. "We both know you're up to something. Something dangerous. I can be a big help to you, even if you don't quite know it yet."

I eyed him. He *had* lifted that dude's wallet. What other latent skills did Hobie possess? More importantly, how much time would I have to waste trying to get rid of him? "Okay. You can come along for the ride. But please keep your arms and legs inside the vehicle."

Hobie's smile could have lit up a dark alley.

Twenty minutes later, we were standing in the reception area of Thurgood's Exquisite Properties, a boutique, high-end realty company. Two leather couches were artfully positioned against one wall, and a grouping of fancy Cherrywood chairs surrounded a marble-topped coffee table. Framed pictures of mega-mansions hung on the wall. If your property wasn't worth at least three million, don't even bother calling.

As we waited for the receptionist, Hobie whispered in my ear. "Thinking about moving?"

"All day long. You see the shithole I live in. But I think I'm out of my price range here."

"We're just window shopping?"

"Actually, we're here to see a friend."

The receptionist hung up and almost blinded us with her smile. "May I help you, gentlemen?"

I tried to match her wattage but had no chance. "We're here to see Antonella de la Verona."

She looked us up and down, gaze settling on Hobie's orange Crocs for a beat too long. "Who shall I say is calling?"

"Chance Winston."

"I'll let her know you're here." She kept smiling at us, and I wondered when she was going to let Ella know we were there. Ten seconds passed until finally she said, "You may have a seat over there." She nodded to one of the leather couches.

"Thank you."

Hobie and I took our seats, and then the receptionist picked up her phone and dialed. She swiveled on her chair so her back was facing us and lowered her voice so we couldn't hear what she was saying. A moment later, she spun around and hung up. "Miss de la Verona will be out shortly. May I get you anything?"

"No thanks," I said.

"Do you have any coffee?" Hobie asked, almost simultaneously.

The receptionist made a face, then said, "Certainly. How do you take it?"

"Four creams, two sugars," Hobie said.

"Just a moment." She got up and came around the desk, then disappeared down a short hallway.

"Coffee? It's almost one o'clock," I said.

"I just wanted to make her get outta that chair," Hobie said. "Did you see the face she made when she saw my shoes?"

"I'm not blind, am I?"

The receptionist returned and glided across the room to deliver Hobie's coffee. "Thanks," he said, taking it and setting it on a wooden side table, sans coaster, as if he really had no use for it. She opened her mouth to say something, then thought better of it and stalked back to her post behind her desk. Every ten seconds or so, she'd glance at us, probably getting more pissed every moment Hobie didn't take a sip.

Five minutes went by, and Hobie didn't reach for his coffee once, nor did he meet her eyes at any point.

My phone buzzed. A text from Sammi. *We're all set for today.*

Sammi and I needed to get Kristal on board, so the plan was to spring it on her during lunch, a two-on-one full-court press. I texted back. *Good. Text me meeting place.*

As I was hitting send, Ella came out to greet us. The last time I'd seen her had been at my trial, when she'd sat in the back of the courtroom providing moral support. She'd looked great then, but she looked even more fabulous now. She wore a cobalt blue wraparound silk dress that accentuated her flawless dark complexion. Her five-inch heels brought her over six feet tall. Trim and fit, expertly applied make-up. One of the few women I knew who could go peep-toe to peep-toe with Kristal in the looks department.

"Chance!" She gave me a hug, and her hair smelled like a meadow of wildflowers. "It's so great to see you." She let me go. "You look terrific." Her words were tinged with an Italian accent.

"And you're full of crap."

She pushed me playfully. "Well, you look terrific to me." She looked over my shoulder. "Who's your dashing friend?"

After Hobie put his eyes back in his head, he extended his hand. "Hobie Harrison. Friend of Chance's. It's a pleasure to meet you."

"Ah, the pleasure is all mine." She glanced at the receptionist and turned back to us. "Why don't we go back to my office? It's more private there."

We followed her down the hall, past half a dozen well-appointed offices. Her perfume acted as a trail guide, and I figured one bottle cost as much as a car payment. Ella's thousand-dollar dresses and thousand-dollar shoes and thousand-dollar earrings enhanced the overall international supermodel image to maximum effect. When you worked in high-end properties—either selling them or ripping them off—appearances mattered a whole lot. Ella was the complete package, all the way down to the fancy nom de guerre.

She stopped at an office at the end of the hall and welcomed us in with a whoosh of the arm. "Here we are."

Her office was about as large as the waiting room. A sleek modern desk faced the door, and from the window you could see most of Tysons Corner— at least the parts that weren't obscured by the ever-present construction cranes.

"Have a seat, over here." Another grand gesture to a designer sofa in front of an angular glass table. Hobie and I shared the couch while she sat opposite in a snow-white ultra-modern chair that looked like it came straight from Italy. "This is certainly a surprise. To what do I owe the pleasure?"

"I need your help, Ella."

"My help? After all these years?"

"I need the best."

"Are you in the market for an *exquisite property*?" Her eyes twinkled.

"I think you know the kind of help I need."

She cut her eyes toward Hobie, who hadn't said a word since he'd said hello out in the reception area.

"He's cool," I said.

She appraised him. "If you say so." Her accent seemed to thicken, and she smiled at Hobie. "Okay, any friend of yours is a pal-o-mine." Her last sentence came out in a Midwestern accent, flat vowels and all. *Arrivederci, Roma!*

When I'd first met Ella, her name had been Monique Clarke, from the South Side of Chicago. She'd been an elite hustler, and together we'd pulled some amazing cons. Even then, she'd always talked about selling real estate as a back-up plan. Back then, though, she never told me about her desire to transform from city girl into international sexpot who spoke with a slight Italian accent. Hell, it wouldn't surprise me to know she'd never even been to Italy.

Hobie shook his head as if his ears were stuffed with cotton.

Ella laughed. "Rich people—men, mostly—respond much better to an Italian flirt than to a Black girl from the projects. Not too many Black Italians, so I've got that exotic thing going for me, too. I adopted this persona when I started in real estate ten years ago. Now I put it on every morning before I go to work, right along with my mascara. It pays off handsomely."

I knew men found Ella very attractive, but it was a one-way street. Ella didn't swing that way, at least not when I worked with her.

"Nice," Hobie said.

"Whatever it takes," she said, reverting back to the accent. "I use it so much, I almost fool myself into believing I'm Italian." She kissed her fingers like a quintessential Italian.

I glanced around the office. "Looks like you're doing quite well."

She laughed again. "I *am* doing great. And it's all legal."

My heart sank. I didn't want to be the guy to mess up her amazing life. I knew how I felt when Sammi asked me to return to the game, and I didn't want to burden Ella. I rose. "You know, I think we'll be going now."

Ella's smile turned into a frown. "Why?"

"Change of plans. This was a mistake."

"Chance Winston, you sit right down." The accent disappeared. "I haven't seen you in years, and you're not waltzing out of here until I know what's going on."

I sat back down. Sighed. "Look, you're doing great. I don't want to drag you down into the mud."

Her eyes flashed. "How about if you tell me why you're here and what you need. Then let *me* decide whether I want to help or not. I'm a big girl. Can't get much fairer than that?" She turned to Hobie, fixed him with her dazzling *belladonna* smile. "Am I right, Hobie?"

"Uh, yes ma'am."

She turned back to me. "Go on. Spill."

I started to tell her about what was going on, but as soon as I mentioned Kristal's name, Ella interrupted me. "You know, I never actually met Kristal. She was before I knew you." Her lips curled funny. "But I know how much she meant to you back then. I wasn't aware you two were back together."

"We're not. In fact, I hadn't even seen her in years."

One of Ella's manicured eyebrows lifted. "Okay. Continue then."

I recapped Kristal's situation, and when I got to the part about the two musclemen accosting us, I played up Hobie's role in the skirmish. Just as I was telling her how Hobie lifted the big dude's wallet, Ella interrupted again.

"So, you and Kristal aren't a thing. Then why are you so invested in helping her?"

I shrugged.

"Something isn't adding up, Chance."

"I don't know what you're getting at." Aside from being slick and gorgeous, Ella was quite intuitive. Next to me on the couch, I could feel Hobie squirming. I hadn't yet mentioned the part about Sammi possibly being my daughter.

"I'm not letting you off the hook so easy." She maintained steady eye contact, until finally I had to look away. "Chance…"

"It looks like I have a daughter," I said, watching for Ella's reaction. And there was one, too. A huge smile, white teeth, and dancing eyes.

"Congratulations. Am I to assume Kristal is the mother?"

"Yeah."

"And you just found out?"

"Yeah."

"Life's weird, ain't it?" Ella said, losing the Italian accent for a second.

"You can say that again."

Hobie piped in. "Chance will make a good father."

"Well, the Chance I knew was a good man," Ella said. "I'm sure he'll make a good father."

"Her name is Sammi, and she's almost twenty. I think it's a bit too late to be any kind of father."

"It's never too late," Ella and Hobie said simultaneously.

There was silence all around as we each got lost in our thoughts. Possibly each of us thinking about our own fathers, and how we turned out. I know I was thinking of mine, and how I didn't want to emulate him, even if I didn't really think I would have much input into Sammi's life.

"What's the plan?" Ella said, bringing me back to the here and now. She shifted positions, and the slit in her dress opened up a bit, exposing a very fit thigh. When I glanced up, her expression said I'd been busted gawking.

I cleared my throat. "I'm not sure I'd call it a plan, just yet, but here's what I was thinking." I proceeded to sketch out a few ideas, thinking as I went along in spots, relying on past cons in other places to provide a foundation for this one. Throughout my discourse, Ella's interest seemed to grow. Weirdly, so did mine.

When I was almost finished, Ella interrupted once again. "You probably need a location, right? Someplace to base your operations. An office or some warehouse space, anonymous, nondescript. I can help you there. Plus, you'll need a glitzier location for meetings with the mark, someplace that looks expensive, but is out of the public spotlight. Someplace without a traceable history. We'll need to gin up some bogus purchasing and ownership history.

Make sure the place is appointed properly—from furnishings and knick-knacks to statement art on the wall. I can help you on all accounts." Her face shone, and her excitement was spilling over, as she spoke faster and faster. "You'll also need people to play some juicy roles. Maybe someone who can represent international participation? Someone who's a whiz with accents? I am *ze fraulein* you require." She said the last part in a German accent. "I'm your Sheila for that, too, mate," she said, switching to a perfect Australian accent.

I shook my head. "I appreciate the offer, but it's all downside risk for you. If you get caught, then all this, all that you've worked so hard to build, goes right down the toilet."

"Chance, my dear." She rose, gestured. "All this is just scorekeeping. It's not about the materialistic trappings for me. It's about the game. The competition. You, of all people, should know this about me. I don't dress or act like I do because I like it. I just like winning and hate, hate, hate losing. Despise it. What you see—all the fakery and bluster—that's what I need to do in order to win." She sighed. "But frankly, I'm getting bored with all this. Too easy. I need more of a challenge. I want to feel my pulse pound." She was working herself up, like an actor on stage delivering the scene-stealing monologue. "Life's too short to waste a second. When it's my time, I want to go out in a blaze of glory, laying it all out there, everything on the line. I want to feel alive!"

I stared at her for a beat, and she stared back, face aflame. Then I started giving her a slow-clap. Hobie joined in, and for a moment, Ella stood still, taking it all in. Then she laughed and took a deep theatrical bow. "How'd I do? Pretty fucking good acting, dontcha think?"

"A real natural," I said. "But I can't ask you to get involved. I could never live with myself if something bad happened."

"You don't have to ask. I volunteer. You'd be doing me a gigantic favor. What I do here isn't exactly boring, but it's not as exciting as what you've got planned. Here, if I screw up, I lose some money. Big deal, I've got plenty. But if we screw up with your plan, something serious happens. Life-and-death serious. And to me, that's the ultimate test. I'm an adrenaline junkie, just like I always was. More so, in fact, because I'm never laying it all out there. Besides, I'd never turn down a *chance* to work with you." She winked. "See what I did there?"

I sat back, looked across the room, and out the window. We needed Ella's skills. We needed her experience. We needed her access to real estate properties. Most of all, we needed her *presence*. Plain and simple, Monique Clarke was a winner, no matter what her name currently was. "Welcome to the team."

"Yes!" She gave a fist pump worthy of a gold medal Olympian, then rushed to her desk. She rifled through a basket of files, plucked a few out, then a few more, and returned to where Hobie and I were still sitting. When we'd first seen her, Ella's eyes twinkled, and she emanated a level of brightness befitting a wheeler-dealer high-end realtor. Exactly how I remembered her, even during the dark time of my trial. But now she seemed positively effervescent. Amazing what the possibility of going to jail will do for one's spirits. Of course, for many people, that would mean abject fear. For Ella, it meant excitement.

She practically threw the files at me. "Check these out. I think they'll be perfect for what we need."

I opened the top file. A glossy photo of some multi-million-dollar mansion. I glanced at the contents of some of the other files. All primo estates. I could feel Hobie's hot breath as he looked at the pictures over my shoulder. "Nice," he said. "But if we could afford these, we wouldn't have to con anyone."

Ella said, "We won't have to pay a cent for these. They're my listings, and they aren't presently occupied. See, when you're rich enough to afford one of these babies, it's not your only house. The owners are all living elsewhere, most of them in even fancier digs. Any of these will work—all we'll need to do is create a different paper trail. One that matches our needs, of course."

"These look great," I said.

"Thank you." Ella beamed. "Let me know which one you think will work best, and I'll get started with the phony paperwork. You know the kind of info I'll need: names, countries of origin, dates of purchase, things like that. This isn't your first rodeo."

"When I figure it out, I'll let you know."

"Don't screw around. I'll also need to get some basic office space. Want me to handle all the logistics, too? Burner phones, business cards, website?"

"Bear is going to do the electronic stuff."

"Bear's involved? I haven't seen him in years."

"He's the same. Except now he scrounges in the trash for doughnuts."

"Sounds about right." Ella laughed. "So, you're getting the band back together. Peck, too?"

I swallowed. "Nope. He's busy with other things."

"And how is your mother?"

"Why don't we concentrate on the task at hand? That should keep us plenty busy." I spit the words out.

Ella looked taken aback. Had I said it too harshly?

"Well, *excuuuuse* me. Just asking about the family. You don't have to bite my head off." Ella glared at me for a second, then returned to glam mode. "What's Hobie's role in all this?"

A good question. I hadn't officially asked him to join in, and I didn't really know his capabilities beyond pickpocketing. For all I knew, he had no desire to get involved, and he was just tagging along because he was bored being home and alone. But before I even had an opportunity to answer, he spoke up.

"I'll do whatever's necessary. Sort of a Jack-of-all-trades, I guess you could say. Like a utility fielder in baseball. Can do everything but hit the curveball."

I smiled weakly. When it came to hustling, most of the pitches we saw *were* curveballs.

Chapter Twelve

I left Hobie with Ella so they could get started on things and headed to my meeting with Kristal and Sammi. We needed to get Kristal's buy-in on some level. Ideally, she'd be all in—willing to participate in the con she and Sammi had already put into motion. If she was still pissed at me working with Sammi, I could understand her reluctance. But at the very least, we needed her permission to allow Sammi to help us continue what they had started. We could easily pull it off without Sammi being an active player, but we couldn't pull it off without all the knowledge and background material she possessed.

As I walked to my car in the Thurgood parking lot, I thought about Kristal and tried to imagine what it would have been like to be nineteen, pregnant, and without much of a support system. With a sometime-asshole as a live-in boyfriend.

I almost deserved getting slugged in the gut by her.

Five yards from my car, someone stepped out from behind a minivan and grabbed me by my arm and twisted it up around my back, like a professional. Then he perp-walked me the rest of the way to my car and slammed my chest down onto the hood. Hard.

"Listen, asswipe. We warned you off. Told you to stop helping this Kristal chick. Did you think we were just screwing around?" He lifted me up six inches, then rammed me into the car again. I tried to arch my neck backward so my face wouldn't hit the hood, but wasn't fully successful. "What do I need to do so you'll hear me this time?"

I craned my head around, got a glimpse of the assailant's face. As I thought, it was one of the guys, K-Bar, who accosted me and Hobie outside the menswear store. "I hear you."

"Yes, but will you *listen* to me? That's the real question, isn't it?"

"Who are you working for?" I struggled to catch my breath, and my ribs ached.

"Mr. None of Your Fucking Business, that's who. If you're still sticking your nose where it don't belong, I just might cut it off. Capisce?" He threw me down and released his grip.

Slowly, I uncurled and turned around.

He sneered at me, then launched forward with a right to my gut, just like Kristal had, except ten times harder. I felt the air whoosh from my lungs, and my knees buckle. I slid down the side of the car until my ass hit the asphalt.

"That was for stealing my buddy's wallet, fuckwad."

He spat at my feet, then spun around and walked off.

I stayed on the ground for a while as I did a quick inventory. Ribs hurt, arm hurt, chin hurt, stomach hurt. Ego definitely hurt. Sitting on my ass driving people around had made me complacent and dulled my reflexes.

Nothing seemed broken, however, and a few beers and a handful of Advil should numb the physical pain. Not sure what would soothe my ego beyond exacting some revenge on the goon. I put that goal on my mental bucket list.

* * *

I arrived at the food court in Westfield Montgomery Mall, fifteen minutes before Kristal and Sammi were due, not wanting to ruin the surprise. I grabbed some dumplings and an egg roll at the Wok Lightly And Carry a Big Chopstick food booth. I hadn't eaten anything except an energy bar I scarfed down in the car after I met with Bear. My jaw was sore from my parking lot encounter, but I'd manage somehow.

I carried my tray to a table way in the back and faced the wall. Sammi wanted to ease into things, so we were following her plan. Claiming she wanted to have a heart-to-heart talk with her mother, she'd persuaded Kristal to do it over lunch at the food court. Sammi was going to call me and leave her phone on the table, face down, so I could overhear their conversation.

When Sammi felt the time was right, she'd call me over, and we'd do our best to get Kristal to see things our way. Sammi thought I'd be able to weave in whatever I overheard during their talk to help alleviate any of Kristal's concerns. To get her to say yes.

It wasn't a terrible plan, but I had a feeling I might end up getting slugged in the gut. And I was getting a little tired of that.

I swallowed some Advil and had taken two bites of my egg roll when my phone buzzed. I put it to my ear quietly and listened in.

"Looks delicious," I heard Kristal say. I refrained from turning around, not wanting to give myself away, if she happened to be looking in my direction.

"Yeah, it does," Sammi answered.

"What do you want to talk about? Sounded important," Kristal said.

"Only our lives," Sammi said, teenage snark oozing through the phone line. I could only imagine what it felt like in person, complete with facial gestures. "Some bad men are after us, Mom, and we have to do something about it."

"Keep your voice down," Kristal said in a harsh whisper. "I am doing something about it. I'm looking for that asshole Granger."

"Come on, Mom, He's probably halfway to Mexico by now. Plus, that's only a small portion of what we need."

"It'll buy us some time. You got a better idea?"

"Actually, I do. A much better way. We need to move forward with the Freeman job."

"That would be nice, but we're not ready. We'd need another three months to shift things around, and find somebody else, now that Granger skipped out. Even then, who knows if Freeman would be interested. And we have less than a week. We'd never be able to pull it off. Too risky to rush it."

"If I told you we could get it done in time, would you change your mind?"

"What's going on, Sammi?" A pause. "Why do I get the feeling I'm being suckered into something?"

"Would I ever do that to you?" I sensed this line was delivered with a huge grin.

"Tell me what this is about, Sammi." Another pause. "This is about Chance, isn't it? I told you to stay away from him, and I told him to stay away from you."

I could practically feel Kristal's gaze on my back as I imagined her scanning the eatery looking for me.

"First off, this is my idea. Second, he's my father. Third, you yourself said how great he is. How he's a master of quick thinking and adapting to any situation. How there's not another person on this planet you would trust with your life."

"That was a long time ago, Sammi. Another lifetime."

"I don't think he's changed."

"Believe me, girl, we've all changed. Besides, he doesn't want any part of this. Following me around is one thing, but actually pulling a job? That's something else entirely. He's gone straight, remember?"

"He'd do it to help me."

"I don't want you to get hurt. You're the only good thing in my life, you know."

"How am I going to get hurt? What, you think he's going to reject me when I ask him?"

Kristal didn't say anything, and I pictured her shrugging.

"How about this? How about we ask him if he's interested? I'd rather risk getting rejected than risk getting my kneecaps blown off. Wouldn't you?" Sammi said.

"Don't you think you're being a bit melodramatic?"

"Mom! If we don't come up with the money, they are going to kill us. After they torture the crap out of us. To make an example for their other clients."

Someone made a sound I couldn't quite identify. Then sobbing. "Oh, Sammi. I've truly fucked this up, haven't I?"

I'd had enough. I turned my head slowly and peered over my shoulder. Kristal and Sammi were sitting about forty feet away, at a table bordering the main concourse. Kristal had her head in her hands, and Sammi used the opportunity to glance around the eatery, trying to spot me. When she looked in my direction, her head stopped moving, and she gave a quick nod. Then it was back to Kristal.

She leaned in close to her mother. "We have a chance to save our skins. All you have to do is say yes. And we can take that scumbag Freeman for all he's worth and live happily ever after."

Kristal raised her head. "No, Sammi, there is no happily ever after. I'm afraid we're fucked."

That was my cue. I weaved my way through the food court tables, making a wide circle so I could approach their table from behind. I didn't want to give Kristal the opportunity to flee if she saw me coming. When I came into Sammi's view, I didn't notice even a flicker in her eyes. I made a mental note to never play poker with her.

I stopped for a beat about ten feet behind Kristal, took a deep breath, then glided right up to their table and pulled out an empty chair. Sat. "Hello, ladies. Mind if I join you?"

Her expression went from surprise to anger to resignation in about two seconds. "If I say yes, will you go away?"

"You always were the comedian."

Her eyes narrowed. "What happened to you? Run into a wall?"

I didn't want to go into details about getting jumped in the parking lot. I'd been hurt a lot worse, a lot of times. "Something like that."

She shook her head. "I knew you were involved in this. You never did listen to me. Never considered what I wanted. It was always the Chance Winston show, and I just had a bit part."

"You know that's not true at all. Then or now. I am considering what's best for you and Sammi. And I came to the conclusion that staying alive is better than not." I nodded to Sammi, who, to her credit, had stayed quiet. "Besides, Sammi came to me and asked for my help. She's an adult, and she's also my daughter. So, I think I'm going to help her. The only question is this: Are you going to help her too?"

Kristal applauded. "Bravo! Terrific speech. Sounds like the end of a cheesy movie, when the main character tries to fire up the downtrodden troops."

I glanced at Sammi, who shrugged. "Sounded good to me. I'd buy what you're selling."

I continued, undeterred. "The way I see it, you really have two choices. Head for the hills or dig in, work the scam on Freeman, and pay back your debt. And you've already told me you have no intention of running and looking over your shoulder the rest of your life." I sat back and offered a smug smile. "Okay. Now I'm done with my speech."

This time, no applause. Kristal sighed loudly, a defeated expression making her entire face sag. A half-hearted shrug. "I know when I'm fighting a losing battle. I suppose we might as well head toward our doom kicking and screaming. I mean, sure, Chance, let's give it the ol' college try."

Sammi turned to me. "We're not going to get a more enthusiastic *yes* than that." She rubbed her hands together, and I could feel the sheer excitement emanating from her body. Mother and father, together again—at long last—working with her on the scam of her life, to *save* her life. Oh, to be nineteen again, before you got kicked in the teeth by reality on a weekly basis. I envied Sammi a bit, but I think the entire situation struck me in a different way. If we failed, my daughter would become a victim of violence. My *daughter*.

"Okay, geniuses, now what?" Kristal asked.

"Pick up right where we left off."

"I don't know." She sighed again.

"In for a penny, you always say." Sammi glanced at me, then back at Kristal. "Come on, you're the best there is. Call Freeman. Turn on your charm. Arrange a meeting with him."

"Finish up your meal, then we can get started," I said to Kristal. "We've got a lot to do before tomorrow."

"I've lost my appetite," Kristal said, but I could sense the hope in her voice.

Despite my pledge to go straight, I felt my own heart race.

The con was on.

Chapter Thirteen

A couple of things.

Everybody had a hustle going on. The scams ranged in scope from big, once-in-a-lifetime cons to penny-ante swindles, from those that were patently illegal to those that were simply on the shady side of the ethical divide. Some targeted a large number of people, other cons focused on merely a gullible few. But all the hustles had two critical things in common: a mark aching to believe—in riches, fame, love, whatever—and a con artist aching to ease that mark's pain.

And there wasn't a big difference between con artists and actors. Both were produced in the same factory, on the same assembly line, from the same misshapen molds. The only difference was at the end of the line, when God—or whoever factory foreperson you believed in—dropped a brain into the empty skull. Actors' brains wanted to entertain, con artists' brains wanted to separate people from their hard-earned money.

Right now, we wanted to separate that scumbag Freeman from a decent portion of his ill-gotten cash.

Kristal and I spent the entire evening at my place, writing our script and rehearsing our lines. We plotted out how we wanted the con to go, but knew things never went according to script. There was a lot of ad-libbing and improv, so we practiced that, too, riffing off each other, coming up with new twists and clever ideas, batting them around, building them up—and tearing them down. All part of the creative process.

We kept at it for hours, fueling ourselves first with coffee and ice cream, then moving on to beer and a late-night pizza, as if we were nineteen again.

Sammi was at home. She'd wanted to come and help, but Kristal and I needed to get back in the groove together, and having to explain things to Sammi would just slow us down. We were under the gun, and we couldn't afford to waste any time.

Finally, around one a.m., we called it a night.

"We made some real progress. I'm beginning to feel like we might actually pull this thing off," Kristal said, pulling me down on the sofa next to her.

I had the same inkling. Working with Kristal again felt nice. Comfortable. And exhilarating, too. "I think you could be right. We make a pretty good team, don't we?"

She took my hand. "Yeah, we do." She fixed her blue eyes on me, and for a moment, I could see all the way to the center of the universe. I leaned in to kiss her, just a short one, but she grabbed me and wouldn't let go, mouth hungrily on mine.

We didn't even make it to the bedroom.

Afterward, we lay on the couch, her lithe body snuggled tight against mine, both of us glistening with sweat. Two people slaking twenty years of thirst for each other. Wild animals in heat coming together to satisfy a primal urge.

Kristal ran a finger across my chest. "Do you believe in people getting a second chance, Chance?" She smiled at her wordplay, exactly like she used to whenever she could double up on the *chances*.

"I do. I really do." And I did.

We stayed there on the couch, basking in the afterglow, for twenty minutes.

Then, wordlessly, we moved to the bedroom. This time, we slowed things down. Took the opportunity to explore each other, to stretch out and luxuriate in the here and now. The passion was still there, too, but so was the patience. This time, it felt like we'd known each other our entire lives. And this time, it felt as if we knew we would remain lovers forever.

* * *

The ability to read a mark was one of the most important skills to have in the con game. Playing a role convincingly was important. Flexibility was vital. Having a well-organized plan was key. But if you didn't know which buttons to press to get your mark to react exactly how you wanted, you were shooting geese at midnight under a moonless sky.

I was damn good at it, but I was strictly junior varsity compared to Kristal.

Kristal and I sat across a ginormous walnut desk from Nathanial Freeman. She'd changed from jeans-and-t-shirt casual into sharp-professional-woman attire. Tailored business suit, nice heels, expensive but understated jewelry. Expertly applied make-up. She had managed to "forget" to button one extra button on her blouse, however, giving Freeman a hint of what lay underneath. From the way Freeman's eyes dilated when she entered his office, I could tell she'd read him perfectly.

Freeman wasn't dressed too shabby either. Custom-tailored five-thousand-dollar suit, shoes shined to a mirror finish, Rolex watch peeking out from under a shirt that cost as much as my entire wardrobe. Perfectly coifed salt-and-pepper hair and a mouth full of even white—perfect—teeth. He could have stepped off a movie set—and not as some anonymous extra. Freeman had panache—and, worse, he knew it.

He was also famously single, and his social antics could be followed in the *Happenings* section of the local papers.

The bigger the ego, the harder the fall. More importantly, the harder it was to admit you'd been swindled and the less likely the mark was to go public. Freeman, like all the other high rollers with mega egos, had a reputation to uphold. We were counting on that.

"You were very persuasive on the phone, Miss…" Freeman glanced down at the card Kristal handed him when we were ushered into his office. "Larsen. Most people would have given up after the first no." He chuckled in a manner he thought was charming. "And certainly by the third one. I admire your persistence."

"I learned long ago that it pays to pursue what you want," Kristal said with a touch of a vague Scandinavian accent. "And please, call me Anna."

"Very well, Anna." He wiped the smile from his face. "I'm quite intrigued by your approach as well as by all the mystery. Tell me, what tremendous business opportunity awaits?"

Kristal had summarized her call with Freeman on the ride over, and I had to hand it to her. She'd managed to paint a picture of a very exciting and lucrative venture without giving any details. But we could only talk in generalities for so long. At some point, we would have to provide Freeman some real numbers and some facts. One of the fundamental rules of running a successful con, though, was to make as much stuff as possible seem to come from the mark himself.

We'd also agreed to let her do most of the talking. She possessed the *it* factor. Compared to her, I was dumpy Uncle Fred with halitosis. Some things never changed.

"I know you're a busy man, so I'll cut right to the heart. We represent a company that wants to build a theme park here, and we need someone to purchase land—on the relative cheap, might be the best way to describe it—without divulging our client's interest. You hold a lot of sway in this market, and you have bought significant parcels of land in the past."

"So, I wouldn't arouse much suspicion, right?" Freeman said.

"That is correct. It's very simple. You buy the land. Then our client buys the land from you, with a healthy profit margin built in. Yet still at a discount to them, if their plans had indeed become public. We hope doing it this way will also sidestep some of the opposition from the local residents affected. The general public hates developers, yes? I do not understand why, exactly. They provide jobs and tax revenue, yet they…" Kristal waved her hand in the air. "Never mind. I don't know why I let them agitate me so." She crossed her legs, and her skirt hiked up a bit. She made a big show of smoothing it back down, somehow leaning over in the process to give Freeman a better look at her cleavage.

He took advantage of that opportunity, too.

Kristal whipped her head up and caught him admiring. Her smile intensified. "As I was saying. This is a win-win situation."

Freeman picked up a gold coin from his desk and toyed with it, running it across the back of his hand from knuckle to knuckle like I'd seen professional poker players do with their chips. "A theme park. Like Disney?"

"I'm not at liberty to divulge details, but let's just say that our clients envision a destination park that caters to families. With broad market appeal. With some very recognizable characters from the world of animation."

"Sounds big. Where is this parcel of land?"

"Not too far. Within forty minutes of Washington and the many millions of people living in the vicinity."

"Maryland? Virginia? DC itself?"

"Yes, you've narrowed it down perfectly." Kristal played coy and fingered a diamond pendant on a gold chain around her neck, drawing Freeman's glance once again toward her cleavage.

Freeman ran the coin across his hand. "Let me guess. You're not going to tell me until I've signed something."

"You didn't get to where you are without being a smart man."

"Really? I'm not used to signing non-disclosures."

"Discretion is crucial to this deal, and if you decide not to move forward, we need to be able to work with some other firms. I'm sure you understand. In fact, if our roles here were reversed, I'm sure you would insist on the same protections." Kristal flashed a blinding smile.

Freeman turned the gold coin around in his hand. "What's the time frame?"

"They hope to break ground within eighteen months. Completion date will vary somewhat on the final scope of the project, yada, yada. But they hope to have the park fully functional within four years or so."

"Fairly ambitious."

"We're talking about one of the world's leading theme park operators. They're looking for this to be their flagship park in North America. All the bells and whistles."

"Flagship, huh? You picked a good underserved market," Freeman said, nodding. "I suppose the area jurisdictions will appreciate the many, many jobs you'll create, too."

Kristal nodded slightly in response, mirroring Freeman's own mannerisms. "Indeed. And they'll need to sub out many services. I imagine some of the companies within your holdings are providers our clients might consider."

Freeman stopped playing with the gold coin and carefully placed it on his desk, next to a marble pen holder. "This opportunity seems more and more interesting."

"I thought you might see it that way."

Freeman suddenly swiveled in his chair to face me. "You're awfully quiet. What's your role in this?"

I cleared my throat. "I'm Miss Larsen's DC rep. Just along to help her negotiate some of the area's zoning laws and regulations. Provide her with some local knowledge."

He held my gaze for a moment, and I could tell he thought I was just some lackey in a suit.

Kristal gave me a pat on the leg. "Charles is an invaluable resource. I'd be lost without him." You didn't have to listen too hard to hear her patronizing undertone.

Freeman shook his head slightly, and I read it as he didn't respect me and my role one bit. I smothered a smile. Kristal and I were falling into our old rhythms, like a well-practiced team. I had to admit, it felt great.

"This definitely sounds like something I'd be interested in pursuing, but I'd need more details, of course, and I'm not sure I want to sign something in order to get them. I think my lawyers would be mad at me." Freeman shot his cuffs and tugged at the sleeve of his suit jacket.

"Some people might interpret that as a sign of mistrust." Kristal crossed her legs. I knew she enjoyed the cat-and-mouse aspect of the con. She once told me that she knew she was doing well when her heart rate entered the red zone. I figured we were pretty close now.

"Prudence, actually. I may be something of a risk-taker, but I'm no fool. There's a certain amount of due diligence required in every deal. I'm sure you would agree, Anna." Freeman made some ridiculous motion with his hand, I'm sure he thought was suave.

"Of course. I understand completely." She paused, pretending to consider something, then, after a long moment of silence, she stood, frowned. "I am truly sorry we couldn't work something out." She extended her arm across the desk for a handshake, and as she did, she dropped the files in her other hand. They tumbled to the ground in a flurry of paper and manila folders.

Exactly as we'd practiced not more than two hours ago.

I laid my leather portfolio on Freeman's desk, open to a calendar page with appointments, tilted in his direction. Hopefully, I'd written the names of a few of Freeman's competitors in bold enough ink on my calendar page.

Then I bent over to help Kristal pick up her files.

Kristal and I took our time collecting all the documents which had spilled from the file folders. It took a while to pick up every single piece of paper.

Except one.

We slid that particular sheet farther under the desk so only one corner was visible.

After a bit more fumbling around on the floor, Kristal and I rose. She squared off the folders in her hand and adjusted her clothes. I ran a hand through my hair and sighed.

"Sorry about that," Kristal said, looking flustered. "Sometimes I can be such a klutz."

Freeman came around the desk, took Kristal's elbow. Concern showed on his face. "You okay?"

"Yes, fine." She offered a small smile. "Embarrassed."

"Don't be silly."

I thrust my hand forward. "Nice meeting you. Thanks for hearing us out."

Freeman frowned at me, pumped my hand quickly. "Of course."

He led us to the door but didn't open it right away. "Your proposal is interesting, so if you would reconsider having to sign the NDA, please contact me. Otherwise, I hope we'll get the chance to do some business together in the future."

Kristal unleashed her most dazzling smile yet and touched him gently on the forearm. "I would love that. Goodbye, Nathaniel."

* * *

We'd set the trap, and at least for the moment, we waited. There was still plenty to do, no matter what Freeman did. If he took the bait, then we'd forge ahead with the plan. If he didn't—or even if he waited too long—we needed to work on Plan B. All while still coming up with more contingency plans on top of that.

Kristal and I returned to our base of operations, where things were humming along. Hobie and Sammi were discussing something, and Jake was on his phone. We'd brought him on over my not-so-strenuous objection. We needed somebody we knew and had worked with before—and while I didn't much like the guy, I had to admit he was reasonably competent.

Most of their energy, so far, had gone toward creating fake prospectuses, real estate documents, web content, social media posts, archived articles, SEC filings, and similar stuff which would substantiate the fictitious entity known as Family Fun Parks International.

They would figure out what was needed, then tell Bear who, in turn, would direct his crew of high school volunteers—using an online app—to actually write the content. Of course, they didn't know the real reason why they were doing it; they thought it was part of a summer internship on corporate marketing and communications. High school credit for hustling!

They seemed to have things under control, and I needed some time to process things, so I borrowed Sammi, who was making a list of real estate companies in District-Maryland-Virginia. For what purpose, I didn't know.

"Want to go for a drive?"

She dropped what she was working on before I even finished the sentence. I guessed I'd be eager to take a break from that kind of drudgery, too.

Out in the car, Sammi asked, "Where are we going?"

"Up for taking a stroll?"

"Sure. Whatever."

The official teenager seal of approval.

Twenty minutes later, I was parking in a gravel lot at the Virginia side of Great Falls.

"We're going hiking?" Sammi made a face as if I'd asked her to scale Mount Everest.

"It's not much of a hike. More like a stroll in the woods."

She kept her face scrunched up.

"Would you rather go back to what you were doing?"

She unbuckled her seat belt. "Let's go."

We found the path that paralleled the Potomac River and headed west. As you might expect on a sunny summer day, it was crowded. Not elbowing-people-in-the-face crowded, but there was a steady flow of people, some going in our direction, others coming toward us. Young people, old people, people of all types. Most walked, but there were a fair number of runners, too, getting their sweat on. There were many things wrong with living in the DC area; going for a walk near Great Falls was not one of them.

"Aside from the current situation your mother has put you both in, are you happy with your life?" From my limited interactions with Sammi, she didn't seem like the sort to need small talk to get the mouth warmed up.

"What are you? My father?"

"You have his sense of humor," I said. "Now, how about answering the question?"

She kicked at a rock, then stopped, bent down, and picked up a twig. We continued walking as she waved the stick like a conductor's baton to some unheard orchestral composition. I recognized avoidance when I saw it. Her reluctance to answer the question gave me *my* answer. Maybe I would have made a great father.

"You know, it's never too late to change the path you're on."

She kept waving her wooden wand, and the butterfly tattoo on the back of her hand fluttered like the real thing. "I get the feeling you're not referring to this hiking path."

"You also got your father's smarts."

"I don't think I'm going to have many choices after this…thing settles out. I'll probably live in a cave in South America, weaving baskets out of straw or something."

"Are you always such a pessimist?" We were walking side-by-side, so I couldn't really see Sammi's face. I turned to speak to her, but she kept her focus on the path, head tilted down so she wouldn't trip over any exposed roots.

"Mom always says so, but compared to her, I'm little miss sunshine."

The Kristal I knew was very dramatic, all right, mood swings like crazy.

Most of the time I'd been able to predict them and act accordingly, but on those occasions when I hadn't been paying attention or had guessed wrong, blammo. They rarely ended well. "A person can work on their attitude."

"Maybe."

"Sammi, you're not even twenty. Maybe you've seen a lot more than most kids your age, but, trust me, there's a whole wide world out there. You can be, and you can do whatever you want. Don't feel like you're trapped by your current situation or by any expectations your mother may have saddled you with."

"You mean, like a father who went to prison?" She stopped on the path, turned, and stared at me, unblinking. Challenging. Sometimes I forgot nineteen-year-olds always thought they were right.

Ouch. I'd hit a nerve, bringing up Kristal's motherly expectations. "I didn't say I was perfect."

"I didn't think you were."

"You should read what happened to me as a cautionary tale, mostly because it's one hundred percent possible. You could get caught and go to jail. I'm a smart, capable guy, and I got caught. You might think it can't happen to you—Lord knows, I thought that—but then you're up against the wall, spreading your legs while they slap some cuffs on you. And in case you weren't sure, prison sucks."

Sammi flung her stick into the adjacent woods and started walking again. "How about if we talk about something else?"

"Sure. Whatever you want."

"Are you and Mom going to get back together?"

Chapter Fourteen

I took a breath. Counted to three. Wasn't sure what the proper *fatherly* response should be. "A lot of time has passed. People go their different ways. Their interests change."

"But now you both have me to be interested in."

I laughed. "True."

"I see how you look at each other now. I'm not an idiot. There's still something between you, I can tell."

In the days since I'd known Sammi, I found her to be especially perceptive. "Let's just focus on what's right in front of us, okay?"

"Whatever." She kicked a rock down the path. "Do you really think we can pull this off?"

The $350,000 question. "I hope so. I think so. But hoping and thinking won't get the job done. We've all got to do our parts, execute the plan properly, and even then, we'll need a few things to fall our way. Let's say I'm cautiously optimistic."

"But what if it doesn't? What if we can't get the money Mom needs to pay back that guy? He said he was going to *kill* us." Her lower lip began to quiver.

"First off, we'll *make* this thing work. Then we'll pay off your mother's, uh, lender, and you'll both be in the clear. And, if by some chance this scheme doesn't succeed, we'll figure out something else. You don't need to worry so much; it will give you ulcers."

Judging by her unwavering look of concern, my pep talk hadn't done anything to alleviate her worry. "Trust me, Sammi. I've been through a lot worse, and I always have managed to come through unscathed."

"Sure. If you call prison being unscathed."

Touché.

We continued walking along the path in silence, passing the occasional hiker coming in the opposite direction, enjoying the smells and sights you can only find among the trees. The woods were fairly thick in spots, and I imagined a wolf in the underbrush next to the path, stalking us, waiting for the opportunity to pounce and rip our throats out.

Sammi broke through my crazy thoughts. "What's my part going to be in this?"

I sensed excitement mixed with anxiety. I had no doubt Kristal had employed Sammi on many of her cons, and I figured Sammi had some decent skills—she had a great teacher, after all, in addition to the bloodline—but this seemed more big-time. Maybe because failure meant disaster. And maybe performing in front of *both* your parents added another layer of stress to the equation. "Don't worry, you'll have something important to do, but it will be something you can handle."

"What's that supposed to mean? I can handle all kinds of shit. More than you know, Chance."

I hadn't meant to sound condescending, but Sammi sounded fired up, all right. "I'm sure you can. But don't forget, we've got a team of people involved, and they all have a lot of experience." I stopped and gently took her arm. Turned her to face me, and she complied, almost robotically.

"I've got experience, too. And my experience has happened in the last decade." She waggled her head, then jutted out her chin, as if she'd scored a major point in a debate contest.

"Listen, Sammi, you don't need to prove anything to me, or to your mother, for that matter. This mess is entirely her doing, and I know that, if she had the choice, you wouldn't be involved at all. At all. Don't take this on as your battle, okay?"

"In case you haven't been paying attention, this does affect me. A lot. What is it with you guys, anyway?"

I wasn't sure what she was referring to, probably some piece of motherly advice she rebelled against. "If we find a place where you can help, we'll be sure to call on you. But if we've got it covered without your participation, just remember that is what your mother wants. She doesn't want to put you in harm's way, not even a bit. And I agree with her, one thousand percent."

Sammi rolled her eyes at me, then wriggled out of my grip. "I'm not a little kid, you know. I've been hustling on my own, for years. You'll see." She stormed ahead, not waiting for me.

Even though she was chronologically nineteen, Sammi was a prisoner of those odd teenage years, when you're stuck between being an adult and a kid, when you think you have more smarts than you really do, when you think all the adults in your life treat you like a child, when you're absolutely convinced you know what's best. Sometimes, flashes of maturity shine through; other times, you are that moody, sullen teenager nobody wants to hang around with—except other moody teens. That transition time is tough, even if you're being raised in a stable, two-parent home. When your single mother is a con artist who never got the responsibility gene, your teenage years must be especially tumultuous.

I jogged after Sammi, searching my brain for some golden nugget of fatherly wisdom, but coming up blank.

* * *

Sammi and I returned to the decrepit office suite from our walk at Great Falls. I'd corralled her without much effort—it was too hot outside to play hide-and-seek—and we'd driven back to our base of operations in dead silence. I'd given her the choice of staying in the car to pout or coming in to join the crew and find something useful to do. After some sighing and eye-rolling, she'd chosen to come in. Probably because it was too hot to stay in a parked car.

I checked in with Kristal to see if I'd missed anything. "Who's that?" I asked, pointing to a woman sitting at a desk across the room, phone to her ear, sporting the biggest blonde hairdo I'd seen since the 1980s. Somehow, she pulled it off well. I guessed there was something to be said for finding a personal style that worked for you and sticking with it.

Kristal looked up from her desk. Lowered her voice so only I could hear. "That is Myndi, spelled with a *y* and an *i*."

"How else do you spell Mindy?"

"She spells it with the *y* first, and the *i* last." Kristal spelled out the entire name, enunciating each letter carefully. "She's one of Bear's charity cases."

"What?" I glanced around. "Where is Bear?"

"He took off about ten minutes after you and Sammi did. On his way out, he said Myndi would be making the faux reporter calls instead of him. Which, I guess, makes sense. I don't think Bear has such great phone manners."

The original plan was for Bear to call up every real estate firm in the area, asking about large tracts of land for sale. Said he'd heard a rumor about a huge development deal coming to town. We figured someone like Freeman would hear about the rumor and be pressured to act quickly so he wouldn't lose out to another investor. Our plan, however, did *not* call for someone named Myndi to be making the calls. The more people who got involved in the scam, the more chance there was for something to go wrong. Especially untrained people.

"Does Myndi have any clue what she's doing? Any experience with this sort of thing?"

Kristal forced a smile and got up. Took several steps off to the side and motioned me over. "I asked that same exact question. Bear said Myndi was an experienced phone operator. I asked what that meant, and he said something about telemarketing, poll taking, and phone sex." Kristal's smile distorted. "If we need to ask anyone if they want a blow job, we're covered."

I ran a hand through my hair, doing some mental calculus on how this latest twist might affect things. "Christ."

"Don't worry, Christ isn't on her call list." Kristal's face hardened. "This operation is hard enough without having to babysit newbies."

"Look, I'll speak with Myndi. Make sure she's doing what we want her to be doing. It wasn't cool how Bear sprang her on us, but Bear has a soft spot for people in need. It'll be okay." I wasn't sure I believed what I was saying.

What *was* Bear thinking?

"Someone very smart once told me that, because there's so much out of our control during a con, it was imperative that we control everything we *could* control. I'm beginning to think that genius might not have known what he was talking about."

I was pretty sure I was the genius who said that, a long time ago. I glanced around. Hobie and Jake were pounding the keys on their laptops. Ella was in the corner talking to Sammi about some aspect of the operation. Even Myndi seemed to be making calls competently. As far as I could tell, everything was breezing along. "You need to trust me."

Kristal just glared at me.

"I don't suppose we've heard anything from Freeman yet," I said.

"Don't you think I would have led with that?" She tapped a lacquered fingernail lightly against her chin. "I'm guessing he's found the piece of paper with the bogus financial projections by now. Probably Googled all the names on it. Read the faked-up websites. He's probably cleared his afternoon schedule and is plotting his first move. The appointment with Loudoun Holdings was scheduled for today at five, right?"

"Yep." We'd created four fake companies in the DC area and developed histories for each. We made three of them seem like plausible companies to partner with on our proposed real estate deal, but the fourth, Loudoun Holdings, seemed ideal. Just sleazy enough to jump at this slightly under-handed deal. Just the kind of company Freeman would hate losing to. Our hope was that he'd read the wildly inflated projections on the piece of paper we'd *accidentally* left behind and realize we had only mentioned the tip of the iceberg. The numbers indicated that tens of millions of dollars were in play, and that we were seriously lowballing him. With his ego, he'd be furious we were trying to take advantage of him. And he'd do whatever he could to try to outsmart us.

"I imagine he'll be hearing from someone soon, asking if he knows anything about the rumor of the development deal. That is, if Myndi is doing her job correctly. Hopefully, by this time tomorrow, Freeman will be back in touch wanting to negotiate." She glanced around the small office suite at everybody working diligently. "We need to make sure we're ready by then. And we sure as hell don't need any more Myndis thrown at us. I mean, did you get a load of that hair? Does she have to duck to get through doorways?" She tore her glance away from Myndi. "I need to run out and take care of something, okay?"

"Now?"

"Won't take long, promise. Text me if something comes up." Kristal didn't wait for any kind of response, just grabbed her purse and bolted.

A minute later, Ella sidled up to me. "Want to join me outside for a cigarette?"

"I don't smoke."

Ella took my arm and guided me toward the door. "Neither do I."

She didn't say anything until we'd left the office and walked past the storefront lawyers and insurance companies all the way down to the far end of the townhouse strip.

"I've got something I want to discuss. Wasn't sure if I should bring it up, and ordinarily I might not, but in this case, with so much riding on it, I thought, well…" Ella seemed more jittery than I had ever seen her.

"Just spit it out, okay?"

"Okay." She drew in a big breath. Exhaled. "I think Kristal is up to something extracurricular."

"What do you mean?"

"I think she's working something else while she's working this job."

When we were together, Kristal always had a few different irons in the fire. She'd been very good at multi-tasking, I had to admit. "What makes you think that?"

"I overheard her on the phone. I got the sense she's searching for someone. Someone who has nothing to do with what we're trying to accomplish. If there's one thing that will wreck a con, it's someone who's not disciplined enough to follow the script."

Granger. I'd mistakenly thought our plan negated the need for Kristal to hunt him down. But I could see Kristal taking things personally and not caring solely about the money. After all, she'd been living with the guy, and he'd ripped her off. Would Kristal risk screwing up our hustle if it meant getting square with Granger? In a heartbeat. "I hear you. I'll talk to her."

"Talk to her? That implies she's going to listen." Ella's engine was running rough. "You've got to rein her in. Make sure she doesn't do anything to derail us. She's a bit of a loose cannon." Ella put a teaspoon of honey in her voice. "We very well might need her skills and experience, so be gentle. But if we can't count on her to deliver…"

"Look, I appreciate your concern, and you and I go back, but you don't really know Kristal very well. You just met her." Two alpha females didn't always play well together.

"I've heard things."

"From who?"

"Stories from the past. From people who knew her. Word travels fast. I've got a good feel for things, and I can tell when something is a bit off."

"She's under a tremendous amount of pressure." I felt the heat rise on my face.

"Yes, she is. And I'm not unsympathetic. It's just…" She averted her eyes for a second, then turned them back on me. "What I'm trying to say is don't let your personal feelings get in the way here. You need to be thinking, pardon the pun, crystal clear."

"I *know* Kristal." The words came out with more force than I'd intended. "She's not like she used to be. She isn't."

Ella inched backward and softened her tone. "Maybe." She put her arm on my shoulder, let it rest there. "This is your gig, I'm here to help however I can. Just thought you should know what I heard. We should go back in. There's still plenty to do."

"Thanks," I said, but I wasn't sure I appreciated Ella's insinuations, even if they did hold a shred of truth.

We headed back to the office in silence, me lost in my head.

I *thought* I knew Kristal. Sure, she used to be unpredictable—that was one of the things that attracted me. And she was moody. And vindictive. And a whole bunch of other things most people did not consider to be positive traits. But she'd changed. Raising Sammi had matured her. She didn't seem as impetuous or as reactive. Did she?

I thought back to her slugging me in the gut.

Were my emotions getting in the way of me seeing things clearly? Was I still harboring feelings for Kristal?

I needed to make sure I was thinking straight, because an error in judgment on my part could easily blow the scam. In many ways, someone who was unreliable—a loose cannon, according to Ella—was worse than a consistent fuck-up. At least with the fuck-up, you can plan work-arounds. With unpredictable hotheads, as Ella considered Kristal to be, you never knew which way things would go, although they usually headed south.

Was Ella right about Kristal?

I couldn't shake the memory of Kristal running out on me twenty years ago, leaving me holding the bag. And not telling me about Sammi.

* * *

We spent the rest of that afternoon and evening preparing for our next meeting with Freeman. Bear returned, and he and his crew worked hard to create the online history we needed to bolster our claims. Jake set up all the Facebook, Twitter, and Instagram accounts for all parties involved, and he made sure our burner phones were all coordinated. All the phone numbers on the websites had to be functional and had to be directed to the correct one of us.

Despite our doubts, Myndi did a fine job acting like a real reporter and creating a ton of interest with her probing questions about large tracts of land. Ella served as the technical resource when it came to the real estate details, and I tried to keep everyone on track.

Sammi moped about, grudgingly serving as our office go-fer, making copies, fetching coffee and food, and pitching in where she could. Outwardly, she projected that vague dissatisfaction most teenagers strived for. Inwardly, I thought I detected a flash or two when she appeared to be happy to help and part of the gang. Mostly, though, it was pouting and eye-rolling and exasperation with how inefficiently the adults were doing things.

I'd considered trying to track down Kristal, but I had no clue where she might have gone, and she wasn't answering my texts. I had Sammi text her, too, of course, and while she didn't flat out ignore those, she mostly answered with I'm fine, or Be Back Soon, or Love Ya, Sweetie, none of which shed any light on where she'd gone or what she was doing.

At six o'clock, Myndi checked out, having completed every single one of the calls we'd given her.

At seven o'clock, Hobie said he needed to take care of a few things and would take an Uber home. When I suggested he take a Ryde instead, he made a face and said Uber was a lot quicker, easier, and cheaper. *Whatever.* I guessed Ryde was the fourth most popular ride-sharing service for a reason. At least they paid their drivers better than Uber did.

Around eleven o'clock, I clapped my hands together. "Okay, everybody. Let's call it a night. Go home, get some sleep, and we'll meet here tomorrow morning, prepared for anything."

Jake and Bear were gone in seconds. Ella straightened up a few things, then gave me a tired smile. "See you tomorrow, boss." She nodded at Sammi. "You did good today." Then she headed for the door, stylish leather attaché bumping against her leg.

Sammi looked at me with pleading eyes. "We're leaving, too, right?"

"Yeah, you can relax. By the way, I agree with Ella. You did good today."

"Thanks."

"Any idea where your mother is?"

"Nah."

"Want to sleep at my place?" I didn't want Kristal's lone wolf shenanigans to impact Sammi, and I sure as shit didn't want to put Sammi into any kind of danger if Kristal had indeed found Granger. Not now. Not when we were—potentially—close to the finish line.

She nodded. "Yeah, that would be cool."

"Okay. Text your mother so she won't worry."

"Fine."

She texted Kristal while I packed up, sliding my laptop into my backpack and stuffing a few papers on top. Work to do in case I couldn't sleep. "Ready?"

"Yup."

We headed home, and she fell asleep on the way to my place.

* * *

The next morning, Sammi and I stopped to get a dozen donuts for the troops. I let her choose them, the only stipulation was that she order no more than three with filling. As she was making her selection, my phone rang. *Trouble.*

"Hang on a second, Ma." With my phone at my ear, I left Sammi's side and paid the woman at the register for a dozen donuts and half a dozen coffees. Then I took up a spot near the door, where I could watch Sammi as she took her sweet time picking donuts. "Okay. What can I do for you so early in the morning?"

"I've been up for hours, dear. I need you to come over."

"Why?"

"I'll explain when you get here."

"I'm kinda busy today. How about tomorrow?" I knew I'd be busy tomorrow, too, but by that time, it was entirely possible Ma would have forgotten what she needed me for.

"It's an emergency, Chance."

"Then call 9-1-1."

She clucked her tongue. "It's not that kind of emergency. It's the kind of emergency only you can help with."

"Why don't you enlist Peck? I'm sure he's not doing anything worthwhile today. He can help you with your emergency."

"Weren't you *listening*? Only *you* can help me."

I didn't answer right away. No way could I spare any time today. We had a decent handle on things, but as soon as Freeman contacted us, things were bound to get crazy. And it wouldn't be good if I were up to my elbows in water fixing her toilet—or whatever the hell only *I* could help her with.

"Hello? Hello? Did I hit the wrong button? Are you still there, Chance? This stupid phone never works right. If I could, I'd...I'd..." Ma sputtered.

About once a week, Ma claimed to have some sort of technical problem with her phone. But I had a feeling it was just a ploy to elicit sympathy from me. On the other hand, Ma and technology weren't the best of friends.

"Chance? Chance? Are you there?"

"I'm still here, Ma."

"I wish we could go back in time before there were cell phones."

So did I, on occasion. Right now, for instance.

Ma barreled on. "You need to come over. It won't take long, I promise. What are you so gosh darn busy with anyway? I mean, what's more important than your mother's life? I carried you for nine months inside of me, and then I raised you, didn't I?"

Lucky me. "How could I forget that when you remind me every opportunity you get?"

"I knew I could count on you. Tell you what, I'll fix you some breakfast while you're here. I know how much you like my poached eggs."

About as much as I liked stomach cramps. "No thanks, Ma. I already ate."

"It's no trouble."

I knew when I was beat. The only thing left to do was cut my losses. "I can spare fifteen minutes. Will I be able to solve your emergency in fifteen minutes?"

"Son, I think that's exactly how long you'll need." She paused. "Give or take."

It was always the give or take that got you.

Chapter Fifteen

nstead of pulling into Ma's driveway, I parked half a block down the street, out of view from the front windows. I turned to Sammi. "Stay here, okay?"

"Why? Where are we?"

"Quick errand. I'll be back in ten minutes or less. Help yourself to a donut."

"I already had one."

"Then have another. Splurge."

She made a face at me as I left her in the car. The last thing I wanted was to have to explain Sammi to Ma this morning. Who knew what kind of reaction she'd have? Ma was nothing if not volatile. Eventually, the truth would come out—that Ma was in fact a Grandma—but I wanted to have my story straight and, besides, I didn't have time to answer the inevitable thousand questions Ma would fire at me. At least not right now.

I jogged across the lawn and knocked on the front door. Ma opened it so quickly, I thought she must have been waiting right on the other side for my arrival.

"Good morning, Chance." She craned her head around me, looking outside through the storm door.

"What's so urgent?" I pushed past her into the house. The smell of cooking onions almost blew me away.

"I need your help with something."

"Yeah, I got that." I stood in the foyer, staring at her. "What?"

"Come in. I'm making an omelet, and I just fried up some onion. Smell it? Have a seat, and we can talk while you eat." She started toward the kitchen, but I blocked her way.

"Sorry, but I don't really have time for that. Tell me what's going on." I paused. "Or I guess I can leave and come back another time."

She narrowed her eyes at me, and the color rose on her cheeks. "When did you become such a smart ass, anyway?"

"Had a good role model."

Ma sighed. "Okay. You wanna skip breakfast, the most important meal of the day, that's your decision. You're a grown boy, after all. Come, let's talk in the living room."

I followed her, and she took her usual seat in a puke-yellow overstuffed chair with threadbare upholstery, while I sat across from her on an even older—and more disgusting—sofa.

"Okay. Hit me," I said.

Ma slowly rubbed her hands together. "So, I..."

A knock on the door interrupted her, before she'd even really gotten going. Ma hopped up. "I'll get it."

She rushed to the door, and as she did, a bad feeling came over me. I jumped up and hustled after her, but she beat me to the door and opened it.

"Is Chance here?" I heard Sammi ask.

"Uh, sure. Come in, dear."

Sammi stepped in, and Ma looked from her to me and back at her. "Chance, someone is here to see you."

"I thought I asked you to wait in the car. Go on, I'll be out in a second."

"I have to go to the bathroom."

"Where are your manners, Chance? Introduce me to your *young* friend." Ma hit the word *young* so hard I thought her fake teeth might break.

"This is Sammi. Sammi, this is Arlene."

"Nice to meet you." Sammi glanced around. "Bathroom?"

Ma pointed down the hallway. "Second door on the left. You can't miss it. It's the one with the toilet."

Sammi followed Ma's finger, and five seconds later, the bathroom door closed. Ma spun toward me. "Who's your friend?"

"I told you. Sammi." I clammed up, hoping the inquisition would blow over, but I knew better. My mind raced with possible explanations why I would be driving around a nineteen-year-old girl.

"Yes, but who is she?"

"She's my landlord's niece. Thinking about becoming a Ryde driver. She wanted to see what it was like." I held my hands out, palms up. *That's that.*

"I could always tell when you were fibbing, Chance." Ma smirked. "Some things never change."

"I don't know what you're talking about," I said.

The toilet flushed, the water ran, and the bathroom door creaked open. Sammi joined us in the foyer.

"Thanks," she said.

"I'll be out in a couple of minutes, okay?" I said as I opened the screen door.

Sammi started to leave, but Ma grabbed her arm. "Are you hungry? Chance and I were about to have breakfast. A nice omelet?"

Sammi looked to me for an answer, and I shook my head, but Ma had Sammi in her grasp and was leading her into the kitchen. If Sammi had known Ma better, she might have had the nerve to break free, but not in this situation. Ma's grip might have been gentle, physically, but her figurative grip was unyielding.

"Have a seat, dear." Ma guided Sammi into a chair at the rickety table, place settings for two laid out. Then she shuffled away and returned with another plate and some silverware. "It will just take me a few minutes to get it all ready."

Resigned, I sat at the table and shrugged at Sammi, praying she didn't call me Dad. Praying she didn't say much of anything. To my relief, she pulled out her phone and started tapping, engrossed in the latest social media postings.

Ma hummed to herself as she started cracking eggs into a bowl. Six eggs later, she got a whisk and started beating the crap out of the eggs, adding a splash of milk and some salt and pepper. Then she poured it all into a hot pan. Seeing Ma in her red-and-white checked apron, humming to herself as she cooked, brought back memories of my childhood, when she would cook for me and Peck on rare occasion, back before things went sideways for us. Back when we acted like a regular family, and we weren't *acting*.

Ah, who was I kidding? We were always acting.

When I was about ten, Ma took me and Chance to the county fair. Most of my friends' parents took them, too, but when my friends went, it was to go on the rides, play carnival games, and eat cotton candy and funnel cakes.

When we went, it was to hone our pickpocketing skills. To be fair, Ma would make it entertaining for us. "Act like those kids in *Oliver*. First one who swipes a total of a hundred bucks gets a frozen lemonade!" or "A gold watch gets a gold star!" My favorite was when Ma told us to go through the haunted house, but hide inside, near the entrance, when people's eyes hadn't yet adjusted to the darkness. "Easy pickin's" is what she used to call it.

If anyone did catch on to what we were doing, they just shooed us away. I mean, we were only little kids! I had to hand it to Ma; she knew the angles.

But that was then. The sharpness of her angles had diminished, a lot, over the past decade. Now, I dreaded the phone call from the local precinct telling me Ma got caught with her hand in the proverbial cookie jar and was in lock-up waiting for a bail hearing.

It was only a matter of time.

Ma dropped her spatula on the floor, and the clatter broke me out of my reverie. She picked it up and kept using it without even a rinse. Typical.

I tried to get Sammi's attention, but she was focused on her phone.

So, I texted her. *Please don't say anything about me being your dad, okay?*

Two seconds later, she looked up at me.

I texted again. *We'll tell her, but at the right time.*

Sammi glanced at her phone, read the message, then looked back at me. Pressed her lips together. I couldn't tell what she meant by that, so I texted her again. *If we tell her now, it might screw up our chance to save you and your mother.*

In the background, Ma changed tunes and started a more upbeat number. I guessed when you lived alone, sometimes off-key humming was better than silence.

Sammi met my gaze and gave one curt nod. Then she went back to her phone.

"Breakfast is served." Ma brought two plates to the table and set one down in front of Sammi and one down in front of me. Then she sat in the chair between us. "Dig in."

"Where's yours?" I asked.

"Already ate."

I thought about giving her a hard time, but decided it was futile. I carefully tasted a small bite. Not very good, but not as bad as most of the stuff she made; I guessed it was hard to screw up eggs. I ate enough to be polite, knowing we still had a box of doughnuts in the car.

To her credit, Sammi forced down a few bites and didn't say anything disparaging. I figured she was thinking about those doughnuts, too.

"How old are you, Sammi?" Ma asked.

"Almost twenty."

"Did you grow up around here?"

"Uh, not really. We moved around a lot."

"But you were born around here, right?"

"Yeah." Sammi tilted her head. "Do I have some kind of local accent or something?"

Ma tapped the side of her head with her index finger. "I know things."

I wasn't sure what kind of scam Ma was trying to work, but I knew from experience it was best to derail it before it gained any steam. "Well, we need to hit the road. Literally." I stood. "Let's go, Sammi. I've got a lot of stuff to show you about being a Ryde driver."

Sammi started to get up, but Ma said, "Sit down, both of you. I've got a few more questions."

"We really need to be going," I said.

"Sit!"

I lowered myself slowly into the chair, and Sammi did the same.

"You look very familiar," Ma said to Sammi. "I never forget a face, you know."

I shook my head at Sammi, trying to get across the message to keep quiet.

"I don't think we've ever met," Sammi said.

"I'm sure we haven't. But you're the spitting image of someone I knew a long time ago."

Oh shit. "Ma, we *really* need to get going."

"If I didn't know better, I'd think you were trying to get out of here before I found out some important piece of information." She raised one eyebrow. "That's not the case, is it?"

"Of course not."

Ma turned back to Sammi, then snapped her fingers. "I know who you look like. Chance's friend, Kristal Johnson. Same smile. Same crinkle around the eyes. Same coloring. Is Kristal a relative, perhaps?"

The color had drained from Sammi's face, and she looked at me, lost.

"Just a coincidence, Ma."

Ma swiveled in my direction, hit me with a creepy grin. "You remember Kristal, don't you? I mean, you lived with her for some time, didn't you?"

"Sure, I remember Kristal. And Sammi does resemble her, but I'm sure Sammi isn't related to Kristal in any fashion."

"Kristal is my mother," Sammi said.

I figured Ma would go ballistic, finding out she had a granddaughter like this, but instead of exploding, she faced me. "How long were you planning to keep this from me? Being a grandmother is a big deal, you know?"

"Why do I feel like I missed part of this movie? You knew Sammi was my daughter, didn't you?"

Ma's grin widened.

"How?"

"Peck told me."

"Peck? How did he know?"

"Said some friend of his told him. Buck or Grizzly or something."

Bear. "And you thought it would be funny to pretend like you didn't know?"

"Well, I was just planning to harass *you*, but fate brought Sammi along for the ride today. I'd say that was some sort of good omen." Ma rose. "Now, if you'll excuse me."

She took two steps toward Sammi and pulled her out of her chair.

Enveloped her in a hug. "This is one of the happiest days of my life, dear. Welcoming a new member of the family to my world. We've got a lot of catching up to do."

I could see Sammi's face over Ma's shoulder, and her expression vacillated between happiness and shock. On the surface, getting a grandmother might seem like a good thing. I'd try not to burst Sammi's bubble for as long as I could.

"Okay, okay. There will be plenty of time to get acquainted, you two. But I wasn't kidding. We need to get going."

Ma released Sammi, but her gigantic grin remained. "Where to? I know she doesn't want to be a Ryde driver. That's not the kind of job for young, smart, attractive winners."

I ignored her jab. "Just something we need to take care of."

"Just something you need to do to save Kristal's skin, you mean."

Damn Peck. Damn Bear. "I don't have time to go into details now. It will all be taken care of in a few days."

Ma bowed her head. "I am at your service."

"What are you talking about?"

"I'm available. To help."

"Thanks, but I think we have it covered."

Ma nodded, the kind of nod you'd give someone who insisted the world was flat. "I was hustling people before you were a gleam in your daddy's eye. I taught you all you know. Don't make the mistake other people have—us old folks can still bring it. Whatever we might have lost in speed, we've made up for in wisdom, five times over." She winked at Sammi. "'Course, I'm not saying *I* lost anything. I'm still as sharp as I was when I was your age."

"Okay, Ma. I hear you. If we have something you can do, I'll let you know." *Over my dead body.*

"Peck said he's available to help, too. He always liked Kristal."

I had no intention of letting Peck get involved, either. We wanted—needed—this thing to go smoothly, and having Peck around would reduce those chances considerably. "Sure, Ma. Thanks for your offer. I'll confer with the others and see what we need, then get back to you. Right now, we gotta go."

"Just one more thing." Ma hugged Sammi again, and even though Sammi saw it coming, she still looked very uncomfortable. Ma had a way of making everyone uncomfortable, no matter the situation.

"Okay, okay. There'll be plenty of time for a family reunion later."

Ma shot me the evil eye.

I practically perp-walked Sammi out of the kitchen and toward the front door, keeping my body between hers and Ma's. I gently pushed Sammi out onto the porch, so Ma wouldn't get another crack at her. "We'll talk to you later. Bye, Ma."

"Bye, son. Bye granddaughter. I sure do like how that sounds!" Ma called after us as we walked across the front yard.

I didn't look back, but I think Sammi stole a peek.

* * *

The second I stepped into our office suite, Kristal came bouncing over, and I could tell something was up. Before she could say a word, Sammi thrust the box of doughnuts into her hand. "Hi, Mom." Then she stalked over to a chair in the corner and pulled out her phone.

"Teenagers," I said, shaking my head at the wild shift in emotions. I guessed I really couldn't blame her. She'd been blindsided with a double whammy—finding out she had a grandmother and then finding out that grandmother happened to be someone like Ma.

Kristal set the box down on a nearby desktop. "Just got the call. Freeman wants to meet to get clarification on a few things." She held up her hand for a high-five, which I gladly completed. "Told him we had another potential investor pitch later this morning, but that we could meet with him around two o'clock."

"We don't have a potential investor pitch this morning," I asked.

"No, we do not. Just making him anxious."

"Well done."

Behind us, Jake and Bear were too busy tapping away on their computers to even notice I'd arrived. I threw them a wave, in case they looked up. I'd give Bear shit later for blabbing to Peck. "Everything ready?"

"Not even close. But I think we're in good enough shape."

"Did Freeman say anything else?"

"Only that he planned to have his finance guy at our meeting." She held up a folder. "Ella worked up some background on him. Lawrence Thane. Interesting character."

I lowered my voice. "Where were you yesterday afternoon? You said it was just a quick errand."

Kristal's face clouded for a moment, then back to sunshine. "Sorry. Took longer than I thought."

I hesitated, then, "Did your errand have anything to do with Granger?"

Our eyes locked, and I could tell I was treading on dangerous ground. "Don't ask questions unless you want to hear answers."

"We're in crunch time here, Kristal. You need to maintain focus."

"I always maintain focus." She poked me in the chest. "I think you know that. But don't worry, my errand had nothing to do with this. It's full speed ahead, matey."

I opened my mouth to say something, but closed it quickly. No sense throwing kerosene on the fire. Kristal was going to do what Kristal was going to do. I just hoped she remembered that her life—and Sammi's life—hung in the balance.

Her phone rang, and she glanced at the caller ID. "I need to take this. Why don't you read up on Thane?" She thrust the folder at me, then stalked off, phone to ear.

I took the folder to an empty desk. Ella had compiled a mini-dossier on the guy, complete with an annual report-style headshot. Mid-forties, ruggedly handsome face, the kind of guy who'd star in an SUV commercial. B.S. from Yale, MBA from Wharton. Finance tool. Started out as a management consultant, then segued into straight finance. Worked for Freeman for the past eight years.

The analytical types were always tougher to crack than those who relied on guts and intuition. Not impossible, just tougher. We needed to find a way to shortcut the process. Our false front company could hold up to a certain level of scrutiny, but any type of prolonged investigation would expose us.

Sometimes getting a little leverage on the mark helped.

I flipped through the rest of the dossier. Thane wasn't a gambler. His name hadn't been associated with any scandals or impropriety. He had a family, served as a volunteer for a couple of local charitable organizations, and was a church elder. Probably was a Boy Scout leader, too.

Just our luck.

I put the folder down and waited until Bear finished up a call. Then I called him over.

"What's up, boss?" he said.

"I understand you've been talking to Peck."

"Yeah. So?" He looked at me, then nodded his head as he realized I wasn't just making small talk. "There a problem?"

"I wish you hadn't told him what you were doing with us."

"Didn't realize it was a secret. I mean, not from him, anyway. He's your brother, right?"

For some reason, I assumed everyone knew I didn't get along with Peck. "We sort of do our own things, you know?"

"Since when?" Bear said.

"Since I went straight."

"You're not so straight now." He smiled. *Got ya!*

"Be that as it may, please don't drag him into this."

Bear shook his head. "Too late. He's been helping us prepare some online copy. He can shovel shit with the best of them. And his prices are very reasonable. Mostly beer and…other stuff."

"I thought your cousin was going to do it."

"She was, but she had to study for her cosmetology exam, or some such nonsense. Wants to be a hairdresser. All that talent, and she only wants to cut hair. Waste, if you ask me."

"So, you asked Peck instead?"

"Yep. I told you, we work together a lot. I do stuff for him, he does stuff for me. He's never failed me yet."

And he fails me all the time. "Fine. But once he's finished, let's not ask him to do anything else, and do me a favor, will you? Don't tell Peck anything else about what's going on. Not about our operation. Not about me. And, please, nothing about Kristal or Sammi or anything else that's personal, okay?"

"Sorry. Won't happen again." He pouted like a schoolboy getting reprimanded by the teacher, but then his expression rebounded. He glanced around, wiggling his nose. "Do I smell doughnuts?"

I pointed to the box on the far table. "Help yourself."

Bear scurried off in search of a chocolate-glazed, or three, and I sat there, trying not to worry that Peck—and, of course, Ma—would infiltrate my life and poison my efforts to go straight.

Chapter Sixteen

Our first meeting with Freeman had been on his home turf. Our second meeting with him would be on ours. Just like in sporting events, having home-field advantage meant something in the con game. More control.

Because our meeting with Freeman wasn't until two, we had time to prepare our digs. We'd told Freeman we'd be meeting at the U.S. residence belonging to one of Family Fun Parks International's board members, without getting too specific. The property *really* belonged to a retired lobbyist who had recently put it on the market and was now vacationing in Greece for two months. Ella had come through for us in a big way, because although the property was listed as an "Exquisite Executive Country Residence," it was like most of the other expensive homes in the neighborhood—a veritable mansion.

Ella made the trip out to McLean in a separate car, while Kristal and I drove her Audi, which we would leave in the impressive circular drive. Ella had suggested a Lamborghini, but I talked her down a bit. We wanted to project wealth and class, but within some limits.

We went about the task of removing all indications that it was for sale. Signage, fake fruit in a bowl, clever notes strategically positioned, pointing out certain features. We'd brought in a couple of bags of groceries and dry goods and filled the fridge and pantry. We scattered a few high-end magazines around, filled the closets with clothing, and, in general, made the place seem lived in. We had no expectations that Freeman and his finance guy would be poking around in closets or in any dark corners, but it paid to be prepared. One false note could sour the deal.

The mansion itself was gorgeous. Modern design. Clean lines. Lots of granite, glass, polished steel. It was fully furnished with stuff that looked sleek but was probably very uncomfortable to actually use. "Staged to the max" was how Ella described it, and I'm sure each piece of furniture cost more than my current net worth.

All types of modern art—paintings, sculpture, mosaics, tapestries—decorated the house, and they looked expensive, but so did anything framed nicely—at least to me. I had to admit most of them weren't really my taste.

After we'd gone through the entire house *untidying*, including the mother-in-law suite in the basement and the pool house, everyone convened in the cavernous family room.

"I could get used to living in a place like this," Kristal said.

"Don't get too comfortable," Ella said. "Unless you've got six million dollars. If that's the case, then by all means, take your shoes off and put your feet up."

Kristal glared at Ella, who glared right back. Was this what it was like when two lionesses tried to prowl the same territory on the veldt?

"Hopefully, this will be the first and last time we'll be using this place," I said, wanting to head off any unpleasantness before it got started. "All set?"

Two curt nods.

A moment of silence, then Ella said, "I guess I'll be going now." She tossed me the keys to the place. "Lock up when you're through."

"Wish us luck," I said.

"Good luck," Ella said, looking directly at Kristal, tension coagulating in the air.

"Luck is only a small factor." Kristal kept her eyes laser-focused on Ella. No other facial expression.

Ella turned on her very high heels and left without a retort.

When she was gone, Kristal turned to me. "What's her problem?"

"Forget it. Just focus on the task at hand, okay?"

"Sure, sure," Kristal said as she stared at the back of the front door.

We'd gone through a host of scenarios earlier, at the office. Our plan called for Bear and Jake to be stationed at their computers, phones at the ready, in case we needed them to look up some info for us or if we needed something posted to a website immediately to somehow cover our asses. Ella would be standing by to answer any detailed real estate questions. Hobie and Sammi would likewise be back at the office waiting to help any way they could.

If we needed help, Kristal or I would simply excuse ourselves, make a quick phone call, or send a text, then return to the meeting. Piece of cake.

We weren't expecting any craziness, but I'd never pulled a job where at least one thing didn't go as planned. And the bigger the con, the more things there were that could go wrong.

"Okay, then. Make one more circuit and take pictures of everything, in case we need to resurrect things somewhere down the line."

We returned to the living room, having documented the positions of everything in the house. The place was library-quiet. It made me nervous. "Okay. Let's do it."

We still had about an hour before our scheduled meeting with Freeman, so Kristal and I took turns freshening up in the master bathroom. For me, that meant combing my hair, brushing my teeth, and making sure there weren't any crumbs on my clothes. For Kristal, it meant a twenty-minute pit stop to touch up her hair and make-up, then changing into a silky dress. The time and effort paid off, because when she emerged, she looked fantastic. Alluring, yet professional. Somehow, I had the feeling I hadn't elicited the same reaction from her.

"Want something to drink?" I asked.

"Water is fine." She glanced at her watch, then at me. "How does it feel to be back in the game?"

"Weird, honestly. Ever since I went away, I vowed to turn over a new leaf. Put my past behind me. Now, I find out I'm a father, and in the same breath, I break that promise to myself in order to save her ass. Not sure what that says about me, but it must say something."

"It says you're a compassionate guy and a caring parent. That's what good parents do for their children, you know—whatever it takes."

I was liking this new Kristal more and more. "Maybe. I think I need to review the file one last time. Then I'll be ready."

I sank into the couch and leafed through the Freeman file, pretending to read the words on the page but thinking of cons gone by.

* * *

Lawrence Thane's more-than-ample gut—not evident from his corporate headshot—stretched his blue dress shirt tight as he maneuvered himself down into a teak patio chair. He ducked at the last minute to avoid hitting his head on the edge of the enormous umbrella shielding our table on the pool deck. Next to him, Nathaniel Freeman had managed to get himself seated without incident, but I didn't think he was fond of our decision to come outside.

Instead of conducting our meeting in the stuffy den behind an ornately carved desk as big as a ping-pong table, we'd decided to go California-style and meet out by the pool. I'd shed my suit jacket, and Kristal's dress was a light fabric, but Freeman and Thane wore suits and ties, and I could already notice a light sheen of perspiration on their faces. I had to hand it to Kristal. Once again, she'd come up with a good strategy to keep our mark off balance.

"I hope this is okay with everyone," she said, rubbing it in a bit, if you asked me. "It's just so stuffy in the house, and I do love the sunshine. Anyone care for some lemonade?"

"Yes, that would be great." Freeman squinted a bit from the brightness. "Lawrence?"

"Sure." Thane tugged at the collar of his shirt. "I'll take some extra ice, too, if you have some."

Kristal poured four glasses of lemonade from a silver pitcher we'd prepared right before Freeman had arrived. I took a nice long pull on mine and set it down on the table, waiting for Freeman to get the ball rolling. I didn't have to wait long.

"Shall we get right to it?"

"Absolutely," Kristal said.

"Very well. After we met yesterday, I did some thinking—and some

149

checking around, I'll admit."

"Find out anything interesting?" Kristal's eyes twinkled. She was a pro at playing people, and, not for the first time, I was glad she was on my side. Her job was to orchestrate the meeting, getting Freeman to enter into the agreement, thinking he was getting the best of it, that he was getting one over on us. My job was to observe the non-verbal clues, to gauge their reactions based on what she was promising—or not promising.

"Oh, there's lots of interesting bits of information floating around. Some of it is probably even true." He gave a half-chuckle, then stopped when he realized he was laughing to himself. "Let's discuss your proposal in more depth."

Next to him, Thane squirmed in his chair, clearly uncomfortable with the setting. I got the impression he wanted to speak but was afraid of stepping on his boss's words.

"What would you like to know?" Kristal asked. "Nothing has changed since yesterday's proposal." She smiled coyly. "Well, that's not exactly true. The terms have changed a bit. We've reduced the margin delta by three percent, and we've increased our fee by a corresponding percentage."

"Oh, really? Why, all of a sudden? Since yesterday?" Freeman's voice had taken on an edge. I'm sure he wasn't used to being strong-armed in his negotiations.

"Market considerations and unforeseen circumstances."

"Market considerations?"

"Well, we've talked with several other parties and think the new numbers are more in line with, in crude terms, what the market will bear."

"We're being punished for not closing the deal yesterday?"

Kristal tipped her head slightly. "The new arrangement is in everyone's best interests."

"Everyone's?"

"Well, ours, mostly." Kristal's smile hadn't dimmed a watt. "But in this deal, if we're happy, then you'll be happy. We only enter into win-win relationships."

"These unforeseen circumstances you mentioned. Is there a problem we should know about?" Thane asked.

Kristal squirmed in her seat and let her smile sag for a moment. Then she perked up. "Not really. Our company insider, uh, increased his asking price a bit."

Freeman's face lit up. "I knew it. I knew this wasn't totally on the up and up. Bribery is involved."

"Is that a bad thing?" Kristal raised one eyebrow, ever so slightly.

"Not necessarily." Freeman smirked. "Sometimes you have to do whatever it takes."

"Let me reassure you. We've worked with this individual on half a dozen development deals. Copenhagen. Tokyo. Vancouver. Sao Paulo. In each case, everything has gone like clockwork. Everybody's been very happy with the results. The company officials know what's going on, but if the scheme is discovered, they will disavow any knowledge of it. The payoff is compensation for the risk our outsider faces for being the scapegoat and going to prison."

"Then why is your insider rocking the boat now?" Thane asked.

"I suspect it's because of the scope of this particular deal. Much larger than the others." Kristal waved her hand in the air dismissively. "The increase is merely a small drop in the bucket. And the logistical change should not be a problem." Kristal pressed her lips together and glanced at me.

"Shouldn't be," I said, with as much trepidation as I could squeeze into those two words.

Freeman exchanged a look with Thane. "Why do I sense there could be a problem here?"

Kristal hesitated. Then, "Simply a cash flow issue."

"Care to explain?" Thane asked.

"In the past, our insider has allowed us to be somewhat flexible with regard to the timing of his fee payment. This time, again, because of the larger scope, he wants fifty percent up front. And he's given us a short timeline."

"And is that a problem for you?"

Kristal said, "No," and I said, "Well," simultaneously. Just as we'd rehearsed. She turned and glared at me. "Charles, I told you there is no problem here.

Really."

I looked away, chastised, and Kristal returned her attention to Freeman. "We're good. All set in that regard."

"How much does your insider need?" Freeman asked.

"I said it's not a problem." Kristal reached for her leather portfolio. "Shall we take a look at the—"

"Hold on," Freeman said. "You may not think it's a problem, but if we're going to be in on this deal, we'd like to know how much we're talking about. You trust your insider, but I think it's important if you and I have a level of trust, too."

"Yes, of course." Kristal sighed. "He wants four hundred fifty thousand upfront, four hundred fifty thousand after the land has been purchased. As I said, in the scheme of things, it's really just noise."

We'd decided to increase our demands so we could pay the crew a small token of our appreciation.

Freeman smiled. "Thank you. Now you may proceed."

"Excellent." Kristal opened her portfolio and removed a single piece of paper, then slid it across the table to Freeman. "Here's a one-sheet outlining our proposal. Now that we've got other interest, I'm afraid it's a take-it-or-leave-it proposition."

Freeman frowned, picked up the paper. Began reading it.

"Do you have another copy for me?" Thane asked.

"Sorry, no," Kristal said. "You'll have to share with Nathaniel."

Anger flashed across Thane's face, then was gone in an instant. He scooted his chair closer to Freeman and peered over his boss's shoulder, like two grade schoolers sharing a book during class. This was another of Kristal's ploys to throw these guys off, and judging by their expressions and body language, it was working. Not every day that two business execs were treated like children.

I did everything I could to prevent a smile from breaking the tension.

Kristal and I remained quiet while they read our proposal. Freeman had started off frowning, and it only deepened the longer he read. Thane, on the other hand, maintained a steady poker face the entire time.

When Freeman finished, he expelled a noisy breath. "Interesting, for sure. But…" He forced a smile that was supposed to be conciliatory but just made him seem constipated. "Surely there must be some room for negotiation."

"I'm sure you understand, Nathaniel. While we would prefer to work with you on this deal, we have certain benchmarks we must hit, and we do have some significant other interest." She tipped her chin at the one-sheet still in Freeman's hand. "Which is all spelled out there. We've already cut things to the bone as it is. I know you probably never enter into any agreement without gaining some concessions, but I assure you this is no ordinary deal." She paused two beats. "I also assure you that, under the terms so dictated, this has the potential to be one of the most lucrative deals you've ever been involved with."

"Could you give us a moment?" Freeman asked.

"Absolutely. Take all the time you need. Charlie and I will stretch our legs." Kristal rose, and I followed, and we strolled away from the table, past the pool, and into the acre of gently rolling landscape beyond. We didn't speak until we were well out of their earshot.

"Think they'll go for it?" I asked.

"They will," Kristal said. "They'd be fools not to."

Famous last words. "Do you think they'll be put off by the change in the terms?"

Kristal patted my arm. "No way. It's only peanuts to them, and with mega-dollar signs floating in front of their eyes, they'll do anything not to let this deal collapse."

Of course, we were going to "collapse" the deal ourselves. We'd claim the company changed its plans and decided against expansion in the DC area. And, unfortunately, there was no way to get back the money paid to the company insider. Not without exposing what had transpired.

We were banking on the fact that Freeman would be too embarrassed to come after us in court, afraid he'd look like a complete fool for getting duped. We were also counting on the fact a billionaire wouldn't miss a few hundred thousand dollars, and that he would realize it was a small price to pay for keeping his public image untarnished.

Kristal positioned herself so she could face me yet still observe Freeman and Thane in the background. "Been a long while, but we both seem to slip so effortlessly back into our roles. I really think we were *meant* to work together. Just like old times."

She had a point. On a professional level, it was almost as if we'd never been apart. "We *do* make a sublime team, don't we?"

"In *many* ways." Kristal twirled her hair. "Can I ask you something?"

"Sure."

"Do you think we have a chance, Chance?" Again, with the cute wordplay smile.

"This scam? Sure, a good shot."

"No, not this." She inched closer, her goddess face only inches from mine. "You and me. Us."

"Us?" My heart skipped a beat. After we'd slept together, we hadn't discussed what had happened. Just kept on going, moving forward, too many other, more pressing things going on to take time to have some sort of conversation or conduct a post-mortem.

Of course, it *could* amount to more than that, and I had *thought* about it plenty since, but not so much about what it meant for the future. Mostly, I thought about it in terms of how it defined the past, when I'd been living with Kristal, and we'd planned on spending our lives together. Right before she disappeared with my unborn child and stayed disappeared for twenty years.

"Chance?"

"Huh?"

"Maybe we should discuss this another time." She nodded toward the two men on the pool deck, who were waving us over. "Time to close this deal. Looks like they're ready to talk business."

We headed back to the deck, but took our time, pretending as if we were in some kind of animated conversation. We laughed and gestured, not a care in the world, and certainly not like two people engaged in a high-stakes business negotiation.

We took our seats, bogus smiles locked in place.

Freeman smiled back at us, and there was a spark in his eyes that wasn't there before. The bottom of my stomach dropped two floors. He took his time pouring himself a glass of lemonade from the pitcher. Most of the ice cubes had melted, but a few small ones still floated on top, and they tumbled into his glass. He took a big sip. Then he spoke. "We've reviewed your proposal, and we'd like to proceed."

"Excell—" Kristal began, but stopped speaking when Freeman held his hand up.

"However," he continued, "there's something we'd like to change."

"This was a take-it-or-leave-it proposition," I said.

"Well, we have a counterproposal." Freeman's smug expression signaled the fact he was going to propose something he felt we wouldn't like, as if he had the upper hand.

"Oh?"

"We want to make sure this deal gets done. I'm very used to getting my way, and I have no intention of stopping now. We'd like to revert back to the original terms of the deal. The original margin deltas. And your corresponding percentage, too, of course." Freeman's dirty grin intensified.

Kristal waited a few crucial beats. "I'm afraid that's unacceptable. There are other investors who would take our deal in a heartbeat." She rose. "We'll show you out now."

Freeman and Thane didn't move.

"There's more," Freeman said.

Kristal remained standing.

"Please, sit. I think you'll be happy with what we propose. And I think it will ensure this deal happens. A bird in the hand, and all that."

Kristal pursed her lips, gave a slight nod, and sat. "Okay. I'll listen."

"In exchange for reducing your cut down to the levels outlined in the original deal, we'll pay the insider's initial fee. Four hundred fifty thousand."

"I don't think that's the direction we want to go," Kristal said. "We'll be able to find the money before Friday. I think we'll be looking for another investor. I'm sorry we couldn't come to some type of agreement."

I cleared my throat. Loudly. Kristal swiveled her head. "Something you wish to say?"

"In private?"

She sighed, exasperated. "Okay. Will you excuse us for a moment, gentlemen?"

Freeman nodded, and Kristal and I walked away from the table, circling the pool to the far side of the back lawn. Put our heads together and conducted a whispered conversation.

"Hook, line, and sinker." She threw a glance over her shoulder at the table.

"People are so predictable. Especially greedy people," I whispered back. We had several contingencies in place if Freeman hadn't proposed fronting the bribery money, but it was always nice when Plan A worked out. "Lovely yard, isn't it? Terrific landscaping."

Kristal nodded, jerked her head up as if I'd suggested she go skinny dipping. I gesticulated, throwing my arms in the air.

"Enough time?" she asked.

"Give it another thirty seconds." We pretended to argue for another half minute. Then we turned and stalked back to the table. Took our seats.

"Okay," Kristal said. "In the name of expediency, we've decided to move forward with your proposal. Congratulations, gentlemen. You have a deal."

"Actually, there's one more tiny thing."

"What's that?"

I felt the hairs prickle on the back of my neck.

"We want to make the payoff ourselves. To the corporate insider. Face to face."

Shit.

Chapter Seventeen

As we planned out the con, we'd brainstormed a myriad of possible scenarios because you always had to think a dozen moves ahead, like a chess match between two grandmasters. So, Freeman wanting to meet the fictional company insider had been discussed, albeit briefly. Most rational people didn't want to be anywhere in the vicinity when bribe money started changing hands, afraid they'd get caught up in some kind of law enforcement sting. Moreover, payoffs like this often conjured up images of nighttime rendezvous with shady characters in dimly lit concrete parking garages. Too dangerous for most people.

In fact, of all the scenarios we considered, we'd ranked this particular one sixth most likely. Unfortunately, we'd only really had time to plan for the top five.

We had some work to do.

Freeman and his lackey Thane had left about an hour ago, and we'd called everyone on our team in for a meeting. Bear, Sammi, and Hobie had come running. We'd called and texted Jake, but he hadn't yet responded, and Ella had a previous business meeting she couldn't reschedule. Which was fine with me. The real estate portion of the con was finished, and despite her general usefulness, the way she and Kristal almost got into it earlier had me fearful of what might happen the next time they were in the same room.

"That's not how it was supposed to go." Bear sprawled on the white couch in the living room.

"Well, that's how it went," Kristal said. "Now it's our move, and the clock is ticking. We need to find a company official to bribe."

"I'll do it," Bear said.

As soon as they'd left, Kristal and I began considering possible people to step up and portray the insider from Family Fun Parks. Ella would have been suitable, but we'd referred to our insider as a "he," and changing that now would most likely squelch the deal. And at this late date, we didn't think it was a very good idea to bring someone new into the con. Which really left us with only two viable options, and neither choice was Bear. "Kristal and I think it should be either Hobie or Jake."

"I could do it, I could," Bear said.

"We need your talents elsewhere."

"Jake's not even here," Bear said, stating the obvious, pout on his face. Knowing Bear, he'd get over his disappointment quickly, especially if we could distract him with a donut.

"No, he isn't, is he?" One of the drawbacks of working with con men and criminals was their unreliability. I turned to Hobie. "You game?"

Hobie glanced around the room at everyone. Shook his head. "Sorry, but I can't."

"Why not?" Kristal asked, a little too pointedly.

"Just don't think it's the best idea."

I'd heard Hobie give sincere answers before, and now wasn't one of those times. I knew him pretty well, and I'd seen him in action, too. He didn't strike me as the kind of guy to be afraid. In fact, he struck me as the kind of guy who would normally arm wrestle you to get an assignment like this. "Can I speak to you in private?"

Hobie sighed, and it took two tries for him to hoist himself off the couch. We ducked into the kitchen out of earshot. "What's going on?"

He swallowed. "The truth? I crossed paths with this Thane guy a while back. He'd recognize me."

"Why didn't you just say that?"

"I didn't want to answer any questions about how I knew him."

"And how did you know him?"

Hobie kept his lips pressed together in a half-grimace, half-smile.

"Oh, you want to play it that way?"

"For everyone's best interests, yeah, I do."

I nodded in the direction of the living room. "They'll think you're afraid to get dirty."

"I learned a long time ago not to care what other people think," Hobie said. "But maybe I can make it up in some other fashion. Behind the scenes, or something."

"Maybe."

We returned to the living room, and three expectant faces. "Hobie's out on this, and he's got a damn good reason. Which he doesn't want to tell you."

All eyes fell on Hobie, and he glared at me.

"We need to find Jake. Let's try contacting him again."

Everyone took out their phones and texted him. Then we all called him. Waited a few minutes, then tried again.

"Surely he knows we're in the middle of something here," Bear said. "He's not a complete asshole, right?"

Not completely.

When we didn't get a response in ten minutes, we all tried again.

While we waited, I joined Sammi, who'd staked out one corner of the cavernous room. She sat cross-legged on the floor, holding her phone in her hand, but she was staring out the window at the pool area, or perhaps she was looking at the expansive lawn beyond. Either way, it was odd to see her *not* paying attention to her tiny screen. When my shadow passed over her, she looked up.

"Hey," she said.

For a moment, I was reminded of the night I met her, when she hopped into the back of my car, when I thought she was simply another Ryde fare. That seemed like another lifetime ago.

"Hey back. You doing all right?" I eased down onto the floor next to her.

"Sure. Why wouldn't I be doing all right? Your plan failed. We'll never get the money we need. Some bad guys are going to beat us to death. Good times, good times."

"Our plan hasn't failed yet." Something went sideways with about ninety percent of scams. And those were the successful ones. "Just hit a tiny bump in the road."

Sammi rolled her eyes and mumbled something that sounded like "delusional" under her breath. Then she pulled out her phone and disappeared into the screen.

I rejoined the others in the main part of the living room, and Kristal popped up from her seat, agitated, as if she was waiting for me to reappear so she could deliver an angry monologue.

"They're just playing chicken with us. They're not going to walk away from this deal. Too much money at stake. I've seen this before, many times. They can't frighten us." Kristal crossed her arms, and I could tell she meant what she was saying, but her assured manner seemed to have cracked, letting a few doubts seep in. "Maybe we don't call their bluff. Maybe we tell them that the insider wishes to remain anonymous, and if they don't like it, they can go screw themselves."

"It's not just about the money," I said.

"It's always about the money." Kristal's voice rose, and if she kept it up, she'd spin out. I'd seen it plenty of times in the distant past, and it wasn't a pretty sight.

I spoke calmly. "Sure, the money is great, and Freeman wouldn't be in it unless he felt he's going to get paid well. But a guy like him wants—needs—to feel like he's in control. Like he's the clear winner in every deal."

Kristal looked as if she was going to continue arguing, but then her entire body seemed to deflate, a balloon getting popped. "I know you're right. It's just…" Kristal stopped midsentence and flopped back onto the couch.

I appraised the group, and everyone exhibited the same symptoms. Slumped shoulders, glassy eyes, slack jaws. Everyone was wiped out. This sudden monkey wrench in our plans had increased the possibility of defeat. I hoped that didn't kill whatever spirit we had left. Some time away—even a handful of hours—would help people recharge. Besides, without Jake and no suitable substitute at hand, there wasn't much we could do anyway. "Okay, everybody. We'll adjourn until we can figure out what to do. We still have a day and a half to come up with a good plan. We'll get it done. Relax, blow off some steam, but stay close. No disappearing acts like Jake, please. And if you have any brilliant ideas, please let me know."

No one even had the energy to respond.

* * *

Sometimes, when you were in the middle of a con, you were so focused on the details, so invested in being someone else, that you forgot who you really were and what was going on in *your* life. On longer jobs, I'd sometimes forget to buy food or pay the bills or water the plants. Everything gets subsumed by the con, and personal neglect was simply an occupational hazard.

As I drove home from the McLean mansion, thoughts ricocheted around my mind like balls in a bingo hopper. Except no matter how many balls came through the chute, I never got bingo. In fact, one ball kept coming up. The one marked: Sammi.

I'd been too focused on the details of the con to really think about what it meant to be her father. And more importantly, was she really my daughter? Or was she simply the bait on Kristal's hook to get me to help her out of this jam?

Had Kristal suckered me in, only to spit me out like a watermelon seed when I'd saved her ass? I'd stepped right into my old multi-faceted role: savior, protector, con artist, man-in-charge. Except maybe I wasn't in charge at all. Maybe it was Kristal pulling all the strings. The grand puppet master.

I drove past the street that led into my neighborhood and kept going until I reached The Krab Shack, the place I'd gone that first night with Sammi. I parked in the back, nose out, motor running.

I hadn't received the results of the DNA test, but the more I thought about it, the more unsure I was about things. I tried to put myself in her shoes. Her mother was in deep shit, in hock to a guy who'd threatened both of their lives. If I were Sammi, I'd do and say anything to get my mother—and myself—out of a jam. Saying I was someone's kid wouldn't even faze me under the circumstances.

Then, in six months when this all blew over, she'd tell me the truth. Or not. By that time, Kristal and Sammi would be on to their next adventure, hustling some poor mark out of his life savings.

A couple came out of the restaurant, holding hands, and crossed the parking lot to their car. The man went around and opened up her door and helped her in before tracking around to the driver's side. Chivalry. Or young love. Whatever happened to people treating each other right?

The car backed out of its space and vanished into the night, leaving me feeling no better. Had Kristal and I ever been in love like that? Memory was a funny thing. Like looking at things reflected in a funhouse mirror. Time and place had such a huge bearing on a person's perceptions. One situation in a different time, different place, could be entirely different. I didn't trust my memories. And really, what did the past matter anyway? You couldn't go back and relive the mythical good ol' days. Not with all the damage done to one's psyche just by growing older.

Did Kristal and I have a future together? After what she'd done to me way back when? I pictured Kristal, Sammi, and I around a kitchen table, laughing and enjoying a meal. A loving family.

Was I insane?

I snapped out of my crazy daydreams. If we didn't figure out a way for Kristal to settle her debt with Norvetch, she and Sammi wouldn't have *any* kind of future, with me or otherwise.

I pulled out my phone and gave Jake another call, but disconnected when it rolled into voicemail. I tried to think of someone who could, reliably, fill the role of company insider. But I'd been out of the business too long to have any great ideas.

Maybe something would come to me after a decent night's sleep.

Somehow, though, I didn't think I'd be getting one.

* * *

I'd just finished watching an episode of Bosch and was getting ready for bed when my phone buzzed with a text from Sammi.

Mom just stormed out.

I texted back. *And?*

And it has something to do with Granger.

Christ. I texted *Call me*. My old man thumbs would get worn out trying to have this conversation by text.

Twenty seconds later, my phone rang, and I picked it up. Sammi was already in mid-sentence. "...Flew right out of here without telling me what was going on."

"Why do you think it has something to do with Granger?"

"I just know. Come on, you have to help."

"Take a deep breath, then tell me exactly how you know." I tried to maintain a level of calmness in my voice, but it was obvious Sammi was in the middle of a freakout.

Her words bubbled over. "The phone rang. She had a brief conversation, and her face got all twisted like it does when she gets angry or excited. She asked whoever called to text her an address. Then she hung up, started talking to herself, and ran into her bedroom to change. I followed, trying to find out what was going on, but she told me to forget about it. She got ready super quick, then ran out of here. You gotta get going, Chance, we're wasting time."

This time I was the one sucking in a deep breath. "Okay, let's take a minute and think this through." Without any specific information, we'd never locate Kristal.

"We don't have a minute."

"Sammi, I'm sure—"

"There's one other thing. She muttered something about getting a gun first."

Shit. "Any idea where she's going?"

"I know *exactly* where she's going. When she went into the bathroom, she left her phone on the bed. I grabbed it and got the address the person texted."

"You got the address? Great, give it to me."

"Come pick me up, and we'll go together."

"Too dangerous. Give me the address."

"You might need help."

I wasn't in the mood to play games. "Goddammit, Sammi, give me the address. If there's a gun involved, it's too dangerous."

"I'm not giving you the address unless you take me with you." Defiant. Brought back memories of some knockdown, drag-out arguments I'd had with Kristal.

"Your mom could be in real trouble. Give me the damn address."

Silence.

"Now you're the one wasting time." I waited. Nothing. "Sammi? The address?"

Finally, "I'm not a little kid. I can help. Drive, call for reinforcements, be a lookout, whatever. We need to do this together, *Dad.*"

What kind of father would involve his daughter in a potentially dangerous situation? "Sammi, if something happened to you, I could never live with myself."

"Then don't let anything happen to me." A pause. "Because you KNOW I'm going to this address, with or without you."

Fuck. She got her ultimatum skills from her mother. "I'll be there in fifteen minutes. Try to reach your mom on the phone, okay? Persuade her to come to her senses?"

"Have you met my mom?" A small pause. "And Chance? Hurry."

Chapter Eighteen

An hour later, I pulled over to the side of the road. We were fifteen miles west of Bumfucksville, and the last vehicle we'd seen was a light blue 1955 pickup truck, bed full of hay. Or some such crap, I was a city boy. And it was dark on these country roads.

"We're here." I turned to look at Sammi in the rearview mirror. She'd put her phone down for the moment, and was looking out the side window, like a kid on a family vacation. I knew she hadn't been too keen on Hobie joining our party, but to her credit, she hadn't complained about it more than a dozen times. I think she felt he was intruding into some valuable father-daughter time. There'd be plenty of time for bonding later, when things settled down. Hopefully.

For my money, I was happy Hobie had insisted on coming along—if this was going to be dangerous, it was nice to have some experienced back-up.

"Why are we stopping? I don't see any house. I don't see anything but trees," she said.

I pointed up the road. "The house is a quarter of a mile away. Down a private drive."

"Then let's go."

"We *are* going." I turned in the seat to face her in the back. "Just me and Hobie. I need you to stay in the car and be our lookout. Let me know if anyone else turns down the driveway."

"Way out here? Nobody's coming. Let's go. I'll be fine."

"I thought you volunteered to be a lookout."

Sammi grunted.

"We might have beaten your mom here, so I need you to stay in the car and text us if you see her. Same goes for anyone else who might show up. Although you can't see the entrance to the driveway from here, you will be able to see any cars that turn into it. We don't know what's going on, so we have to be prepared for the worst."

"I'm coming, too." She pouted, and her words had lost a bit of their bluster. I think the stark reality of being in the dark woods facing the unknown had eroded some of her youthful—naïve—confidence.

"No, you're not. You're staying in the car. If we don't call or text in forty-five minutes, call 911. You're our safety valve, Sammi. Think you can do that?"

She bit her lip and nodded, and I thought I sensed a wave of relief wash over her. Smart girl.

Using Maglites to light the way, Hobie and I hustled down the road. I was glad he'd exchanged his Crocs for normal shoes.

When we reached the mouth of the private drive, I turned and waved to Sammi. I had no idea if she was paying attention, but I pictured her in the car, watching every step of our progress and waving a teary goodbye in return.

In reality, she was probably messing with her phone.

We turned down the secluded lane. From the street, the gravel driveway rose, then dipped and zig-zagged out of sight. Just trees, trees, and more trees. No structure in sight. A pretty remote hiding place. We were assuming it was Granger's hideout, but we didn't have any confirmation—just seemed like the most prudent assumption to make. If we were wrong, and Kristal was only meeting a friend in need or scoring some weed, then we'd look like assholes. But at least Kristal wouldn't be in danger.

We made our way down the drive, keeping to the edge of the gravel, ready to jump into the woods if a car came along—or if Granger somehow got tipped off and decided to make a getaway.

"Hang on. Wait here a sec." Hobie crept forward, stopping every few steps and examining the driveway and surrounding trees, looking for what, I didn't know. After about a minute, he turned around and waved me forward.

When I got next to him, I asked, "Anything?"

"No cameras that I can detect. No sign of any monitoring at all. Hopefully, being this secluded has given him a false sense of security."

We continued along the winding driveway slowly, not wanting to make any noise that would announce our arrival. Trees closed in all around us and shut out any meager moonlight. If we didn't have our Maglites, we'd be blind.

We kept our hands cupped over the head of the flashlight, but if Granger somehow spotted us, he wouldn't be able to drive out this way without having to go through us. Of course, if Granger was smart, he'd have prepared another emergency escape path.

Finally, we broke through the woods and came upon the cabin. It wasn't made out of logs, like old Abe Lincoln's, but it was small and boxy. A satellite dish protruded from the roof, another difference between Abe's place and Granger's.

It could have been as old as Abe's, however.

A beat-up Chevy parked at an odd angle. I'd seen that car before, recently, although I couldn't quite place it. There was no sign of Kristal's ride, and I took that to be a very good sign. Maybe we'd gotten here in time to head off trouble. Kristal was unpredictable and dangerous *without* a gun. With a gun, holy hell was liable to break out.

"What's the plan?" Hobie asked.

If circumstances were different, I'd say we should sit tight and watch the house. Wait until Granger came out for air or groceries. But we didn't have that luxury now, not with Kristal on the way. "Let's go in. Maybe we can surprise him and get Kristal's money back without anyone getting hurt." *And before she gets here.*

"I'll follow your lead." Hobie drew a gun from somewhere under his shirt. He must have seen my eyes dilate. "Never hurts to be prepared. Don't worry, I know how to use it."

Nothing about Hobie should have surprised me anymore, but he still managed to get me, just for a second. "Hopefully, you won't need to demonstrate that fact. Let's go." We crossed the small clearing quickly and hopped up onto the front porch, flattening ourselves against the wall on either side of the door.

I pointed to my chest, *I'll go in first*, then very slowly pulled open the flimsy screen door in a smooth motion to minimize any squeaking. Barely a *whisp*, but I still held my breath for a few seconds, waiting for a shotgun blast to come roaring through the front door.

Nothing.

I nodded, more to myself than to Hobie, and reached for the knob of the front door. I expected it to be locked, but it turned easily. I guess you didn't worry about nosy neighbors this far in the woods.

I turned the knob fully and pushed the door open a hair. Dark inside. I glanced at Hobie, who stood stock still, gun by his side. I aimed my light through the narrow opening, taking every precaution in case Granger had somehow booby-trapped the front entrance. No evident trip wires or anything else suspicious, but when it came to staying alive, you couldn't be too careful.

From my angle, all I could see inside was the corner of a couch and a small table.

I tilted my head toward the house, and Hobie gave a quick nod in response. Time to enter.

I pushed the door open farther and was about to step over the threshold when I heard the faint sounds of a car crunching up the gravel driveway. Hobie must have heard it, too, because he tugged on my sleeve and motioned me to follow him.

He darted off the porch toward the woods on the side opposite the driveway, and I was fast on his heels. We found a hiding spot behind some bushes that gave us a view of the front of the house. Hobie crouched next to me, his full attention on the driveway, weapon still in his hand.

My pulse pounded as I thought about Sammi. Obviously, someone had gotten past her. Had they hurt her? An image of her inert body lying in the front seat flashed through my mind.

I pulled out my phone to text her when a pair of headlights washed across the front of the house. The car skidded to a stop on the gravel behind the

Chevy, but the engine and headlights stayed on.

There was enough ambient light to tell it was Kristal's car.

The driver's door swung open, and a fraction of a second later, so did the passenger door.

Kristal and Sammi.

I rose and felt Hobie's hand on my arm, tugging me down. I shrugged it off and burst through the underbrush. "Kristal," I called out in a harsh whisper. "Over here."

She spun in my direction. When she did, I noticed a gun in her hand, too.

"Don't shoot. It's me, Chance. Get your ass over here."

She turned back to the house, took a step in that direction, then paused. Veered back toward me. I motioned her over more urgently. "Come on. We'll do this together."

She grabbed Sammi with her free hand, and they hurried over. I ushered them into the bushes, hoping Granger was a sound sleeper.

"That fucker is here, Chance. I want a piece of him. And I want my money back." I knew Kristal was baring her fangs even though I couldn't see them.

"Why do you think we're here?" I turned to Sammi. "I told you to stay in the car."

"Lay off her," Kristal said. "She's got a stake in this, too. She'll be fine. In case you can't count, it's four against one." She held up her gun. "Make that five."

"Please put that away," I said, noticing Hobie no longer held his weapon. "Like you said, it's four against one. And from what Sammi told me, Granger isn't the violent type."

"Neither am I. Usually." Kristal waved her gun and laughed, and it sounded a lot like an evil serial killer laugh at the end of a bad movie. Disconcerting coming out of Kristal's mouth, to say the least.

"Kristal, put that away, and we'll go in. Sammi, you stay out here and call the cops if something goes sideways." I glared at Kristal until she tucked her gun away. "Okay, then. Follow me. And try to keep quiet."

We left Sammi in the bushes and approached the house. With all the commotion and the car's headlights shining through the front windows, we figured we'd lost any chance of surprise, unless Granger was a *really* sound sleeper.

Nonetheless, we entered the house carefully and didn't turn on the overhead lights, relying instead on our flashlights. I led the way, followed by Kristal, and Hobie brought up the rear.

We moved through the main living area, and there was no sign of Granger. But an overturned floor lamp caught my attention. I pointed it out to Hobie as we passed. For all we knew, it could have fallen over months ago.

Or it could have been tipped over thirty minutes ago.

After the main living area, we filed through the kitchen. Dirty dishes everywhere. Kristal muttered, "Always was a pig."

Down a short hallway. Bedroom on the right. I called a halt to our procession with an upraised hand. Pointed at my chest again, *me first*. I took a step in, focused my flashlight on the narrow bed in the corner. Empty.

Took a step farther into the room to check out the closet and half-stumbled over something on the floor.

I directed my Maglite beam down at my feet.

A body.

"Shit," I called out, and Hobie was there in a flash, followed by Kristal. And Sammi had joined us, too. *Why wouldn't that girl listen to me?* I held them back with an arm so they wouldn't trip over Granger.

I moved the flashlight beam toward his face.

But it wasn't Granger's face it illuminated.

Chapter Nineteen

We were looking right into Jake's face. And he blinked a couple of times as a noise gurgled from his mouth.

"He's still alive," Kristal said.

"I'm calling 911." I pulled out my phone.

"Wait," I thought I heard Jake say.

"What?"

"Wait," he said, stronger. "Don't call. I'm..."

I stepped over to the wall and flipped the light switch. A small bedside lamp popped on. Jake lay on the floor, hair matted with blood. He blinked rapidly against the light. "I'll be all right. Head hurts, though. A lot."

Jake struggled to get up, and we helped him get to a sitting position, more or less. We propped him up against the side of the bed, and Hobie grabbed a couple of pillows and stuffed them under Jake's head. He looked as if he'd just gone twelve rounds in a boxing match that should have been stopped after seven. In addition to a knot on his head, the beginnings of a black eye were forming. And the way he held his side and winced when he moved made me think he'd broken a rib or two.

"What the hell happened?"

Jake licked his lips, tried to speak, but no words came out. Only croaking.

"Get him some water."

Kristal ran off to get some water, and Hobie and I exchanged glances. Whatever had happened wasn't good. Especially for Jake.

Kristal returned with a beer. Twisted off the cap and handed it to Jake. He tried grabbing it with his left hand, but his fingers didn't seem to be working too well, so he switched to his right. Downed a long gulp. Spoke again. "Got blindsided."

I knelt next to him. "By who?"

Jake shrugged, not very convincingly.

"It was Granger, wasn't it?" Kristal asked.

Jake winced as if he'd been struck again. He mumbled something.

Kristal kicked him in the leg.

"Shit! Watch out," Jake said.

I put my hand on Kristal's arm and tried to pull her away, but she shook me off. Kicked Jake again, and he yelped in pain. "You were in on it, weren't you? You were working with that asshole!"

Jake's eyes fluttered, and he slumped. I thought his head was going to hit the metal bed frame, but he caught himself an inch before that happened. He took a moment to collect himself. "It wasn't like that."

Kristal reared back to kick him again, but this time I grabbed both of her arms and pulled her out of range. Held on tight. She put up some token opposition—I think she wanted to see what Jake had to say for himself before really tearing into him. "Explain yourself, and it better be damn good."

"Duane came to me, completely on his own. Said you and him had been having a few, uh, problems." Jake glanced apologetically at Kristal. "He also wasn't very confident the scam you were working on would pay off."

"So, he took my money instead?" Kristal said.

I still held her, and I felt every muscle in her body tense. Out of the corner of my eyes, I could see Sammi paying close attention, too.

"I didn't know he was going to rip you off. He said something about taking the money and using it in a different con. One with a smaller payoff, but a higher likelihood of success."

"And what was that?" Kristal demanded.

"He didn't tell me."

"What are you doing here?" I asked, trying to get things moving along. Jake needed to get medical attention, and unless he had a damn good reason not to, I was going to call 911 as soon as we were done debriefing him.

"When the shit really hit the fan—after Norvetch threatened you—I tried contacting Granger to explain what was going on. He didn't answer, at all, and I thought he'd skipped town. One reason I decided to help you guys. I felt bad for knowing what he did and not telling you."

"Why didn't you come clean, dipshit?" Kristal squirmed in my hold.

"What good would it do? You'd get pissed at me, kick me out of the operation, and I was just trying to help you get the money you need." Jake took a deep breath. "Anyway, he finally contacted me—kind of a drunk dial, I think—said he'd heard some shit about you being squeezed by Norvetch."

"And he offered to give me my money back?"

"That's exactly what I asked him. He laughed, cackled really. Like I said, he was pretty wasted. Then told me he needed my help in that con he was talking about. I asked if that meant he still had your dough. He didn't answer directly, just told me he'd return your money to you after he scored. Told me to meet him here—I think it's some buddy's hangout—so we could talk about the whole situation. I did, with the goal of getting your money back, but..." Jake shrugged, winced, and took another slug of beer.

Jake had been acting a little uptight before he'd disappeared, but I'd chalked it down to the jitters we all felt when doing a job.

Hobie stood in the doorway, still and quiet. Only his eyes seemed alive, and I knew he was taking everything in and analyzing the situation. I'd grown up in this world of back-stabbing and double-dealing bullshit, so I was used to it, but I wondered what he thought about it all.

"That's bullshit. He was never going to return my money," Kristal said.

On this, I agreed with her. "How did he get the drop on you?"

"We started out by talking about the job he wanted to pull. It was some kind of deal where he was going to buy some manufacturer seconds at a deep discount, then turn it around to a chain of sketchy boutiques who would sell them as unblemished. Or some such shit, we never got to the details."

"What happened next?"

"I told him I didn't believe he still had your money, and that I wasn't going to even hear him out unless I saw it. He got this weird expression on his face. Then he popped up out of his chair, ran into the back, returned with the duffel bag. Showed me. It was full of cash, all right. I told him okay, I was in. He started to take the duffel bag back, and I followed him. Tried to grab it from him, and we started brawling. I think he hit me on the head with an old bowling trophy." He touched his head. "Did I mention it fucking hurts?"

"And now he's gone, with my money."

I felt Kristal deflate, so I let her out of my grasp.

She stood there for a second, then sprang forward and kicked Jake again. Hard. He cried out, and Kristal turned and fled from the room. Sammi rushed out after her.

Finally, Hobie spoke. "What now?"

I exhaled. "Get Jake here to an ER."

"No, I don't need—" He started coughing and sputtering.

I raised my voice to be heard over him. "Drop him off at a hospital. Then we need to find someone to pose as our company insider. Know any prospects?"

Hobie just shook his head.

We performed a quick search of the place, but didn't uncover any other duffel bags full of money, or anything else of value. Even all of Granger's clothes were gone, which meant he had no intention of returning.

Hobie and I drove Jake to the Fairfax Hospital ER, while Kristal and Sammi went home, probably feeling as dejected as we did. I told them to get a good night's sleep, and we'd regroup in the morning, but I wasn't hopeful. Our last option was a terrible one—having Bear portray the company insider. What kind of company would hire a guy who presented like Bear?

I fell into bed without even changing my clothes. I barely had enough energy to take my shoes off.

* * *

I awoke to the sound of great claps of thunder. Loud. Relentless. Nearby. I glanced at the clock on my nightstand: 8:42 am. After another fifteen seconds of cursing Mother Nature, I realized it wasn't storming outside.

Someone was banging on my door.

I hopped out of bed. "I'm coming. Shut up, I'm coming."

I peered through the peephole, then threw the door open. Sammi came barging in. "Is she here?"

"Who?"

"Mom. Is she here?" Sammi elbowed her way past me and went straight to the bedroom. A moment later, she came rushing back to where I stood. "Where is she?"

"She's not here."

"I don't believe you."

"Want to look in the attic? Or the basement?"

Sammi's eyes smoldered. "This isn't funny. When I woke up, she wasn't there."

"Maybe she went out for coffee."

"I waited an hour. Texted her. Called her. Nothing. No answer."

"So, you figured she was here?"

"Yeah, I did. I know what's going on."

"And what is that, exactly?"

"You two." She smirked. "I'm okay with it. Mom and Dad back together. I just wish she'd let me know she was coming over."

"I told you, she's not here." My anxiety level was rising. That's all we needed was for Kristal to go missing now. A terrible thought struck me— would I ever see Kristal again?

"Then where is she?" Sammi's voice quivered, and a few tears formed. "Goddamn it, where is she? Something's not right. She got super panicky when we got home last night. Was saying stuff about how much she loved me, in a super serious, sad way. Totally out of character. We need to find her! My whole world is going to shit!"

"Have a seat." I guided Sammi over to the sofa and sat next to her. Put my arm around her shoulder. "I'm going to make sure nothing bad happens to you."

"Right. And Mom, too?" She glared at me with red eyes. "I'm not a dummy. I know the score. We are screwed."

"Why don't we try to locate your mom? I'm sure there's a very innocent explanation. Was her car gone?"

"Yeah."

"Then she went somewhere of her own free will. That's a good thing. Maybe she went to visit a friend?"

"Sure. Or maybe she's singing in the Mormon Tabernacle Choir."

"Stranger things have happened." Although I was at a loss right now to name any, at least concerning Kristal.

"Look, I know my mother isn't the most reliable person around, but she never disappears without telling me where she's going. Especially now, with Norvetch on her case and all. And she always answers my texts, even if it's just some stupid heart-face emoji."

Sammi was spinning some revisionist history. In the few days since Kristal and Sammi had airlifted into my life, I could think of several times Kristal hadn't clued Sammi in on things. No need to correct my sweet innocent child, though. "Could be anything. Maybe her phone crapped out."

Sammi stared at me, not buying what I was selling. "Something bad happened, I just know it."

I tried to make my words sound comforting, but my mind was following Sammi's down the path of worry. "Why don't you make a list of her friends? Other places she might have gone?"

Sammi opened her mouth, and I could tell she was about to blast me with another round of teenage sarcasm, but snapped it shut and looked the other way, out the window. I crossed over to the kitchen junk drawer and pulled out a pad of paper and a pen. Walked back and handed it to Sammi. "Make a list. We'll go through it together. We'll find her, have some faith."

She delivered a vicious eye roll, then set aside the paper and pen and picked up her phone. Thumbs started flying.

I took a quick shower and was ready to go in ten minutes.

"While you were singing in the shower, I made a list." She showed it to me on her phone. "Six possibles, and ten unlikelies. I only listed the local ones."

"Great. How should we do this? Call or text?"

She speared me with another disdainful expression. "I put everyone in a group. We can text them all at once."

"I know that." When I'd gotten out of prison, I found myself behind the eight ball, technology-wise. Amazing how only a few years made such a difference. I never really caught up, although driving for Ryde forced me to learn the bare minimum.

Her thumbs danced on the screen, and she sent off the message with a final press.

A moment later, her phone buzzed, and she checked the text. "Shit. It's nothing. I was hoping it was…"

"I know. Me too."

She rose, smoothed her clothes. Her lower lip quivered. In a small voice, she said, "Chance, I'm scared."

She stood a foot away from me, my daughter, but I didn't know whether to hug her or not. I was beginning to get a little scared myself, and I wasn't sure why exactly. Was it Kristal's unknown whereabouts, or was it the fact we were one step closer to Norvetch bringing the hammer down?

I didn't have to figure out what to do because Sammi hugged me.

I put my arms around her and held her close. How many hugs had I missed, not being there as she grew up? Skinned knees? Teasings on the playground? Mean girls' insults? Boys breaking her heart? How many times had she wondered where the hell her father was, to comfort her, provide her with guidance, help her out with homework, give her rides, to laugh with her? To tell her he loved her?

Would I ever be able to make up even a small percentage of what I'd missed, for my own benefit, or for Sammi's?

We held each other, me reassuring her, while she gave me the smallest taste of what it would have been like to be a father.

Then her phone buzzed again, and she backed out of the embrace as if I'd burst on fire. She looked at the message and shook her head. "Another person who hasn't seen her. Something is terribly wrong."

I resisted the urge to pat her head, as if I were comforting a panicked dog. "Perhaps. But until we get some more information, there's no need to imagine the worst. The sooner we find her, the sooner we can stop worrying."

She sighed. "Fine. I know where we can start. Mom's favorite breakfast place."

"Lead on, girl. Lead on."

Kristal's diner of choice was nearer her home in Maryland, of course, so we got on the Beltway and fought rush-hour traffic. I made my living driving all day, yet I still couldn't fathom how anyone could fight this insane traffic every morning and every afternoon on their way to and from work without going insane themselves.

An hour and some minutes later, we pulled up to a greasy spoon in Hyattsville. "Mom likes the waffles here," Sammi said. "And the coffee. Says it cures her hangovers pretty good."

"Does she come here often?"

"Often enough."

We went inside, and a quick scan of the place told us Kristal wasn't there. "I don't see her. Why don't we grab something to eat while we're here? Ask the server if she's seen your mother while we're at it?"

A sign on a metal stand said to seat yourself, so we did. We grabbed an empty booth toward the back, near the restrooms. Two laminated menus that had seen better days were stuck between the napkin holder and the window. I gave one to Sammi and took one for myself.

She gave it a glance, then slid it aside.

"That was quick."

"I'll get what I always get. Number three. Eggs and bacon, with toast."

"Huh. I figured you for a French toast girl."

Sammi didn't answer me but pulled out her phone instead.

I set my menu down. "I don't suppose your mother just texted you."

"Oh, sure, she did. About an hour ago. I didn't tell you?" She widened her eyes. "She's fine. Decided to go to Disney World."

"Okay. Stupid question." I had a lot to learn about being a father, that was clear. "If you care, I'm having the waffles."

Our server arrived a few minutes later, and she recognized Sammi. I guessed Kristal came here quite frequently; she really wasn't much of a cook, and she did like to go out for breakfast a fair amount. At least more than I did. Although, again, I was remembering things that happened in another lifetime. I wondered when I'd stop projecting the behavior of long-ago Kristal onto the actions of current Kristal.

"Hey, hon. Where's your mom?" the server asked Sammi, not taking her eyes off me for a second.

"You haven't seen her?"

"Not since you were both in here, couple weeks back, I guess." Her gaze bored into my skull. "Everything okay?"

"Just looking for Mom."

"This guy's not holding you against your will or something, is he?"

"No. He's okay," Sammi said. "In fact, he's my father."

The server's eyes dilated to the size of saucers, then shrank back to normal. She smiled. "Well, then. Nice to meet you. Now, what'll you both have?"

We placed our orders, and she returned to the kitchen to put them in.

"What now?" Sammi asked.

"We eat breakfast, then we start in on your list. We'll go right down the line until we find her. She's got to be somewhere, right?"

"Sometimes I wonder what my mom ever saw in you." Sammi rolled her eyes for the fiftieth time. "Of course, she was my age when you were together, right? Sometimes people my age don't make the best decisions." She picked up her phone and started swiping and tapping. I was dismissed.

I pulled out my own phone, ran through some unimportant emails. Scrolled through Facebook. I was on Facebook, but I never posted anything and never responded to other people's posts. I wasn't proud of my life and had no need to enter into political discourse with a bunch of trolls.

Our food arrived, and we ate in silence. Every time I tried to open up a line of conversation with Sammi—ask about her friends, about her likes and dislikes, about her dreams—she shut me down with a grunt or a dismissive shrug. I guessed there were many aspects of fatherhood that weren't so appealing.

Kristal was right on one count—the waffles were delicious.

Chapter Twenty

Going by the radio silence, we figured Kristal might not want to be found, not by us, not yet, so we decided to skip calling or texting the friends on Sammi's list again. Just showing up might be a better way to corral Kristal. When we finished breakfast, Sammi directed me to the first name on the list, Jerri Adkins. Jerri and Kristal had met at a club a few years ago, and, according to Sammi, Jerri was Kristal's BFF.

Sammi had picked Kristal up at Jerri's once after a night of too much partying, so she knew the way. We'd hoped to spot Kristal's car parked at the curb when we pulled up, but no dice. I sent Sammi up to the townhouse to see if her mom had spent the night. No sense showing my face at the door to complicate things.

Sammi jogged to the door, long coltish legs covering the ground fast, hair flowing behind her. She'd be breaking a lot of hearts, I imagined, especially once she shed her age-appropriate snarky attitude. Of course, that probably made her *more* attractive to the multitude of snarky boys her age.

Someone came to the door, and Sammi spoke to her, gesturing with her hands. After a moment, Sammi's body slumped, and I had my answer. Kristal wasn't here. Sammi trudged back to the car, and her hair fell limply on her shoulders.

She got in, slammed the door. "She's not here."

"We'll find her." I had no idea if we would or not, but it seemed the adult thing to say.

"I don't need any pep talks. Let's just go, okay?"

We repeated this pattern for the next four hours, texting and calling Kristal from the car as we drove to our next stop. The longer we searched, and the more potential places we crossed off our list, the higher my anxiety rose. Pretty soon, we'd be out of possibilities. Or should I say, we'd be out of *good* possibilities. A bunch of terrible possibilities still loomed before us.

Where could she have gone?

She wouldn't have gone to visit Norvetch on her own to plead for more time, would she?

* * *

Later that afternoon, as we were headed to the next-to-last place on the list, a nail salon, Sammi got a text. "We gotta go."

"What is it? That your mother?"

"Close. My grandmother."

Alarm bells went off. "What? What does she want?"

"Can't a grandmother just want to see her granddaughter?"

"Not your grandmother. She's always got some ulterior motive." I considered what that might be, came up empty. "She actually texted you? Usually, she calls me. In fact, I wasn't aware she knew how to text."

"I taught her."

I wasn't sure when or how that had taken place, but I let it go. "Did she say why she wants to see you?"

Sammi examined her phone. "Nope, not why. And she said she wanted to see *us*."

"How does she know you're with me?"

A shrug. "She said it was urgent."

Ma's urgent wasn't a typical person's urgent. Probably just wanted me to kill a mosquito that got into the house. "Why don't we finish your list first? Locating your mom is *actually* urgent."

Sammi shifted in her seat to face me. "I'll call the nail salon, see if Mom's there. If not, we'll go see Grandma. Deal?" She made the call, and no one had seen Kristal. "No sign of her."

"Okay, then. Over the river and through the woods."

"Huh?"

"Never mind." I changed lanes to make the next right turn up ahead, the quickest way to Ma's house. Time to see what was so urgent in her world.

A half mile before the turnoff onto Ma's street, Sammi told me to stop the car, with a hitch in her voice, so I pulled over to the curb and shifted into Park. "What's wrong?"

"I'm so sorry, Chance." She spoke so softly I could barely make out her words.

"About what?"

She started the waterworks, again, and the fact that I might be getting played slowly dawned on me. The more time I spent with Sammi, the more I believed she inherited Kristal's acting ability. This girl could turn it on and off with the best of them.

But I wasn't sure, and I didn't want to come off like an insensitive ass, so I tried again, gentler. "What are you sorry about?"

She picked her head up, took a few gulping breaths. "For leading you on. A wild goose chase. Mom told me to keep you occupied today. She said it was our best hope. Our *only* hope. She said if you found out what we were doing, you'd try to stop us. I'm sorry, I should have told you earlier."

"What exactly are you two doing?"

Sammi just started crying again.

Only one way to find out for sure. I shifted into Drive, mashed my foot on the gas pedal, and sped the remaining blocks to Ma's house. When I got there, I had to park on the street because the driveway was occupied.

With Kristal's car.

I got out, slammed my door, and jogged to the front door. Flung it open without even knocking. Ma, Kristal, and Peck were watching some inane comedy on Netflix at an insane volume. You could barely hear Ma's loud hooting over the abrasive laugh track.

Sammi had followed me in and stood by my side. The TV was so loud, no one had heard us enter. I practically had to shout, "Hello!"

Their heads swiveled my way, and Ma hit the mute button. "Lookie what the cat drug in. C'mere, Sammi, have a seat, hon. The show's almost over."

She waved Sammi over, then hit the mute button again, and the screeching continued. Ma and Peck went back to their show, now with Sammi watching, too, but Kristal kept her eyes locked on mine. I jerked my head, motioning outside. She gave me a curt nod, then got up as I headed to the porch. Outside, she closed the door behind her so we could hear each other talk.

"What the fuck is going on?"

"We're watching some TV to lighten the mood."

"Have you lost your mind? Norvetch's going to kill you. Both of you. And you're here, watching *Friends*?"

"It's *Will & Grace*. One of your mother's favorites."

"I don't care if it's a rerun of *America's Most Wanted*; we should be figuring out a solution to your problem. And why did you coerce Sammi into wasting my time? What the hell is going on?"

"We're just taking a little break."

"A break from what?"

Kristal twirled her hair. "I found a substitute for Jake."

It took me a few seconds, but then Kristal's solution hit me like a sucker punch in the gut. "Peck."

"Yes, Peck. We spent today going over his role. He's got it down pretty good, I think." Kristal's eyes twinkled.

Fuck, fuck fuck. "And you had Sammi distract me because you thought I wouldn't approve?"

"Would you have?"

"Hell no. Peck isn't the man for the job. The only thing he's good at is fucking things up. And he's *real* good at that."

"Beggars can't be choosers. Besides, we went over it for hours, all kinds of contingencies, all kinds of possibilities. I really think he's got a good handle on this. You're way too hard on your brother, always have been. And he's happy to help if it means his niece stays safe." More twinkling.

I wanted to blow my top, tear into Kristal. Yell, scream, carry on. But our meeting with Freeman was tomorrow morning, and we had no other options. Maybe this time, this one time, Peck wouldn't screw the pooch. Yeah, and maybe talking armadillos would come crawling out of my butt.

I exhaled. "You think he understands the play?"

"I do."

"You think he'll be able to pull it off?"

"I do."

"Do you have any other, better options?" I asked.

"I don't."

I exhaled again. I didn't like when things didn't go as I planned. Sometimes, though, you had to play the hand you were dealt, no matter how bad the cards were. "Okay, why don't we all go through it together, so I can see for myself?"

Kristal beamed. "Sure."

I turned to go back inside, but she caught my sleeve. I spun back around. "Yeah?"

She stepped closer, and I could smell the Tic-Tacs on her breath. "I've been thinking about something. A lot."

"What?"

"What I mentioned the other day."

"You'll have to be more specific."

"You and me."

"Me and you?"

"Yes. I think we should try again."

I opened my mouth, but she pressed her index finger against my lips.

"Hear me out. You and me, we had a great thing. We were soulmates, for Christ's sake. You know that's true. But I got scared and bolted. I was afraid to give myself up to you completely back then, especially with Sammi on the way. I was so immature. But I've changed, a lot. Having a kid will do that to you. And Sammi is an awesome kid. Wouldn't it be great to reunite as a family? Live together?" She removed her finger from my lips. "According to my Kristal Ball, we'll live happily ever after."

My emotions felt as if they'd been dumped into a blender, and someone had hit the puree button. How many years had I dreamed that someday I'd get back together with Kristal? Even after she'd run out on me? Love was a crazy, crazy thing. And so far, our reunion had been going great. But then, for her to pull what she did today? "You just used her in your plan to deceive me. And you expect me to trust you?"

"I knew you'd feel that way, and it's totally expected. But only because you haven't been a father. Because if you had, if you'd watched your daughter grow, tended to her bumps and bruises, soothed her after nightmares, rejoiced with her during good times, you would have done exactly the same thing I did today."

She was overselling it. Proof of how anxious she was? "I'm not sure I follow."

"I feel terrible that I deceived you. But I'd do it again every day of the week and twice on Sunday. I did it because I thought it was the best shot we have for saving Sammi's skin. She's the only reason I'm doing this. The *only* reason. If it were up to me, I'd just sit back and let Norvetch beat the crap out of me. Or I'd try to run. Whatever. But I need to fix this for Sammi's sake. Don't you see? I'd do *anything* for that kid." Kristal hit me with an expression I didn't ever recall seeing. One that reflected the unvarnished truth.

"I hear you." On some level, Kristal made a lot of sense. Still…

"In fact, if you don't see eye to eye with me about this, about putting your own life on the line to save your child's, then I *don't* think we have a future together." She smiled and put the flat of her hand against my chest, against my heart. "But I know you, Chance, better than I've ever known anyone in the world, and I know you would have done *exactly* the same thing I did, if our roles were reversed. Tell me that isn't true."

I swallowed, tried to take it all in. Tried to imagine how I'd feel and how I'd react if someone threatened my child. Actually, someone *was* threatening my child, and I was pissed. There was a reason I was doing all of this. To save Sammi from harm. "You're right, of course."

Her smile grew. "I know I am."

"But what about your career? I'm through with all this. I can't be in the game anymore. And you, well, you still seem to be on the make. Living for the next hustle."

She put her hands on my chest again and moved close. Her lips grazed mine as she spoke. "That's the thing. After this job, I'm going straight, too. We can stay straight together, Chance. You, me, and Sammi. Together."

"Working regular jobs? In a regular house?"

She laughed. "Sounds good, doesn't it? Happily ever after?"

Sounded like pie in the sky. But it did sound good. Was it so wrong to let a little hope creep into my life?

* * *

We went back inside, and the TV was blessedly off. Sammi was snuggled up next to Ma, and it seemed like Ma was explaining some kind of scheme involving insurance fraud and fake IDs. Sammi was transfixed, eating it all up, as if my mother was spouting gospel and Sammi was itching to be born again.

"Enough with the stories, Ma. No need to corrupt Sammi."

"If a grandmother can't corrupt her own granddaughter, then what's this world coming to?" Ma rose from the couch. "Who's hungry?"

"Nobody's hungry."

"Sammi looks hungry."

"You're confusing hunger with boredom."

Ma glared at me.

"Where's Peck?" I asked.

"He said he needed to go talk to a guy about a thing. Slipped out the back door, I think. Said he'd see you guys tomorrow and not to worry. He's got it all down pat."

I exchanged glances with Kristal, and if she knew me as well as she thought she did, she knew I wasn't a happy camper. And if she could read my mind, she was getting an earful.

* * *

In the best of times, I wasn't a good sleeper. When I was younger, I was too busy worrying about something—everything—to drift off into slumber. Did

I pull off the last job as efficiently as possible? Was the current job going to go without a hitch? What fabulous rewards will the next con bring? My mind was always racing, and I learned early on that wasn't conducive to getting a good night's sleep.

In prison, things weren't any better sleepwise, that was for sure, but my worries shifted from the hustles I was working on to staying alive and undamaged. Even though I was sentenced to time in a relatively low-security facility, my roommates were tough guys with no futures. A bad combination.

Once I'd decided to go straight, it took about six months until my body relaxed enough to get better sleep. I still had plenty of worries—like where my next paycheck would be coming from—but the pressures seemed different. Maybe not worrying about getting caught and going back to jail was the key.

Now, however, on the eve of arguably the most important con of my life, I found myself staring at the ceiling, unable to sleep. I rolled out of bed and went into the other room. Pulled a chair up to my fish tank. They weren't sleeping either. Instead, they just swam around in an ever-changing kaleidoscope of movement and color.

Unfortunately, the fish only provided a momentary respite from my worries.

There were a million ways things could go wrong. Unlike my fish, we were definitely sailing in uncharted waters. And we had a deckhand I didn't trust at all—Peck. Would he surprise me and come through? Or would he meet my expectations and take the entire ship down in flames?

I hadn't even had the opportunity to run through it with him. Kristal said he knew his part, and when it came to stuff like this, she was a pretty good judge, but it would have been nice to see for myself.

Of course, worrying about tomorrow's con wasn't the only thing keeping me awake.

I still felt Kristal's finger on my lips.

Her breath on my cheeks.

Had she gone around the bend? Did she really, truly, honestly think we could make a go of it? Or was this all some part of a gigantic con, with me as the sucker?

I tried to picture us in a cute house somewhere, with a yard and a dog, Kristal wearing some gardening gloves as she fussed with her flower garden, hair tied back in a messy ponytail.

And Sammi. She was there, too, sitting sideways in an overstuffed chair, long legs dangling over the arms, tip-tapping on her phone, serving up the occasional grunt or eye roll.

Could life be like that?

How would we make our living? Neither Kristal nor I were 9-to-5 office types. What kind of legal side hustles would we cobble together to make ends meet? Would I still be driving for Ryde? Would Kristal get a job as a checker at the grocery store? A receptionist scheduling kids at the orthodontist's? Maybe we'd start a family-owned pet grooming service.

And where did Sammi fit into my fantasy life? Would she stay home and go with Kristal and me when we went off to pick strawberries or go antique shopping? Would she watch Wheel of Fortune with us and solve the puzzles before we could? Or would she head off to college, get a degree in computer science, and develop apps for her phone, make a million dollars the legal way? Buy her parents a big house right on the beach?

Would we all be happy if Kristal and I tried to make things work? Or would we be inviting disaster?

On the other hand, what did we have to lose by trying?

My emotional well-being? Overrated.

My nighttime daydreams were wiped out by an image of Kristal and Sammi, lying on the ground in some dark alley, bloodied and beaten.

I went back to bed and tried to shut down my brain so I could get some sleep.

Fat fucking chance.

Chapter Twenty-One

The next day, Kristal picked me up, and we drove to the McLean mansion together. Ella was already there doing some final preparations—plumping couch pillows, hiding personal knick-knacks—to restore it to the state it was in when we'd first met Freeman and Thane there.

We'd recruited Ella to serve as Peck's assistant, for two reasons. We figured her Italian accent would add some international flavor to the meeting—Family Fun Parks International was a worldwide concern—and more importantly, we figured she might be able to step up if Peck started foundering, for whatever reason. Ella was as polished as Peck was raw.

Kristal and Ella greeted each other cordially, but there wasn't much warmth beneath the surface. Which was fine. Once this con was in the bag and we had Kristal's dough, they wouldn't ever have to interact again.

"Where is Peck?" I asked. We'd all agreed to meet at the house an hour before Freeman was due, so we could go over things one last time.

"Relax, he'll be here," Kristal said.

Ella flashed me a sideways look, but kept her mouth shut. She'd never met Peck, only heard about him from my bitching all those years ago.

"Can you contact him and make sure he hasn't overslept or something?" I tried to hold my temper in check.

Kristal rolled her eyes, and I saw where Sammi got it from. She made a big show of texting him. "Okay. Done. Probably stuck in traffic. I'm sure he'll walk through that door any minute now."

Fifty minutes later, Peck walked through the door. He wore a pin-striped suit and conservative silk tie. I couldn't remember the last time I'd seen him dressed up like that, but it must have been at some distant relative's funeral.

Before he could even open his mouth, Ella swooped in. "No, no, no. You're based in Europe. At a theme park company. And you're not really here on official business. You wouldn't be wearing a stodgy suit like that." Without waiting for an okay from Peck, she removed his suit jacket and had her hands untying his tie before anyone could blink. "Now, unbutton your top shirt button, okay?"

Peck did as instructed, then smoothed out his shirt. "Good. Feels better. Looser." Then he looked around as if he was seeing Kristal and me for the first time. "Hey there. Ready to fleece Herr Freeman?" he said in a thick accent I'm sure he thought was German.

"Cut the crap, Peck. This is serious."

"I am being serious. I thought I was supposed to be vaguely continental."

I waved him off. "You were *supposed* to be here an hour ago so we could run through it again. Freeman will be here any minute."

"Sorry I was late. The Uber driver got lost. I guess I should have taken a Ryde, instead." He winked at me. "Now, which way to the negotiation table?"

This time, we chose to hold our meeting in the study instead of outside. We figured having walls and a door would lend more of an air of privacy, important when shady dealings were being discussed. Peck would sit behind the enormous mahogany desk, and we moved two chairs facing the desk, for Freeman and Thane. Kristal, Ella, and I would sit in a small sofa/loveseat grouping off to one side of the large room.

Our plan was for Peck to explain the deal again, lay it out in simple terms, then ask for a down payment to show Freeman's intention to follow through with things. If that was unacceptable, there were other players more than willing to step in on these terms.

Once everyone agreed, Freeman would hand over the money—cash, of course, no paper trail here—and Peck would hand over the listing of the tracts of land he wished to be purchased. If everything went according to plan, we'd be out of there within an hour.

Things never went according to plan. Witness Peck pretending like he knew what was going on.

While we were busy arranging the seating, he'd taken his post behind the desk in a tall leather executive chair. With his hands clasped behind his head, he kicked his feet up onto the glass-topped surface. Started riffing in his faux-German accent. "Bow before me, peons, I'm a pillar of capitalism and greed. Pay me your American dollars, and I shall give you your crumbs. All kneel before Peck the Great!"

"Your name is Peter Becker," Kristal said.

"I know that. Just testing you."

I glanced at Kristal and Ella, and judging by the expressions on their faces, I wasn't the only one Peck was making nervous. "Okay, then. Anybody have any questions?"

The two women shook their heads, and everyone's gaze shifted to Peck. He had a way of controlling the room, that was for sure.

"Peck? Any questions?"

"Just one." He removed his feet from the desktop. "What the hell am I supposed to do again?" He paused a beat, then treated us to his biggest shit-eating grin yet.

I couldn't take it anymore. "Swear to god, Peck, if you screw this up, I will rip off one of your arms and beat you silly with it. And cut out that stupid accent!"

Peck pouted, but I could tell by his eyes he was laughing inside. He always relished getting my goat, and I should have known better than to give it to him. I was a little rusty, and I prayed I wouldn't screw up myself.

The doorbell chimes rang, echoing ominously in the cavernous house.

"Let's do this," I said, glancing around. No more smirks to be seen.

* * *

After the requisite pleasantries and after we'd introduced Ella as Becker's assistant, we all settled into the den. Peck slid into the chair behind the desk, this time keeping his feet on the ground and his smirk in check. Across from him, Freeman and Thane got comfortable, and both seemed less uptight than the last time when we sweltered out by the pool. Air conditioning had a way of cooling both air and anxiety.

"Let's get right down to business, shall we, Mr. Becker?" Corporate tool Thane spoke first, no doubt accustomed to controlling any meeting he was in.

"Of course," Peck said. He'd toned down his ridiculous accent, but he'd kept a wisp of a foreign sound to it. I had to admit, it seemed to fit the situation. "First, I've just flown in from Geneva, so please forgive my rumpled appearance." Peck fussed with his open collar, knowing all eyes were on him. Even in his grade school productions, he'd hogged the stage. After a final adjustment, he continued. "Mr. Freeman, are you sure you have not been followed here? My presence in this country must be kept secretive. If it gets out, then all types of speculations occur, and the land prices will be skyrocketing." He gave Freeman the stink-eye.

"I'm sure we weren't followed," Thane said in a tone that implied Peck was being utterly ridiculous for asking.

Peck glanced suspiciously around the room, then got up and walked over to the windows facing the backyard and pool, where he noisily lowered the blinds and drew the curtains. "One must always take the precautions."

He returned to his seat behind the desk. Leaned forward and placed his elbows on the top and steepled his hands. "I know my representatives have already laid this out for you, but if you don't mind, I'd like to go over the basics of the agreement again. I don't want there to be any misunderstandings. In my experience, it never hurts to be too careful. Would you not agree, yes?"

"Right. Can't be too careful," Freeman said before Thane could respond.

"Wonderful." Peck cleared his throat, a raspy, phlegmy sound, and for some reason, I pictured this entire con going up in smoke in a matter of seconds. He continued, "I'm here on a scouting trip with my lovely assistant to narrow down the possible tracts of land upon which we intend to build our United States flagship park. At least that is what my company thinks I am doing here." Peck raised one eyebrow theatrically. "However, we know that is not the case, yes?"

Peck stopped talking, evidently waiting for Freeman or Thane to answer his rhetorical question. Finally, Freeman realized Peck wasn't going to continue until he got some kind of affirmation, so he responded with a terse "Yes. Go on."

"Yes, we do know that is not the case. Thank you," Peck said.

Kristal had told Peck to speak as if English wasn't Becker's mother tongue. It was just like him to push things to the very brink.

"I have, in fact, already identified the land we wish to purchase. My goal here is to get the best possible price for that land for my company. To do that, we are using a method we have used numerous times in the past, which has furnished us with excellent results. So, we are using the same strategies in this case. As they say, do not fix what has not been broken, yes?"

I tried to gauge how Peck's act was going over with Freeman and Thane, but I couldn't see their faces from my angle. From our earlier meeting, and from what I'd read about him, I knew Freeman was an impatient man. I also knew that when big money was involved, people's tolerance for bullshit grew accordingly.

Freeman took advantage of Peck's pause to interject. "I think we know the score here. You tell us which tracts to purchase at a slight market premium. Then you buy those tracts from us for another markup. Everyone is happy. The original landowner, who makes a profit. We, who also make a profit. And your company, which doesn't have to pay the exorbitant prices they would have to if your interests had become public at the outset. And you personally, of course, who will make a nice payday for putting this entire deal together. That pretty much sums it up, yes?"

Peck tilted his head, and a small smile formed on his face, tacitly acknowledging Freeman's mirroring of his sentence pattern. "Yes, I do say that sums it up. Well done. Do you have any last-minute hesitations?"

Thane leaned forward in his chair, but Freeman put a hand on the man's forearm. "Nope. We are ready. But I have one request."

"Yes? What is that?"

"I'd like to speak to you privately."

Next to me, I felt Kristal tense. This was off script. I hoped Kristal and Peck had discussed this possibility.

Peck chuckled. "We are all friends here. I trust my representatives fully. You can say whatever you wish to say in front of them. They are very discreet."

"I'm sure they are, but where I come from, when two people enter into a business deal, they should be one hundred percent invested in it. And right now, I'm only ninety-nine percent on board. I prefer to do business mano-a-mano, sealed with a simple handshake. No need for assistants and aides and suck-ups all looking to cover their own asses."

I couldn't see Thane, but I imagined his face turning purple at being called a suck-up. I could see Peck, however, and a vein in his neck had started throbbing noticeably.

"Well, if that is what you wish, so it will be so." Peck gestured at us. "Would you mind waiting outside? Mr. Freeman has something he wishes to discuss with me in privacy."

Peck/Becker was running the show, so there wasn't much we could do about it. We should have anticipated this and hidden a microphone somewhere in the desk. I cursed myself for being rusty, and I hoped it wouldn't come back to bite us in the ass.

The three of us shuffled out, with Thane on our heels. The door clicked shut behind us. Peck and Freeman were alone, discussing who knew what. Everything now rested with Peck, and I felt slightly nauseated.

"Why don't we wait in the living room?" I suggested.

"If it's all the same to you, I think I'll wait outside by the pool," Thane said, face still a little shaded.

"Sure," Ella said. "Would you like some company?"

Good thinking on Ella's part—it was always better to have some eyes and ears on the mark in the middle of the con.

"Thanks, but I'm okay. Let me know when they're done, will you?" Thane stepped off briskly.

When he was outside, Ella shrugged. "I tried."

The three of us huddled on the white leather couch. "What do you think

CHAPTER TWENTY-ONE

Freeman wants?" Kristal asked.

"He's probably quizzing him about corporate details, trying to see if Peck is on the up-and-up. That's what I'd be doing."

"Shit," Ella said.

Kristal gave her the side-eye. "Have faith. Peck and I went over a lot of background about our fictitious company. Everything that Bear and his crew put up on the website. And even a few other random tidbits to add a little verisimilitude."

I eyed Kristal. "Verisimilitude?"

"Yes. It means—"

"I know what it means. I just don't think I've ever heard you use it before."

She smiled. "Trying to broaden my horizons."

"I like your horizons just fine," I said.

Ella elbowed me. "Chance? The job? Aren't you always telling us to focus?"

"Sorry." I swallowed. "It will all be fine as long as Peck doesn't relinquish the landowner contact records before getting the payoff. He's not always so good at keeping his eyes on the prize. Sometimes he gets distracted by shiny things."

By some sort of mutual unspoken agreement, we refrained from any more speculation while we waited. After what seemed like an hour, the door to the study opened. Freeman came charging out, face screwed up in anger. He stormed past us without a word.

My stomach dropped three floors.

A moment later, Peck emerged, poker-faced.

I started to go after Freeman, to see if there was some way to save the obviously screwed-up deal. But he was too fast, striding right across the living area, through the foyer, and out the front door, ignoring my pleas to slow down.

I hoped he remembered to collect Thane before he departed. I glanced out the huge picture windows facing the back, and Thane was no longer out by the pool.

What the hell had just happened?

I gathered with the others, who were standing in the living room waiting for Peck to explain.

"So?" I asked.

"Bad news, I'm afraid," Peck said. "The deal is off. Fini. Kaput. As in 'your services are no longer needed.'"

Chapter Twenty-Two

"Goddammit, Peck. I knew this wasn't going to work." I tried to control my emotions. Losing my temper here wouldn't do a bit of good. I'm not even sure it would make me feel better. My mind immediately shifted into salvage mode. What could we do to try to resurrect things?

Peck held up his hand. "I should have said, the deal, as it was *originally proposed*, is off." A small smile tugged at the corners of his mouth.

"What are you talking about?" Kristal's face blanched. "You're telling me we're screwed?"

"You're screwed," Peck said. "But I'm not."

Some color returned to Kristal's cheeks. "Please tell me what the hell you're talking about. Now."

Peck didn't answer right away. Instead, he took a leisurely stroll around the room, stopping to admire the knick-knacks on the marble mantel, pausing to pretend to smell some fake flowers in an ornate vase on a fancy side table. Part of me wanted to charge across the room and wrap my two hands around his neck, squeezing until he passed out. The other part of me wanted the posing to stop so he could tell us what the fuck happened.

"Peck!" Kristal shouted. "Tell us what is going on!"

Evidently, Kristal felt the same way I did.

"Oh, sorry," Peck said, as he sauntered over to the couch and plopped into the middle of it. "I suppose you'd like to know about Freeman's counterproposal."

"That would be nice," I said through gritted teeth.

"Freeman is cutting out the middleman. He's going to be dealing with me directly. He's paying me an extra thirty percent, too. We make more, he pays less. A win for him. A win for us." His tiny smile transformed into a Joker-level grin.

Getting cut out of the deal wasn't a bad thing—we were never going to see the payout for our facilitator's share regardless. As long as the money ended up in Kristal's bank account—and subsequently in Norvetch's—it didn't matter what route it took. So, this was a win for us, too.

In fact, this way was better, because it included the thirty percent bump Freeman was giving to Beckcr, in addition to the original sum. More money for us.

I ran through it aloud with the others to make sure I wasn't missing anything. They all agreed. Freeman's greed was our good fortune. Literally.

Unless Freeman had some sort of double-cross up his sleeve, which I thought was a very real possibility.

I grabbed Peck's hand and gave it a hearty shake. "Well, Bro, I have to admit, you did all right. Better than all right, really. You done good."

Kristal and Ella also congratulated him, and Peck was all smiles. "You know, I pretended to be offended on your behalf, but not too offended. If I do say so myself, I think I played it to perfection." He took a mock bow with a gigantic arm flourish.

Always the actor.

"I hate to spoil the fun, but where's the money?" Kristal cut right to the chase.

"I don't have it. Not yet," Peck said. "But it's as good as a done deal."

If I had a dollar for every time I heard that, I'd be lounging by the pool at my villa on the French Riviera.

The temperature of the room dropped.

Kristal fumed. "Shit. You were supposed to get the money. Today."

Peck shrugged. "He said he didn't want to give it to me here, with you all standing around. See, in his twisted scheme, I wasn't supposed to tell you he went around your back to deal with me. I was just supposed to say the deal fell through. I guess he didn't want you and me to get into it or something.

You saw him storm out of here. All part of his charade."

"I wish you'd gotten the money," Kristal said.

"You know how it is. Got to follow the mark's lead. Make him think he's calling the shots. If I had demanded something different, Freeman would have walked. I could feel it."

Peck had a point.

"Okay, then. When are you supposed to get the money?" Kristal's tone was harsh.

Peck seemed taken aback. "Don't lose sight of the big picture. This is a good thing. More. Money. For. Us. I told him I had an early flight tomorrow morning, so he said he'd arrange a meeting for tonight. You know, I could have told you he blew us off, then met with him in secret and taken all the dough for myself."

"And I could have pulled out your fingernails one by one," I said.

Peck glared at me for a second, then grinned. "Relax, everyone. We're golden here, I tell you. Golden. Now all we have to do is wait for his text with the meeting details, then go pick up our money. Piece of cake."

* * *

For the hand-off, Freeman had chosen a bench in the middle of Seven Oaks Mall, right by a children's play area. Lots of commotion, lots of moving bodies. Out in public, but plenty of chaos around to allow for a relatively private payoff.

Not trusting Peck to get there on time, Hobie and I had picked him up at Ma's and brought him with us to the mall, where we'd met Kristal, who'd driven in her own car. Always nice to have a second set of wheels in case some unforeseen crisis occurred.

Which happened way too often.

Now, we'd taken our positions in the mall. Kristal, Hobie, and I had spread out, finding spots with line-of-sight to the exchange point so we could see all the action.

Peck was waiting for Freeman patiently with his messenger bag next to him on the bench.

I was up on the second floor, leaning on a rail, watching the bench from above. Hobie was on the south side of Peck, about forty yards away on another bench, and Kristal was closer to the action, on the north side. Both of them wore hats and glasses to alter their appearance, although I didn't think Freeman was really keyed in to looking for them. He didn't have the same instincts as a con artist, born and bred. He was simply a greedy opportunist with no sense of panache.

They generally made the best marks.

We were connected on a three-way call, me, Hobie, and Kristal, and when Freeman approached, Peck was going to call my second phone and put his phone in the pocket of his windbreaker so I could hear the entire exchange play out. We'd discussed having others from the team join us, but we didn't want to run the risk of getting spotted, so we decided three lookouts were enough.

I spoke into my phone to Kristal and Hobie. "Any sign of Freeman?"

"Not here," Hobie said.

"Not yet. Do you really think this is going to go off without a hitch?" Kristal asked. She'd been asking me some variation of that since Peck had received Freeman's text with the instructions three hours ago.

"Yes, I do. We've still got a few minutes before blast-off. Keep your eyes peeled and relax. We'll be at home, counting our money within an hour." We'd put our heads together and tried to figure out all the ways Freeman could sour the deal. First and foremost, he could show up without the money, or he could try to shortchange us somehow. To make sure that didn't happen, we instructed Peck to count it all, very carefully. Freeman must surely be expecting that, so it seemed unlikely he'd try it, but you never knew how some people responded in high-pressure situations. If Peck didn't get every cent he was due, he wasn't going to hand over the document containing the land tract information.

We discussed the possibility that Freeman might try to pass along counterfeit bills, but came to the conclusion that would be a long shot. Why take such a risk when, if everything were to go right with the land deal, you stood to make a shitload of money?

Of course, that was the answer to just about every wacky scenario we could imagine Freeman pulling. Why take the risk when such easy money was within grasp? And when the amount of the bribe, while a decent chunk of money, was only pocket change to a guy like Freeman.

One possibility did have me concerned. What if Freeman was part of a government sting? None of us thought it likely. *We'd* approached *him*. Peck, portraying Peter Becker, worked for an international firm, based in another country. None of us thought it likely, but it niggled at the back of my mind. Stranger things had happened.

"Here he comes," Hobie said. "Right on time."

Below, Peck reached into his pocket and called my other phone. He said, "I trust you can hear me. Don't worry, little brother. It will all go fine."

I sure hoped so.

Thirty seconds later, Freeman entered my field of vision. He wore a large gray hoodie and carried a backpack slung over one shoulder. Walked at an even pace. Didn't look around. Didn't appear fidgety. As if he'd made kickback payoffs all the time. For all I knew, maybe this was a weekly thing.

Without any indication of recognition, Freeman took a seat at the opposite end of the bench and dumped his backpack next to Peck's messenger bag.

Peck glanced at Freeman exactly the way you'd look at a stranger sitting next to you on a bench, then faced forward again.

The two men sat like that for a full three minutes. Then, according to the pre-arranged plan, Peck reached over and pulled Freeman's backpack onto his lap. Casually unzipped the large pocket and began counting the money. It took a while, and from my vantage, it seemed as if Peck counted it twice, although I could have been imagining it.

"What's going on?" Kristal asked over the phone. "This is taking too long."

"Peck is simply being thorough." Which was unlike Peck.

Finally, Peck zipped up the backpack. But instead of keeping it on his lap, which was the signal for Freeman to examine the list of land tract owners, Peck hoisted it back onto the bench next to Freeman. Then he shielded his mouth with his hands like football coaches sometimes did when calling in the plays from the sideline.

"I counted it twice, and it came up short each time. What is your explanation?" I heard Peck say via the phone in his pocket.

Freeman put his hand in front of his mouth, too. "Well, Mr. Becker, I've reconsidered my offer and decided to revert back to the original terms. No thirty percent bonus. I don't like to reward disloyalty."

"We had a deal. You cut my associates out of the deal, so you really should not be talking to me about the disloyalties."

"Deals change. Good businessmen adapt." Freeman turned his head away from Peck toward the raucous play area but kept his hand in front of his mouth. I'm not sure who they were afraid was watching their little payoff. All most observers would notice—and hear—were the eighty kids running around and shrieking nearby.

"This is unacceptable," Peck said.

"I'm betting you won't walk away, considering this is what you wanted originally," Freeman said.

On the three-way call, Kristal said, "Chance, he needs to take it. The original amount is fine. That'll cover what I need to pay back Norvetch. If he walks, then I end up with nothing. And Sammi and I get our legs broken. Or worse. He has to take the money!"

I hoped Peck would come to the same conclusion Kristal had. We didn't need the extra money. It would have been nice, of course, but we didn't *need* it. In fact, the bump was something Freeman had offered up on his own. If he wanted to renege to make him feel like he had won some competition, then we should be fine with that.

Peck rose and made a show of picking up his messenger bag. "I am sorry, truly. But that is not how I do business."

"Chance! Do something! Peck's going to walk away!" Kristal said.

"Like what?"

"I'm going over there," Kristal said.

"Sit tight. There's nothing we can do right now. It's Peck's play." Leaving money behind was sometimes necessary in a long con, but that wasn't the case here. I hoped Peck was just playing some perverse game of chicken. I scanned the area where Kristal was supposed to be stationed, but she was no longer there. My pulse quickened. If she showed her face, the con would be blown, for sure.

"Kristal, where are you?"

No answer.

"Hobie, do you see her?" I scanned the lower concourse, trying to spot her, mind racing with contingency plans. All I saw were shoppers and kids. No Kristal.

"Nope," Hobie said. "No sign of her."

I returned my attention to Peck. He had the messenger bag looped over his shoulder and turned to speak directly to Freeman. "Nice almost doing business with you, Mr. Freeman. Be assured, if I have anything to say about any future dealings with your company or any of your company's business partners, that will not be advantageous to you." His faux European accent came through a bit more here. I wished he'd thought through the ramifications of his actions more than his acting technique.

Peck turned on his heels to go.

About thirty feet away, Kristal came into view, charging hard.

"Hold on there, hoss," Freeman said. "Have a seat. I was just testing you. I figured if you had bullshit information, you'd jump at whatever I was offering rather than lose out on the deal. Now I know you got the real goods."

"Stop, Kristal! The deal's back on," I said, hoping she was still listening and hadn't let her emotions take over completely. I felt my heart in my throat. She took three more long strides, then veered off into a gaggle of kids before getting too close to Freeman, and my entire body unwound. I spoke to her, guiding her from my viewpoint above, still concerned she could be spotted. "Listen, you can't turn around now, in case he saw you out of the corner of his eyes. It will look too unusual. Keep going and head out to your car, nice and smooth. We'll meet you there when this is over."

Kristal threw a hand up in the air over her shoulder, middle finger extended, knowing I was watching. But she headed toward the mall's exit, leading out to the parking deck.

I focused again on the action below. Peck now faced Freeman, but he didn't sit as requested. "And the rest of my money?"

Freeman stood and unzipped his bulky hoodie. Underneath was some kind of homemade harness, like a baby carrier. He reached in and removed three or four large Tyvek envelopes. Handed them over to Peck and sat down again. "Count these. You'll find all the money there."

"Thank God," Kristal said over the phone.

Peck undid his messenger bag and lowered himself onto the bench. Went through each envelope, counting and recounting. I had no doubt the money was correct now, but it never hurt to double-check.

When Peck finished his tally, he stuffed the envelopes into the backpack with the rest of the dough. "Okay, then," he said. "The information you want is in the main pocket of the messenger bag. Paper and electronic."

For some reason, Freeman wanted the information in both forms. I didn't know whether he felt better actually looking at the names before consummating the deal, or what, but it didn't matter to us. The names were bogus, whether they were printed on a sheet of paper or stored on a thumb drive.

Freeman snatched the messenger bag off the bench and unzipped it. Removed a folder and leafed through the pages inside. A minute later, he closed the folder and slid it into the messenger bag.

"All set?" Peck asked.

"All set," Freeman responded.

"Very well. Please wait five minutes before you are leaving. Less suspicious that way." Peck rose, slung the backpack over one shoulder, and saluted with two fingers to the bill of an imaginary cap. He snapped off a nod to Freeman. "Pleasure. Perhaps we shall be doing business together one day again."

Then he strode toward the exit.

"We've got the money. Let's roll," I said into the phone, then jogged toward the nearest staircase, needing to beat Freeman out the door in case he didn't wait the full five minutes. I dodged a few people and hit the stairs, descending two steps at a time.

"We've got some trouble," Hobie said, over the still-open phone line. "Big trouble."

Chapter Twenty-Three

"What kind of trouble?" I asked, still weaving through the shoppers toward the exit.

"Granger's here with his goons, and they just grabbed Peck. They're escorting him out the door now," Hobie said.

Shit! "Can you stop them?"

"Doubtful. Too far back and too many people in the way. But I'll try."

A dozen thoughts raced through my mind, none of them good. I shouted into the phone, "Kristal, get the car started and pick us up by the door. We need to follow them."

I had no idea how they knew about our scam or about today's payoff. Figuring that out could come later. If they took the money, we were screwed. More importantly, Kristal and Sammi were doomed.

We needed to keep that backpack in sight.

I dodged a few pokey shoppers and sped toward the exit. Banged through the doors.

To my right, ten yards away, Peck was sprawled on the concrete floor, lip bloodied. I rushed to his side and bent over him. "You okay?"

He nodded, tried to say something, but coughed instead. After almost hacking up a lung, he managed to clear his throat. "Hobie went after them." Peck pointed. "Thataway."

I sprang to my feet. In the distance, at the far end of the parking lot, I saw Granger and his hired help just making it to their car. And if I wasn't mistaken, Granger was toting the backpack.

Where the hell was Hobie?

As if on cue, Hobie appeared from around a van, walking toward us, looking a bit dazed. I rushed over. "What happened?"

"I saw them attack Peck, and I went after them. Caught 'em, too. Got in a few good licks before they escaped." He grabbed his jaw with his thumb and forefinger and gave it a massage, evidently to see if it still worked. He spoke to Peck. "You okay?"

"I'll live." Peck grunted as he got to his feet, then dusted himself off and patted his body to make sure all his parts were still there, all in the right place.

I glanced around, looking for Kristal's car. "Where is she? We need to follow them. If they get away, we are completely fucked." With every passing second, our window of success got smaller.

"Relax, Chance," Hobie said. "Before they—"

All I saw was red. My pulse raced, and I struggled to catch my breath. Without the dough, Kristal and Sammi were doomed. I saw my life together with them dissolve before my eyes.

"Listen, Chance," Hobie said, gripping my arm.

I spun around to face him. "What?"

"We don't need to follow them," he said.

"What are you talking about?"

"While they were knocking me around, I managed to slip a GPS tracker into a pocket of the backpack. We'll know exactly where they're going."

A GPS tracker? It sure was nice to have an extremely well-prepared wingman. Once again, I wondered exactly who Hobie had worked for as a younger man.

A moment later, Kristal came roaring up.

We piled into her car and explained the situation. Hobie opened the tracking app on his phone, and after a moment, we had our quarry located. An actual blinking dot on a map overlay.

We set out in pursuit.

* * *

We caught up with their car in about fifteen minutes. They performed a number of what I'm sure they thought were evasive maneuvers, but with the tracking app were able to pick them right up again. Of course, we could stay far enough back—out of sight completely—so they never even knew we were following them. I'm sure they figured they were free and clear.

Their ultimate destination turned out to be a townhouse complex, four groupings of six units each, a couple miles west of Chantilly. The area had been growing rapidly as the suburbs continued their sprawl toward the Shenandoah, and it was full of strip shopping malls, car dealerships with enormous flags out front, chain restaurants serving bland food, and other evidence of societal progress. Or decline, depending on your viewpoint.

During the drive, we'd kept quiet, letting Hobie direct Kristal so we wouldn't lose their vehicle. Every once in a while, she'd mutter about some other creative orifice she was planning to open up in Granger's body.

We parked under a leafy tree at the back part of the lot, with a view of Granger's unit, which we could narrow down thanks to the GPS tracker. Of course, Granger's car sitting in the parking space out front helped, too.

"Let's just walk up to the door, barge right in. They won't be expecting us at all." The words came out like dragon fire from Kristal's mouth. "I call dibs on Duane first."

"They'd never open the door," Peck said. "Of course, we could just wait on their doorstep until they had to come out. Lay siege to them."

"Let's think this through." I turned to Kristal. "Do you think they all live here together?"

Kristal snorted. "No way. Not Duane's style. The Neanderthals are probably going to split once they get their share and have a celebratory beer."

"Agreed," Hobie said. "And when they step out of the house, we make our move."

"Wouldn't it be easier to let them leave the premises completely before charging in?" I asked, knowing full well it was, but I wanted to make sure we were all on the same page.

"Sure, it'd be easier," Peck said. "But I owe those bastards a little something."

"As do I," Hobie said.

"Me, three," Kristal added.

Come to think of it, I owed them some payback, too. My gut still ached from getting jumped by K-Bar. Nice to know we *were* all on the same page.

We moved the car to a different parking spot, closer to Granger's unit, but down the row far enough not to be seen from any of his windows. Kristal and Hobie still wore their wigs, so they hopped out of the car and started taking pictures of some plants and flowers bordering the walkway. Just two nature lovers. We figured they could do this for a while without seeming too out of place.

Peck also got out, but he circled back around and took up a position behind a tree with a clear view of the front door. As soon as he saw the front door begin to open, he would let us know. He'd remain there as lookout, alerting us if anybody else showed up. All we needed was for Granger to be calling some type of gangland staff meeting to plot his next heist.

I waited in the car, slumped down in my seat, pretending to be enthralled with something on my phone, but ready to bolt as soon as I got the signal from Peck.

There were four concrete steps leading up to Granger's door, and our goal was to meet his heavies before they'd descended all the way to the sidewalk.

Hobie and I would neutralize them, while Kristal went to the door in case Granger heard some commotion on his front steps and poked his head out. If he did, we figured he'd be less likely to clobber Kristal than one of us.

We didn't have to wait long. My phone buzzed with a text from Peck—I didn't even read it—and I jumped into action. I flew from the car and, ahead of me, Hobie and Kristal were in motion, too, dashing for Granger's townhouse.

His lackeys were too busy laughing with each other about their big heist to notice they were being ambushed. As their feet hit the last step before the sidewalk, they finally heard us, and their heads snapped up—just in time to get creamed.

As we'd planned, Hobie attacked the one on the left, who happened to be Ulrich, and I aimed for the one on the right—K-Bar.

My first punch connected with K-Bar's lower jaw, and my second clocked him square in the face. He stumbled backward and cracked his head on a concrete step. I couldn't actually see them, but I imagined his eyes rolling back inside his head. Out for the count.

I spun around to help Hobie, but he already had Ulrich down, immobilized in a half nelson. From his back pocket, Hobie produced a zip-tie and had his man hogtied in a matter of seconds. Then he whipped out another zip-tie and bound Ulrich's feet. Out of a side pocket, he pulled out a rag and stuffed it into Ulrich's mouth. "If you somehow get this out of your mouth and scream, I'll come back for you and cut out your tongue. Got it?"

Wide-eyed, Ulrich simply nodded. Then he rolled over on the grass into a fetal position. Hobie moved on to K-Bar and tied him up, too, along with another rag in the mouth. Hobie had come *ultra*-prepared.

"Come on," I said. "Help me hide these guys in the bushes before some nosy neighbor notices."

Hobie and I dragged the two guys off the sidewalk and rolled them behind a row of thick shrubs. The still-conscious Ulrich winced as we bumped him along but didn't cry out. When Hobie made a threat, people seemed to listen. The unconscious K-Bar didn't complain at all.

Our handiwork now hidden, we bounded up the stairs and got ready to enter. We figured Granger would open the door, thinking his pals had forgotten something, but if not, we'd just kick the door in.

Kristal put her finger over the peephole and rapped three times on the door, hard.

A moment later, a voice from within. "Hold your fucking horses."

The door swung open, and Kristal put her shoulder down and rammed into Granger, a linebacker smashing into the running back. He flew backward into the main room and went sprawling on the floor. Kristal managed to keep her balance, and she loomed over Granger, practically daring him to get up.

Hobie and I streamed in after her. Once Granger saw us, any thoughts of getting up to fight Kristal must have evaporated, because he remained on the floor.

"Oh, hello. Why don't you come on in?" he said. "I'm just lying around waiting for you."

On one hand, I had to give him credit for not whimpering and for showing a little snark after having just been knocked on his ass by Kristal. On the other hand, I wasn't sure how wise it was to talk back to people who were in a position to mess you up like you'd never been messed up before.

I'd seen pictures, and I'd seen him from a distance, but up close, Granger was a wiry dude, full sleeve of tatts running down his left arm. Long, stringy hair with about a week's worth of stubble covering his sunburned face. Not bad looking, on the whole, if he got cleaned up a bit. I could see him fitting Kristal's bad boy preference.

Still breathing hard, Kristal reared back and kicked Granger, catching him on the outside of his knee.

"Hey," he said, scooting backward.

"Where's my money?" she demanded.

"What are you talking about?"

Kristal took a step toward Granger and kicked him again, landing a hard blow on his hip. Granger crawled backward until he bumped up against the wall behind him. I guessed he was afraid of what might happen if he tried to stand. With good reason—I think Hobie and I would have put him down again, unless Kristal beat us to it.

"Let's start with the money you stole from me. The money I trusted you with. Yeah, let's start there." She started to move closer to Granger, but I gently held her by the waist. If we let her pummel Granger as much as she wanted, we'd never get out of there.

Granger smirked. I wasn't sure if that was his normal expression, or if he'd become emboldened now that I was restraining Kristal. "Oh, that money. It's gone. Blew it gambling."

"Bullshit. You don't gamble." Kristal struggled in my grasp, so I held on a bit tighter.

"Blew it on a bad con, I should have said. All gone."

I glanced around the townhouse. Huge TV on the wall. Three separate game systems. Two laptops resting on a table. A shiny guitar on a shiny metal stand. New furnishings scattered about. I think I knew where a good chunk of Kristal's money had gone. He'd spent it quickly, too, if he'd been living with Kristal up until recently. Maybe he'd been planning to rip her off for a while and had only been waiting for the right time.

Kristal didn't seem to know how to process Granger's bullshit. "And what about the money your robot fuckers just took from us? Huh? I know you didn't have time to blow through that. Where is it?"

"Robot fuckers? What are you talking about?" Granger said.

"Those two goons. With muscles on muscles."

"I have no idea what you're talking about."

I'd had enough of this nonsense. I released Kristal and hauled Granger up off the ground. Perp-walked him over to the front window. With my hand on the back of his neck, I swiveled his head like a puppeteer to face the guys we'd dumped in the bushes. You could see their legs sticking out from underneath some branches. "Those two. We followed them from the mall where they mugged my brother. Took off with some money that belongs to us."

"I seriously don't know what the hell you're talking about." I manhandled Granger away from the window, back into the living room, and gave him a shove in Hobie's direction. Hobie gathered him up and pinned one arm in another old-school wrestling hold.

"You were always an asshole, but you weren't always so stupid," Kristal said.

"Let's turn this place upside down and inside out. If we have to break a few things, that's the way it goes. Too bad, because it looks like you have a lot of nice stuff. Or should I say *had*." I said, tiring of this game.

"Okay, wait," Granger blurted out.

"You sure rolled over easy," Kristal said.

He shrugged. "You'll find it anyway. This way, you won't break all my stuff."

"Yes, we will." Kristal picked up a lamp, took a three-step running start, and smashed it into the TV screen hanging on the wall. The sound of glass shattering was drowned out by Granger's moaning.

Granger strained against Hobie's hold, but Hobie tightened his grip, and Granger stopped squirming with a whimper. "Christ, you didn't have to do that."

"I know," Kristal said. "But it sure felt good."

"Listen, Duane. All you have to do is relax. We'll get what belongs to us, and we'll be out of your hair." I paused, then spoke to Hobie. "Would you mind?"

I didn't need to elaborate. Hobie pulled out another zip-tie—good lord, was he prepared—and although Granger put up a struggle, the three of us managed to get him neutralized without catching an elbow in the face. When we were done, we deposited him on the couch.

I nodded to Kristal and Hobie. "I don't trust this clown. Go find the money and grab whatever else of value. According to my calculations, he owes Kristal plenty," I said. "I have something I need to discuss with our host."

Kristal and Hobie left the room.

Granger eyed me, with good reason, I supposed. "What do you want?"

"How did you find out about our con?"

His obnoxious smirk returned, but lying sidewise on the couch in zip-ties seemed to take some of the bite out of it. "A little birdie told me."

"Who's the birdie?"

He tried to shrug, but he was tilted over on one shoulder, so it came out as more of a muscle spasm. "I don't remember."

I snatched the matching lamp and smashed it into the glass-topped end table. A few shards of glass ended up on Granger's shirt. "Is your memory coming back to you now?"

Granger stared at me, smirk gone, replaced by hate. I took my time walking across the room and picked up Granger's guitar from its stand. Slowly raised it over my head like Pete Townshend of The Who used to do before he smashed his instrument to smithereens on stage. "Duane? Who tipped you off?"

Beads of sweat had accumulated on Granger's forehead. "My guys. They told me about the payoff."

"Those two in the bushes?"

"Yeah."

I noodled that through. Those two didn't look like they'd know which end of a spoon to use. They certainly didn't stumble upon us on their own. "Who told them?"

"Can you put my guitar down now?"

I kept it aloft. "Tell me how they knew."

Granger swallowed. "Jake Petrucci."

Why would Jake tell Granger's muscle? Last I heard, Granger brained him so bad it put him in the hospital. I'd think Granger would be the *last* person Jake would want to clue in to what he thought was an easy score. "That doesn't make sense."

"How about putting the guitar down, and I'll explain?"

I set the guitar back on the stand carefully. It wasn't the guitar's fault its owner was an asshole. "Talk."

"Petrucci and I did a lot of work together over the years. At various times, we used some of the same crew, on different jobs, here and there, you know how it is. I guess he wasn't aware I'd been working a lot with these two lately, had them on my payroll as a matter of fact. They alerted me to the deal, figuring I'd take care of them better than Petrucci would. And they were right. Petrucci's a cheap bastard. Besides, last I heard, Petrucci wasn't in any shape to be telling anybody what to do." He chuckled a bit, evidently thinking about clobbering Jake.

I reached over and slapped him across the face.

Getting double-crossed in this business was an everyday occurrence, and I figured Jake to be kind of a skunk anyway. It all made perfect sense to me, except for one thing. After we took him to the hospital, we'd cut Jake out of the loop. He claimed he was trying to get Granger to return Kristal's money to her, but none of us fully believed that. We didn't trust him, he was persona non grata. Put bluntly, Jake had no way of knowing the spot Freeman had chosen for the payoff, nor the time.

And it sure as hell wasn't simply a lucky guess.

But somebody—one of us—*had* tipped him off.

I needed to figure out who. And why.

My phone buzzed with a text from Peck. *How's it going in there? Get the cash back?*

I responded. *Out soon. Keep an eye out.*

Roger that.

I slipped my phone back in my pocket just as Hobie and Kristal returned from their treasure hunt. Kristal had our treasure, the backpack full of Freeman's money, slung over her shoulder, while Hobie carried an old gym bag with the word Adidas printed on the side in white letters.

"Success?"

"Success." Kristal entered the room with one eye on me and the other on Granger, who was still tied up and leaning uncomfortably on the couch. I got the feeling she was going to tee off on Granger again, so I inched in front of him to ward her off. She frowned but didn't press the issue. Then her face brightened as she seemed to remember what she'd recovered. "We got our money back from today, and we got some of my money back. Not all of it, not most of it, but some of it."

She stepped around the coffee table and elbowed me just far enough aside so she could see Granger. "I'll be back for the rest, asshole. And I'll take it out in flesh, if I have to. Count on it."

"Come on, we need to get out of here. No telling when those two yahoos out front will wriggle free." I opened my arms and tried to corral Kristal out the door, but she dodged past me. Instead of heading for Granger, though, she went straight for his prized guitar. Snatched it up and smashed it into the already-busted TV. Kept hammering it against the TV—and wall—until all that remained in her hand was the guitar's splintered neck. She tossed it onto the rapidly growing heap of debris. "Sorry about that, Duane. Accidents happen." She hustled past me and out the door. Hobie followed her out.

I shrugged at Granger before I left. He might have been crying, I couldn't tell for sure.

Chapter Twenty-Four

We'd done it.

We'd conned Freeman for more than we'd aimed for. And as a bonus, we'd recovered a portion of the money Granger had stolen from Kristal, which seemed to satisfy some weird internal need of Kristal's. All we had to do now was pay back Norvetch, so Kristal and Sammi would be free.

We had Kristal's car, so she swung by the mall to drop Hobie at his car, and Peck and me at mine. Kristal wanted to go home so she could have a brief celebration with Sammi before we arranged our meeting with Norvetch to pay him back. They asked me to join in the fun, but I had something I needed to discuss with Peck. I asked for a rain check on the celebration, and I drove Peck to Ma's. I parked on the street, and we walked across the lawn to the house. I stopped on the porch.

"How about if we talk out here?" I asked. "I'm not quite ready to face up to Ma and her inquisition just yet."

"Sure. Let me go in and hit the head, and I'll be right out." Peck started to reach for the door, but I grabbed his sleeve.

"That can wait."

"Not really." He did an exaggerated bathroom dance for effect, like he used to do when he was five years old.

"Have a seat, Peck," I said.

My tone must have scared him because he plopped down into one of Ma's old beach chairs. I was afraid the webbing would give way, and I'd end up on the concrete porch, so I lowered myself gently. It held, eliciting a sigh of relief.

"We did good, Bro, didn't we?" Peck put his hands behind his head and kicked his legs out, as if he was really at the beach.

"Yeah, we did. You came through for us."

He closed his eyes, bowed his head. "You're welcome."

"I'm sure Kristal is most appreciative." I didn't say anything else, preferring to let the silence eat at Peck a bit.

"Okay, what's so important I can't take a leak first?"

I kept mum.

Peck fidgeted. I knew which buttons to push and how hard to push them. Of course, he knew the same about me, but now I had the upper hand. I knew Peck never felt comfortable in silence. Rising, he said, "Look, if you're not going to talk, I'm going inside."

"Fine. You can go inside. Just leave the money here with me before you do."

He sat back down. "What money?"

"The money you skimmed out of our deal."

"I don't know what you're talking about. Kristal counted it at Granger's. All there." He cocked his head at me. "Am I missing something?"

"I know you, and I know you're always working an angle. Took me a while to figure it out, but I did. Stand up."

"Fuck you."

"Stand up, take off your windbreaker—it's almost eighty degrees, by the way—and lift up your shirt."

"I said fuck you."

"I know you've got an envelope tucked away under there. You hid it right after the exchange. When you disappeared from our sight behind the play area."

"You're crazy."

"You weren't out of sight long—just long enough to reach into the backpack, remove an envelope, and hide it away. You need to hand it over."

Peck stared at me for the longest time. I wasn't sure if he was trying to think up a different way of telling me to fuck off, or if he was trying to figure out a way to persuade me to split his take. Finally, he said, "Shit, Chance. I was going to fess up and give it to Kristal. I was going to make a big production out of it and present it to her as a gift. For going straight. Like an old retiree getting a gold watch for all those years of service."

"Sure you were." I gestured with my hand. "Fork it over."

Peck sighed and stood. Took off his windbreaker, then reached behind him and removed an envelope he'd tucked into his waistband under his shirt. He handed it to me.

"Thanks. I'll take the other one, too."

Peck grinned and pulled out another envelope. Tossed it over. "You always were smarter than me."

"How much extra did Freeman offer you?" I asked. Peck had been the one to tell us Freeman had offered him a thirty percent increase over the original bribe—we'd never heard it from Freeman's mouth directly. The real amount of the increase could have been anything.

"Fifty percent."

"And you thought you'd deceive us and take the extra twenty percent."

"Come on, it was extra! Kristal had what she needed to pay off Norvetch. And a man needs to get paid for his efforts. That's fair."

"Yeah, if we had agreed to it. Stealing is not fair."

"Bro, stealing is what we do." Peck smiled. "Stealing is how you were raised. It's what you still should be doing. Ma's right, you know. You're a genius when it comes to stealing."

I wanted to pop Peck in the face. "Ripping off your own brother is low, even for you."

"Turning on your own brother is low, even for you."

"You think I turned on you? That implies I was *with* you." I softened my voice. "It's been a long time since I've been with you on anything."

Everybody had a hustle going on.

Some worked. Some didn't.

* * *

I killed an hour before driving to Kristal's. I wanted to give her some time to celebrate something good—for a change—with Sammi, before I confronted her.

When I got there, I asked Sammi for some privacy with her mother, and she gave me a face, thinking I wanted a certain kind of privacy. I didn't say anything to change her mind, but I wasn't there for that.

I was there to find out why she told Jake about the payoff location.

"I'll go for a walk," Sammi said, then disappeared out the front door.

As soon as the door clicked shut, Kristal threw her arms around me and hugged me tight, her long hair tickling my cheeks. "We did it, Chance. We saved my ass. And Sammi's, more importantly. I owe you so much. I think this could be the start of something good. With us. With all of us."

I enjoyed the embrace without saying a word. After a minute, I gently pushed her away. On the floor were a couple of small suitcases, packed and ready to go. "What are those for?"

"Those *were* Plan B. Despite my protests otherwise, I'd come to the decision that it would be safer to flee than to stay and get brutalized. Thankfully, we won't be needing those." Kristal was beaming, and I couldn't remember the last time I'd seen her so happy. She was gorgeous normally, but now, she was positively effervescent. I hoped she had a good explanation. I really did want this to be the start of something good. She grabbed hold of my belt and tugged me close again. "You know, we have about an hour before we meet with Norvetch. I have a terrific idea."

Ordinarily, I loved Kristal's terrific ideas. But I wouldn't be able to focus until I knew the score. "I need to ask you something." I licked my lips, unsure how to proceed. I could stop talking now, quash my gut feeling, move on with life, with Kristal, with Sammi. But that wasn't who I was. I needed to know the truth.

"Okay." Kristal stared at me with bright eyes, twirling her hair, still riding the high of pulling off a successful con. "What?"

"Don't you wonder how Granger knew about the payoff?"

"I figured that asshole had those guys following me for a while. Just to make sure I didn't get close to him. Or to jump in when I found a way to get the money I needed." Her smile dimmed a notch. "How do *you* think he found out?"

I swallowed. "According to Granger, he—"

"Granger? That lying scumbag? You can't believe a word he says."

"He said that Jake heard about the payoff and told his guys to rip us off. Then those two goons flipped on Jake and clued Granger in about the deal."

Her face contorted as she considered this. "You think Jake turned on us?"

"Seems like it."

"Suppose you're right. Then who told Jake about the payoff? After he went to thc hospital?"

"Did you?"

She stepped back abruptly. "What?"

"Did you tell Jake about the payoff?"

"No. Why would I do that? He was out of commission. And I wasn't positive he was on the up-and-up. Not sure I fully believed his story about his dealings with Granger." A cloud came over her. "Why are you asking me that, anyway? Are you accusing me of something?"

We *had* ended up finding Granger and some of Kristal's missing dough, so if she somehow orchestrated the whole thing, she'd played her cards right. "Just trying to discover the truth."

"Fuck you, Chance." She didn't smile when she said it. "What difference does it make now, anyway? We got the money." She stepped closer and tried to hug me again, but I inched backward. "Seriously? You think I had something to do with this? You think I would somehow jeopardize our con? For what purpose?"

"Because you couldn't stand getting ripped off by Granger, and you'd do anything in an attempt to get back at him. You're vindictive like that." I regretted the words the moment they escaped my mouth.

Anger flashed across her face, but then her lower lip started quivering. A tear dripped down her cheek. "Get out. Just get out. I thought you'd changed. I thought we had something."

"I have changed."

"Not enough. You're still an asshole."

I tried to focus, tried to figure this out logically. "Okay, if you didn't talk to Jake, who did?"

"Get out of my house." She stared at me, eyes now red. "I mean it. Get out. And don't come back."

I turned to go, hoping this outburst was just one of Kristal's emotional demonstrations, to be completely forgotten in an hour or two. This time, though, I wasn't so sure. I'd been counting on trying to make a go of it with her. With Sammi.

She threw open the door for me, and as I stepped over the threshold, she said, "By the way, Peck talked to Jake. He called him in the hospital to see how he was doing. Maybe he slipped somehow. You really are an asshole."

I was about to defend myself, but she slammed the door in my face.

Chapter Twenty-Five

I sat in my car outside of Kristal's place. Had I jumped to a wrong conclusion? Had I destroyed any chance of a future with Kristal? I pulled out my phone and called Peck.

"What do you want?" He answered without his usual, "What's up, Bro?"

He was pissed at me, too. Lot of that going around. "One simple question: did you call Jake when he was in the hospital and tell him about the con? How it had changed since he'd become incapacitated?"

"Yeah. I called him to see how he was doing. He's a friend of mine—of ours—you know." A long pause. "I also wanted to get some insight about how he might play the role of Peter Becker, Company Insider, since that was going to be his role. Just doing a little thespian research."

"Did you mention the payoff details? The exchange at the mall?"

"I thought you said one simple question."

"Just answer me, Peck."

Another pause. "Yeah, I asked him how he would play it."

"More thespian research?"

"That's right. In fact, he was very help—"

I disconnected the call. Peck was the leak, inadvertently, it seemed.

I called Jake and was surprised when he picked up. Somehow, I figured he hated me, too. "Hey," he said. From his tone, it sounded like he didn't have a clue what transpired.

"How are you doing?" I asked.

"Sore, but I'll live. How did the payoff go?"

"Peck told you about that, huh?"

"Yeah. Said he was trying to get into the role, wanted to become Herr Becker, head to toe. Called me for some pointers. He's very invested in making his roles authentic. So, go okay? Did Peck work out?"

I explained what had happened.

"Christ! Those two double-crossing sheepfuckers! I paid them two hundred each to watch the action and make sure it didn't go south. Some extra protection for you guys. I felt bad for Kristal that I hadn't been able to get her money back from Granger, and I felt bad I couldn't do my part. Didn't tell you or her because I knew you wouldn't approve." He coughed. "Shit! If I see those guys, I'm going to rip their balls off. Granger, too. By the way, I never knew what Kristal saw in that guy."

"I thought you worked with him a lot."

"Oh, I did. He's a shithead, all right, but sometimes you gotta work with shitheads to get the job done. You know the score."

"All we need to do now is pay off Norvetch, and we'll be done with this nightmare. Later." I hung up.

Before we did that, though, there was something I needed to do. Until this very moment, the idea of spending the rest of my life with Kristal, and Sammi, had been a pipe dream. Something I'd love to come true, but it had seemed out of my control.

But it wasn't. My future was entirely within my control, if I didn't screw it up. I needed to apologize to Kristal and make her see the new—real—me. She was wrong; I *had* changed. And I desperately wanted to be a part of her life and my daughter's life.

I sat in the car another ten minutes, mentally trying out different scripts, different approaches. Finally, I discarded all the cutesy, clever ones and decided to go with a straightforward mea culpa. *I fucked up, Kristal. Will you forgive me?*

I got out and went to her door. Rang the bell and heard it ding-dong inside. A moment later, the door opened, and I was staring into the face I wanted to spend the rest of my life with.

"I thought I told you to get lost." She didn't make a move toward slamming the door in my face, and I took that as a good sign.

"May I come in? I'd like to apologize."

One eyebrow shot up. "Then by all means." She swung the door open, and I entered.

We settled at her dining table. She didn't offer me anything to eat or drink, although I could see a half-empty bottle of champagne over her shoulder on the kitchen counter. Remnants of her celebration with Sammi.

"So?"

"I'm sorry for accusing you of tipping Jake off. I was really pissed we had a leak in our operation, and I jumped to a very, very wrong conclusion. I should have figured it was my dipshit brother from the get-go."

Kristal didn't say anything, and I couldn't read anything on her face. When she wanted to, she could maintain a poker face with the best of them. I got the feeling she wanted more.

"I, uh, sincerely apologize. You had too much riding on this, and to think you would do anything to jeopardize things was ludicrous. I let my warped imagination run away with me, and I messed up. I won't do it again." I swallowed, hard. "If I get the opportunity, I mean. I've been thinking an awful lot about us—all three of us—and if things are to work out as much as I hope they will, I know I need to do better in trusting you."

Still no words. No expression. Stone-faced Kristal.

I reached for her hand and nearly fell out of my chair when she didn't pull it back. I squeezed it, and I swore I felt her squeeze back. "Am I forgiven?"

A small smile cracked her veneer. "I'll think about it."

It felt as if a boulder had been removed from my chest. "That's all I can ask for."

"Maybe we do have a shot. I hope we do, too." She squeezed my hand harder.

Our intimate moment was interrupted by the front door opening. Sammi waltzed in and pulled the earbuds from her ears. "You guys done yet?"

"What if we're never done?" Kristal said.

Sammi shrugged, but there was a gleam in her eyes. "Whatever. Don't we need to repay some money or something?"

"Yeah, we do. BRB." Kristal got up and left the dining area.

Sammi flopped down in her seat. Lowered her voice to a whisper. "Before she gets back, I need to tell you something."

"What?" I whispered back.

"Mom's scared."

"About what?"

"About *who*. Norvetch. Seems she owes him more than she originally said."

"What do you mean?" The butterflies began gathering in my belly.

"Norvetch started charging her interest or late fees or some bullshit. Totally against their agreement. He's trying to screw us. Mom said she'd have the extra, today, but obviously, we don't have it—even if you add in the extra money we got from Freeman and the money we got back from Duane the Douche—we'll still be a little short. She thinks he'll accept what we have and call it square—I mean, it's more than the original loan but less than if you add in his extra interest bullshit—but she's still afraid of what might happen if he doesn't. Like, 'I'll accept your money while I break one of your legs to make up the difference.' And I'm also afraid what Mom will do or say if he *doesn't* accept the money. I don't know if you've noticed, but Mom's mouth sometimes gets her into trouble."

I leaned back in my chair and tried to absorb it all. Didn't surprise me that Norvetch tried to pull some shady shit. When you rule the roost and you've got the muscle, you can pretty much dictate the terms. And I assumed Norvetch didn't see Kristal as a returning customer he needed to make happy. Would Norvetch tee off on Kristal and Sammi for coming up short, even though he'd get *most* of his money?

Frankly, I had no idea.

"How much short, do you know?"

"Mom said fifty thousand. *If* you throw in all the extra money."

I did some calculations. I had the money I'd taken off of Peck in the car. I'd planned to split it up and give it to our crew as a token of thanks, but I'm sure they would understand if I gave it to Kristal instead. Counting that, we'd still be short, but close. "Do you know if your mom told Norvetch I'd be coming along for the payoff?"

"I don't think so. Seems like something Mom would want to keep in her back pocket, right?"

It did. "Maybe he won't try anything if I'm there. Especially if it's only a tiny bit short."

Sammi's head whipped up as Kristal entered the room carrying a duffel bag. "Here it is. Bag Full O' Benjamins. Let's count it to make sure we got it all." She hoisted it up onto the table.

"Hang on," I said. "Sammi filled me in on Norvetch's demands. I've got some money in the car we can add to the total. That way, you'll be close. Close enough, I hope."

"Money from where?"

"Some of the extra money Freeman threw in. I was going to split it up for the crew, but I'm sure they'd rather donate their shares to the cause."

Kristal shot daggers at Sammi, who averted her eyes. Then Kristal turned to me. "I can't do that, Chance. You guys earned that money."

I waved her off. "Look, it's not that much. And with it, you'll be pretty close to what Norvetch wants."

Kristal stared at me for the longest time. Then threw her arms around me. "Thank you."

After a moment, she let go, and emotional Kristal vanished. "Let's get counting."

She removed the money from the bag, stack by stack. She gave it a first counting, then, in piles of ten thousand, she slid the money to me, and I counted it. When we finished, our counts agreed, and we put it back in the bag. Kristal zipped it up ceremoniously. "Okay. Let's go. Let's do this."

I held up my hand. "One thing, though. In exchange for my— our—generosity, you need to do me one favor."

Her eyes narrowed. "What's that?"

"You need to let me handle the payoff." In for a penny, in for a pound, Kristal always used to say.

"What? No way, not in a—"

I held up my hand again. "I'll take Hobie with me. You may not know it, but Hobie can be a very persuasive fellow."

"No way. This is my mess. I should be involved in straightening it out. I should be the one who deals with Norvetch." She took a couple of quick breaths, and her jaw clenched.

I imagined Kristal throwing the bag of money into Norvetch's face, then attacking him just as she'd attacked Granger, kicking and screaming and smashing guitars. Sammi was right in being afraid of what Kristal might say or do. "Kristal, you need to trust me. I am the person best suited to make this payoff. Like we've always said, go with the high percentage play. In this case, I'm that play."

Again, Kristal stared at me for the longest time, trying to read something in my face. Then she sighed. "Shit, Chance. Fine. But I owe you. And I owe Hobie, too. Thank you, both."

After Kristal finished thanking me, Sammi wrapped me up in a hug. Whispered in my ear. "Thanks. Good luck and be careful, *Dad*."

I went out to get the envelopes of money from my trunk, hoping Kristal's thanks would be warranted.

* * *

On the way to pick up Hobie, I had a thought. What if I just kept driving? Halfway around the Beltway, west on I-66, into the hinterlands, across the Midwest, up into the hills of North Dakota, with the duffel bag of money? There was plenty to keep me going, especially if I laid low and lived within my means. I wouldn't have to live in somebody's converted garage. I wouldn't have to drive idiots around for rent money. I wouldn't have to contend with Ma and Peck's perpetual bullshit.

On the other hand, I wouldn't have the opportunity to reconnect with Kristal and really get to know my daughter.

I vanquished that thought as quickly as it popped up in my brain.

I called Hobie from the car. "Want to accompany me on a field trip?"

"Is it dangerous?"

"I should think so."

"Then by all means."

"I was hoping you'd say that. I'll pick you up in about fifteen minutes."

"I'll be here."

I barely had slowed to a stop before Hobie was buckled into the passenger seat. He sported an expression I'd never seen before, and it made my stomach clench. "What's up?"

"Drive, and I'll fill you in."

I slapped the car in gear, and we took off. Kristal had given me the directions to Norvetch's usual hangout, a bowling alley in Alexandria, so we had about twenty minutes. Hopefully, that would give Hobie enough time to get whatever it was off his chest.

"I've gone up against Norvetch in the past."

Now he had my full attention. "Oh?"

"About twenty years ago, I was an independent contractor. Not exactly a mercenary, but not official law enforcement either, although I always—*always*—worked for the good guys. Sometimes there would be a situation where, for whatever reason, law enforcement couldn't perform essential operations without bending the rules. That's where I came in. I was bound by my morals and ethics, but not necessarily by the laws of the land. I conducted clandestine ops, what some might call illegal searches—without probable cause, for instance—or whatever the detectives or DAs might require to put away the bad guys." He paused, glanced at me, evidently waiting for a question.

I obliged. "How long did you do this?"

"Long time. Paid well, and I was good at it. *Very* good at it. I guess I was an activist who liked to get things done without waiting for the glacial grinding of the gears of justice."

"You mean a rabble rouser?"

"No. My targets were well-defined, and I operated with surgical precision. One of the things I prided myself on was my ability to take down the bad guys with an absolute minimal amount of collateral damage to innocent people."

"Admirable." I was afraid to learn more, afraid things would go down a much darker path, but I needed to know. "How did your interaction with

CHAPTER TWENTY-FIVE

Norvetch go?"

"Feds were after him for racketeering, but they couldn't get any real evidence, at least not using legal means. Brought me in to run a black ops team to get them their evidence. Took eight months, but we finally got what the prosecutors needed. Norvetch went away for ten years. I never actually met him, face-to-face. But I was at his trial on the last day, when they read his verdict. Always nice to know your work has paid off, because so often it doesn't."

Over the past week, I'd realized Hobie had some skills ordinary civilians didn't possess, but I never would have guessed his backstory. I just figured he'd been a two-bit hustler like me. "And now you're a landlord and patron of the less fortunate."

"I do what I can."

"You didn't think to tell me—or any of us—about your dealing with Norvetch before now?"

He laughed. "Sure, I thought about it. Kept me up at night, thinking about it. But in the end, I figured it wouldn't change a thing. We still needed the money to get Kristal and Sammi off the hook. Believe me, if I thought I had any juice left with the authorities who could have helped her, I would have pursued that."

We drove in silence for a few minutes.

"You spent some time inside, didn't you?" I asked. He'd never said as much, per se, but I'd gleaned enough intimations from previous conversations to think he had. One huge reason why he now looked out for many others of us who'd also been incarcerated.

He laughed again. "Not much gets by you, huh? Yeah, I did three years. Would have been more, but my law enforcement contacts stepped in, got me an early release."

"Would have been nice if they'd stepped in *before* you did time."

"Politics, politics, politics. They couldn't be seen helping me—by the way, I was clearly guilty—without giving up all the many operations I'd been instrumental in. I knew the score going in, and I was duly compensated for that risk from the get-go. Occupational hazard, as it were. Anyway, now I can justify it all as a small price I paid for an early, comfortable retirement."

"Then why aren't you in Florida? Or San Diego? Or the Bahamas?"

"Thought about Southern France." He shrugged. "I've always liked helping others. Felt I could do more here than lying on a beach someplace. And from my time inside, I know ex-cons need more help than others. At least those who are really trying to stay straight."

"Well, I appreciate your help."

"Wish I could do more. Norvetch is a mean SOB. A whole lot of evil residing in an ordinary man's body. I hate giving him the cash, but I've thought about it from every angle, and it's the best course of action. You don't want to screw with him, not unless you have a good-sized army and a stomach to take some heavy losses."

When we got to the Annandale Bowl 'N Brew, I popped the trunk and grabbed the duffel bag full of cash. "Ready?"

Hobie answered with a curt nod, and we traipsed across the parking lot and into the building.

Chapter Twenty-Six

The Bowl 'N Brew smelled like every bowling alley, everywhere. Lane grease, French fries, foot odor. We stood inside the entrance waiting for our eyes to adjust to the cave-like darkness. Dim lighting was another bowling alley staple. At least it was well air-conditioned.

"Wait here."

I left Hobie by the door and walked over to the counter. A guy in a sweatshirt with cutoff sleeves was spraying deodorant into rental shoes. I rapped on the countertop, and he lifted his head. "Help you?"

"I'm looking for Yelton Norvetch."

"He's where he always is."

"Which is?"

The guy jerked his head to the right. "Snack bar. All the way at the end. Follow the smell. Ask the big guy sitting there."

I thanked him and motioned to Hobie. We walked the length of the bowling alley. About half of the lanes were occupied, and the sounds of the balls smashing the pins echoed in the large building, along with the occasional shout of glee when someone rolled a strike.

There were ten booths in the snack bar, but only one was occupied. A guy with an unruly mop of dark hair sat in one of the booths in front. "Big" was an understatement. This guy was huge, with two of the largest arms I'd ever seen. He was engrossed in something on his phone, so we stood there patiently, waiting for him to acknowledge us.

After a minute, I cleared my throat.

Slowly, the giant raised his head and appraised us with hooded eyes. "Yeah?"

"Is Mr. Norvetch around?" I asked.

"He is. But he doesn't like to be disturbed."

"He's expecting us."

"Oh, yeah?" He gave us a more thorough visual examination, then made a call on his phone. "Two guys. Say you're expecting them. Okay." He sighed, once, twice, then very slowly slid out of the booth and rose. "Follow me."

He was even larger standing up.

We followed him through a door in the back of the snack bar area into a short hallway, and then through another door into a medium-sized room. One wall had a few shelves with bowling trophies, and the opposite wall was covered with posters of dinosaurs and castles and football players. At one point, the bowling alley must have used this room to house birthday parties.

Now it served as the office of Yelton Norvetch, who sat behind a beat-up metal desk in the center of the room, eating a burger. He was average in every respect. Brown hair, brown eyes, not fat, not thin. Not great looking, but not ugly. About fifty years old. Glasses. Looked like the kind of actor who'd be cast as a barber in a movie.

He didn't get up to greet us.

The Sasquatch who escorted us lowered his bulk into a chair by the door. He folded his arms, tilted his head down, and closed his eyes.

We stood in front of Norvetch's desk, staring at him. He stared back at us. Finally, he spoke. "Who are you?" Average voice.

"I'm Chance Winston, and this is—"

"I know who *this* is." For a second, I pictured Norvetch as a cobra about to strike. Then my vision dissolved, and he was just an average-looking guy looking vaguely nauseated. "It's been a while, hasn't it?"

Hobie said, "It has. Wasn't sure you'd remember me."

"Hard to forget the sonofabitch who took me down." Norvetch's lips curled into something halfway between a smile and a sneer.

"Wasn't only me. Part of a team."

"You're still a cocksucker." He pushed aside his plate and stared at us with dead eyes. "Fuck you want? And talk fast, I'm in the middle of my dinner."

I glanced over at the guy by the door. Still appeared to be snoozing. I stepped forward and talked quietly, not wanting to be the one to wake the sleeping gorilla. I didn't see any reason to stretch this out.

"Here's your money." I lifted the duffel bag and placed it on his desk, next to his plate of food. "From Kristal Young. Her original loan, plus the interest you laid out in the original agreement. Plus a little extra, too, for goodwill." I said it all with confidence, and I could sense Hobie nodding next to me, trying to sell it, too.

"Is that right?"

"Look, she borrowed money from you. And now she's paying it back. With interest. I'd say you two were even."

"Are you implying something here?"

"No. Just telling you how I see it."

Norvetch bared his teeth. Snakes smiled more warmly. "Well, then, let's give it a count, okay?" He unzipped the duffel bag, took out a few stacks of money, set them on his desk. Then his face contorted. First, wide eyes in surprise, followed by the knitted brow of confusion. He pulled out another handful of stacks but didn't put these on the desk. These, he held up in the air so we could see.

He riffed through one.

A few bills on the top. Cut newspaper on the bottom.

My heart slammed against my rib cage. Next to me, I heard a sound escape from Hobie's mouth, but if he was talking, I couldn't make out any words. Norvetch was saying something, too. None of it registered. None of it really mattered. Someone had switched out the money for worthless paper. Someone had stolen virtually all of the money we'd conned from Freeman.

And that someone was Kristal.

My mind raced. She must have switched to an identical duffel bag when I went out to my car to get the money I'd recovered from Peck. I recalled she'd taken that money from me and stuffed it into the duffel bag without giving me a glance inside. Of course, if I had gotten a glimpse, I'd probably have seen only the top few stacks with real bills.

My legs felt like they were filled with jelly.

Hobie's hand gripped my upper arm. He squeezed and spoke until I finally heard his words. "Chance, take a breath. I'm sure there's a good explanation."

There was an explanation all right, but it wasn't good. I'd been taken by one of the best in the business. She'd stolen my heart, and then she'd suckered me in to help steal her windfall. I had to hand it to her. She played me like Stradivarius played his fiddle.

"Hey. Hey!" Norvetch's voice broke through my fog. "Looks like you got ripped off, buddy. Life's tough in the big city." He brayed like a donkey.

I sucked in a deep breath. Exhaled. Repeated it. Slowly, everything swam back into focus, and I could speak. "Fuck you" were the first words that came out. I sprayed them at Norvetch, but they were directed at someone else.

Norvetch laughed some more. "Ordinarily, I'd take offense, but given the situation, I'll let it slide. By the way, I never heard of nobody named Kristal. Needless to say, I never loaned her any money, neither."

Now his bodyguard had gotten off his ass and was standing next to Norvetch, laughing right along with him.

"Let's get out of here, Chance," Hobie said, mouth close to my ear. He still held me by my arm, as if I'd keel over if he let go. Maybe he was right, I still wasn't feeling too steady on my feet.

"Give me a sec, okay?" I tried to regain my balance.

Norvetch and his minion kept on laughing.

Anger began pulsing through me, and that helped snap me out of my daze. I thought about lunging across the desk and slapping the laughter right out of Norvetch's mouth, but reconsidered quickly. I needed to lick my wounds in private. A fifth of scotch would help.

I nodded to Hobie. "Okay. Let's go." I reached for the stacks of money on the desk, but Norvetch's muscleman clamped his enormous mitt on top of them. I addressed Norvetch. "I thought you said Kristal didn't owe you any money."

"That's right, she doesn't," Norvetch said. "But my time ain't free. And I guess you could say your buddy owes me, too. You two are free to go, but the bag stays. Got it?"

I glanced at Hobie, looking for some support, but he slowly shook his head.

"Thanks for your donation," Norvetch said. "Now, get the fucking fuck out of here, cocksuckers."

Norvetch was average in many regards, but he was gifted at cursing.

I had a few curses I was planning to hurl at Kristal.

If I ever saw her again, that was.

* * *

In the car, in the Bowl 'N Brew parking lot, I tried calling Kristal. No answer. I tried Sammi's phone. No answer. I texted both of them. No answer.

No surprise.

Hobie had gently guided me out of Norvetch's back office and through the bowling alley. Out to the car. He'd been quiet while I had frantically tried to reach Kristal. Now he spoke in a soft voice. "I didn't see that one coming."

Neither had I, obviously. I should have, but I didn't. It was a good thing I was out of the game, because I had become a loser at it.

"I'm sorry," Hobie said, giving me a pat on the shoulder. "You deserve better."

I did.

I knew I'd miss Kristal. But I think I felt worse about Sammi getting yanked right out of my life again, without really getting the chance to know her.

I drove home and declined Hobie's offer to get drunk with him. I was going to get drunk all by myself and wallow in pity until I couldn't take it anymore. I figured I had a good five or six days in me, at least.

Alone, I shut the door to my hovel and went straight for the bottle of scotch I kept in the cabinet above the fridge. Thought about getting a glass but decided that would just slow me down. I took the bottle to the couch, unscrewed the top, and brought it to my lips.

My phone buzzed.

Kristal? With a perfectly plausible explanation?

I set down the bottle, checked the display. *Ma.* I hit ignore and picked up the bottle. Almost had it to my lips again when the phone buzzed, again.

Ma. Again.

I hit ignore and took a swig of scotch. It burnt going down, but that was the least of the pain I'd be feeling for the next...day? Month? Year?

The phone rang once more. *Ma.*

My day couldn't get any worse. I picked up. "What?"

"This is your mother."

"What do you want?"

"I'm at a diner outside of Hagerstown."

"So? Order the meatloaf."

"Kristal and Sammi are here."

Chapter Twenty-Seven

I bolted fully upright, almost tipping over my bottle of scotch. "What?"

"I said that Kristal and Sammi are here."

I'd only had a sip of booze, but things weren't making any sense. "I'm not following, Ma."

"Ha! But I was. Following Kristal, that is. And she's here. They stopped for some food, looks like."

"Are you sure it's them?"

"Do you doubt your mother?"

I did, often. "Why would you be following them?"

"I can fill you in, but don't you think you should get your butt up here?"

She had a point. "Give me the name of the place."

She did, and I was on the road ninety seconds later.

I jumped on the Beltway, then I-270, going as fast as I dared without getting pulled over. On the ride, I called Ma back and tried to get her to explain what was going on. She said she got a text from Sammi after Kristal got home from the mall with the money, and it triggered one of Ma's *feelings*. So, she decided to keep an eye on Kristal and Sammi, just to see what they were up to. Ma said she arrived a few minutes before I left Kristal's—saw me drive off, in fact. About twenty minutes later, she watched from her car in the parking lot as Kristal and Sammi loaded up their car with bags and suitcases, then sped off.

"You didn't think to call me then?"

"I wasn't sure what was going on. Besides, I was following them. They weren't going to get away from me. I'm an old pro at this."

"You've got eyes on them?"

"I'm sitting on a bench under some trees, about twenty yards from the front door of Dave's Deadwood Diner. I called you right when they went in."

"And they haven't spotted you?"

"Feh. I told you, I'm an old pro at this. Now, hang up and concentrate on your driving. If anything changes or if they get done before you get here, I'll let you know. And don't worry, I've got this." She clicked off.

I hit the gas.

* * *

It took me just under an hour and a half to get to the diner. I parked, nose out, at the far end of the lot and hurried to where Ma was waiting. She patted the bench next to her. "Have a seat. They're still in there."

I didn't sit. "Are you sure?"

"Child, I've been sitting here the whole time, and they haven't come out." She glanced at her watch, a fake Rolex. "'Course, they should be getting done pretty soon now."

Something didn't smell right. An hour and a half in a greasy diner when they were on the run? "I'm going inside."

I rushed into the small restaurant and scanned the dining room. A few couples, half a dozen solo diners. One larger party of six. No Kristal or Sammi. I hustled through the main area to an alcove with the restrooms. Knocked on the door to the Ladies room. When no one answered, I barged in. One empty stall, nobody at the sink. I left the bathroom and continued down the hall toward the back.

Around a short corner, there was a service entrance. I pushed open the flimsy door and found myself next to a smelly dumpster. The parking lot stretched out to my right.

They'd given Ma the slip, and who knew how long they'd been back on the road.

I re-entered the restaurant, and a skinny guy with black-rimmed round glasses pointed at me. "Can I help you with something?"

"Did you happen to see two blonde women leave, probably out the back?"

"Sure did. They skipped out on their check." He narrowed his eyes at me. "Know them?"

"How long ago did they leave?"

"'Bout forty minutes, maybe more." His gaze intensified. "They friends of yours?"

"They were." I pulled a twenty out of my wallet and held it out to him. "Here you go."

He plucked it from my grasp. "They ordered fancy desserts, you know."

I gave him another ten.

Ma was waiting for me by the cash register.

"They're gone. Out the back. I thought you were an old pro at this," I said. "You sure?"

"Yes, I'm sure. Don't believe me? Go check for yourself."

Her face sagged. "I'm sorry, Chance. Maybe I'm losing a step, after all."

"You think?" I practically yelled it at her.

"On the other hand, all is not lost." Ma's expression brightened.

"What now?" I'd had enough of Ma's shenanigans. I just wanted to get back to my scotch-drinking self-flagellation project. I pushed past her, out the front door of the diner. I headed for my car, not even waiting for Ma.

"Hold your horses, Chance," Ma called to me.

I spun around. "You have ten seconds, then I'm going home."

She held up ten fingers, counted down until she got to one. "I found something."

"What? Where?"

"Well, judging from all the stuff they packed in their car, I figured they might be bugging out, so I went through her car right after I called you, while they were ordering their food."

"You broke into their car?"

"I did. To see if I could figure out why they were leaving and where they were going, of course."

"And did you?"

"Not exactly." Pause. "But I did find a duffel bag full of money."

My heart skipped a beat. "What did you do with it?"

"I did what anyone would have done. I took it. It's in my car. But finders keepers, sonny!"

"Where are you parked?"

Ma smiled, then shuffled toward her car, me right beside her. I didn't want the money, per se, but I thought that maybe Kristal—and more importantly, Sammi—might return if they knew we had it. I didn't think they could go very far, or live very long on the lam, without it.

When we got to Ma's car, she fumbled with her keys and every fiber in my body wanted to shout *Hurry up!*

"Here they are," Ma finally said, holding up her key ring. She clicked the button for the trunk release, and the trunk popped open. I stepped forward and lifted the lid all the way up.

Ma's trunk was empty.

"Oh, give me a break, Ma. What nonsense are you trying to pull on me?"

She shoved me aside, stared at the empty trunk. "It was here, I swear. She must have broken in and taken it back while I was guarding the front door. That bitch!"

I took another look. No duffel bag.

But I did find an old receipt.

With a note scribbled on the back of it.

Nice try, Ma! I knew there was a reason we got along so well. Take care of Chance, will you? Ta ta! P.S. Sammi says bye, too!

Chapter Twenty-Eight

Three days later

Hobie and I sat in my place, drinking. I'd finished all the scotch, vodka, and gin on my own since Kristal had skipped out, and I'd invited Hobie over to help me polish off the last of the beer.

"Do you think Kristal had you in her sights the whole time?"

I shrugged, took a chug.

"Why did she involve you, though? Couldn't she have pulled the Freeman scam off on her own?"

I'd been pondering that, too. "I think she needed my team to get involved. I don't think she had the technical expertise to create all the website material and online trail that Bear had. I don't think she had the access to a mansion that Ella had. I think she needed someone she trusted to play her assistant and keep things on track. And I'm not sure she felt comfortable working with anyone else, but me." I knew that sounded a bit egocentric, but Kristal and I sure had fallen back into our familiar—and effective—patterns.

"Well, you did a great job, that's for sure."

"I think it went beyond that. I think she really thought that maybe we *could* make a life together and was hedging her bets."

"Not sure I follow."

"Well, if after we'd completed the con, she felt the same connection I did, namely that if she felt we could make a go of it, then she would have fessed up about not owing Norvetch any money. I might have been pissed when I found out about the ruse, but I would have put it behind me." I took a breath. "And I think she was undecided until the very last moment, too. I mean, she could have taken off right after she dropped us off at the mall to get our cars."

Hobie shook his head.

"Don't believe me?"

"I dunno. You knew her better than I did." Hobie put a size ten orange Croc up on the coffee table.

"I think that ultimately, Kristal was Kristal. Afraid of commitment. She ditched me now, just as she ditched me then. Some people change—*I've* changed. Other people don't." I felt bad for her, stuck as she was. And still running, from the present, from herself.

Hobie took a sip from his beer. Swallowed. "And Sammi? Do you think she was involved from the beginning?"

I'd been thinking about that question a lot, too. "I'm going to choose to believe she didn't understand what was going on. That she wasn't involved. I think Kristal lied to her from the beginning in order to get her to really believe their lives were in danger. So she could be that much more persuasive, when it came to luring me in." I finished my can of beer, crushed it in my hand, and tossed it in the general direction of the kitchen. "Of course, we'll have no way of knowing for sure, will we?"

Hobie belched in response.

* * *

Three weeks later

After I'd emerged from my alcoholic stupor, a few things became clear to me. First and foremost, I'd dodged a bullet. Or, more accurately, a mortar shell. Once the initial pain—and embarrassment—of getting ditched and hustled subsided, I realized just how crazy the idea of me and Kristal making a life together was. She hadn't changed a bit, and while we might have had some fun in the short term, living together would have been a monumental train wreck. Funny how love can blind a person.

I was glad that the episode of "Kristal, The Return" had been a short, if painful, one.

Of course, one regret loomed large. I wouldn't get to know my daughter. I didn't know if I'd ever be able to get over that.

Life was cruel sometimes.

Things had taken a fortuitous turn on the job front. Ella had offered to assist me in getting my real estate license. She was willing to take me under her wing and shepherd me all the way through the process: Get me enrolled in the proper courses. Tutor me for the exam. Hook me up on a sales team and do whatever else necessary for me to get my bona fides. After I paid my dues, I'd be able to make a nice living for myself. It was a very generous—and tempting—offer, and one I was very, very grateful for.

I almost said yes.

But Hobie had a different proposal. One of his buddies, Fareed Qasim, had just started a nonprofit organization with the goal of easing the transition of people like me—ex-cons—back into the real world. Provide job skills training. Assistance with housing. Access to affordable health care. In short, things that were essential to improve the odds of success for those who wanted to redeem themselves and contribute to society in a meaningful fashion.

They'd received a grant for some seed money from a local charitable foundation, but they'd need a lot more cash to develop all their programs and keep them running. That's where I came in. Thanks to Hobie's sparkling endorsement, Qasim wanted to bring me on as the Assistant Director of Development, which was just a fancy name for Sales Guy. At the moment, there was no *Director* of Development, so if things went well, there was opportunity for advancement.

I could use my skills and talent for persuasion to do good for a segment of the population that could use all the help they could get.

The pay was decent—enough for me to stay in Hobie's garage and even sock away something for a future place of my own. And I'd have health care and a place to go every day where I could make a real difference in a positive way.

The position was full-time, so there'd be no more driving for Ryde, hanging drywall, or working landscaping jobs.

No more side hustles.

I started next week.

* * *

Three months later

I'd just gotten home from the office when my phone buzzed with a text. From Sammi. *Hey, Dad! Sorry about everything that happened. Out of my control, as you might imagine. Mom and I are pretty good, but she needs me right now. I'm sure you understand. The time you and I had together was special, even though it didn't last long. Tell Grandma that I'll be back to see her. And, of course, I'll be back to see you, too! (you didn't think you were getting rid of me so easily, did you?)*

I thought about texting her back, telling her that I'd love to see her. But was she playing me? Laying some groundwork for some long con? That would be just like her mother. Was Kristal pulling the strings here? My brain hurt, like it had every time over the past few months when I thought about how things had ended.

At some point, I might respond to Sammi. But not now. Instead, I put my phone down and retrieved an unopened envelope from the drawer in my nightstand, brought it back to where I was sitting on the couch.

Set it on the coffee table and stared at it.

Kept staring at it for five full minutes.

The envelope contained the results of my paternity test—was Sammi really, truly my daughter? When I'd gotten the results back a month or so ago—I'd checked the *physical copy requested* box on the order form—I'd tossed it into my drawer, emotionally unable to deal with it.

I'd kept it there since. I'd been tempted a couple of times, but it didn't take much effort to talk myself out of opening it. Afraid to know the truth? You bet.

And now?

I had to deal with it sometime, didn't I?

I picked up the envelope and took it into the kitchen. Got a plastic lighter from a cabinet and, holding it over the sink, lit the envelope on fire. Watched it burn for a few seconds, then dropped it into the sink basin as it turned to ash.

When it had been entirely consumed, I ran the water and turned on the garbage disposal.

Because deep in my heart, I *knew* the truth.

Acknowledgments

So many people have helped me with my writing and career over the years!

My sincerest thanks go to:

The great folks (and good friends) at Level Best Books.

The many readers and critique partners I've worked with through the years: Dan Phythyon and Ayesha Court. Dorothy Patton. Mark Skehan. Doug Bell. John Stevenson, Jill Balboni, Kim Stevenson, and Samantha Stevenson. Andy Heyman, Todd Hall. Lorraine Storms. Fred Rexroad. Tara Laskowski. Barb Goffman. John Betancourt, Carla Coupe, Bonner Menking, Adam Meyer, Megan Plyler. Ed Aymar. Eric Smith.

The Rumpi: Donna Andrews, Ellen Crosby, John Gilstrap, and Art Taylor. Amazing writers and friends.

My awesome crime fiction community: Mystery Writers of America, International Thriller Writers, and Sisters in Crime. My pals throughout cyberspace.

The P.J. Parrish sisters (Kris Montee and Kelly Nichols), Reed Farrel Coleman, Elaine Raco Chase, Jeff Deaver, Jim Grady, Hank Phillippi Ryan, Lori Rader-Day, Eli Cranor, Catriona McPherson. Supportive teachers, mentors, and blurbers!

Booksellers, librarians, and, of course, my faithful readers.

My terrific, terrific agent, Michelle Richter, and the entire group at Fuse Literary.

My extended family.

My parents, for everything.

My children, Mark and Stuart, and my wife, Janet. My inspirations—in fiction and in life.

Thanks everyone!

About the Author

Alan Orloff has published thirteen novels and more than sixty short stories. His work has won an Anthony, an Agatha, a Derringer, and two ITW Thriller Awards. He's also been a finalist for the Shamus Award and has had a story selected for *The Best American Mystery Stories* anthology. He loves cake and arugula, but not together. Never together. He lives and writes in South Florida, where the examples of hijinks are endless.

AUTHOR WEBSITE:

  www.alanorloff.com

SOCIAL MEDIA HANDLES:

  https://www.facebook.com/alanorloff
  https://bsky.app/profile/alanorloff.bsky.social
  https://www.threads.net/@alanorloff
  https://www.instagram.com/alanorloff/

Also by Alan Orloff

Novels

Diamonds for the Dead, Midnight Ink 2010 (Agatha Award Finalist)

Killer Routine, Midnight Ink 2011

Deadly Campaign, Midnight Ink 2012

The Taste, 2011

First Time Killer, 2012

Ride-Along, 2013

Running From the Past, Kindle Press/Amazon Publishing, 2015

Pray for the Innocent, Kindle Press/Amazon Publishing, 2018 (ITW Thriller Award Winner)

I Know Where You Sleep, Down & Out Books, February 2020 (Shamus Award Finalist)

I Play One On TV, Down & Out Books, July 2021 (Agatha Award Winner, Anthony Award Winner)

Sanctuary Motel, Level Best Books, October 2023

Late Checkout, Level Best Books, October 2024 (Anthony Award Finalist)

Driving the Bugmobile, May 2025

Short Stories (*60+ including one in five consecutive* Best New England Crime Stories *anthos*)

Notable ones:

"Rule Number One" appeared in *Snowbound* and was selected for *Best American Mystery Stories 2018*

"Dying in Dokesville" appeared in Malice Presents: *Mystery Most Geographical* and won a Derringer Award

"Rent Due" appeared in *Mickey Finn: 21st Century Noir*, Vol. 1 and won an ITW Thriller Award